ATLAS
THE CHAOS DEMONS MC
NICOLA JANE

Copyright © 2025
Atlas
The Chaos Demons MC

By
Nicola Jane

All rights are reserved.

No part of this book may be used or reproduced in any manner without written permission from the author,
except in the case of brief quotations used in articles or reviews.
For information, contact Nicola Jane.

This book is a work of fiction. The names, characters, places, and incidents are all products of the author's imagination and are not to be construed as real. Any similarities are entirely coincidental.

No AI has been used in creating the cover or contents of this book.

Cover Designer: Wingfield Designs
Editor: Rebecca Vazquez, Dark Syde Books
Formatting: V.R. Formatting

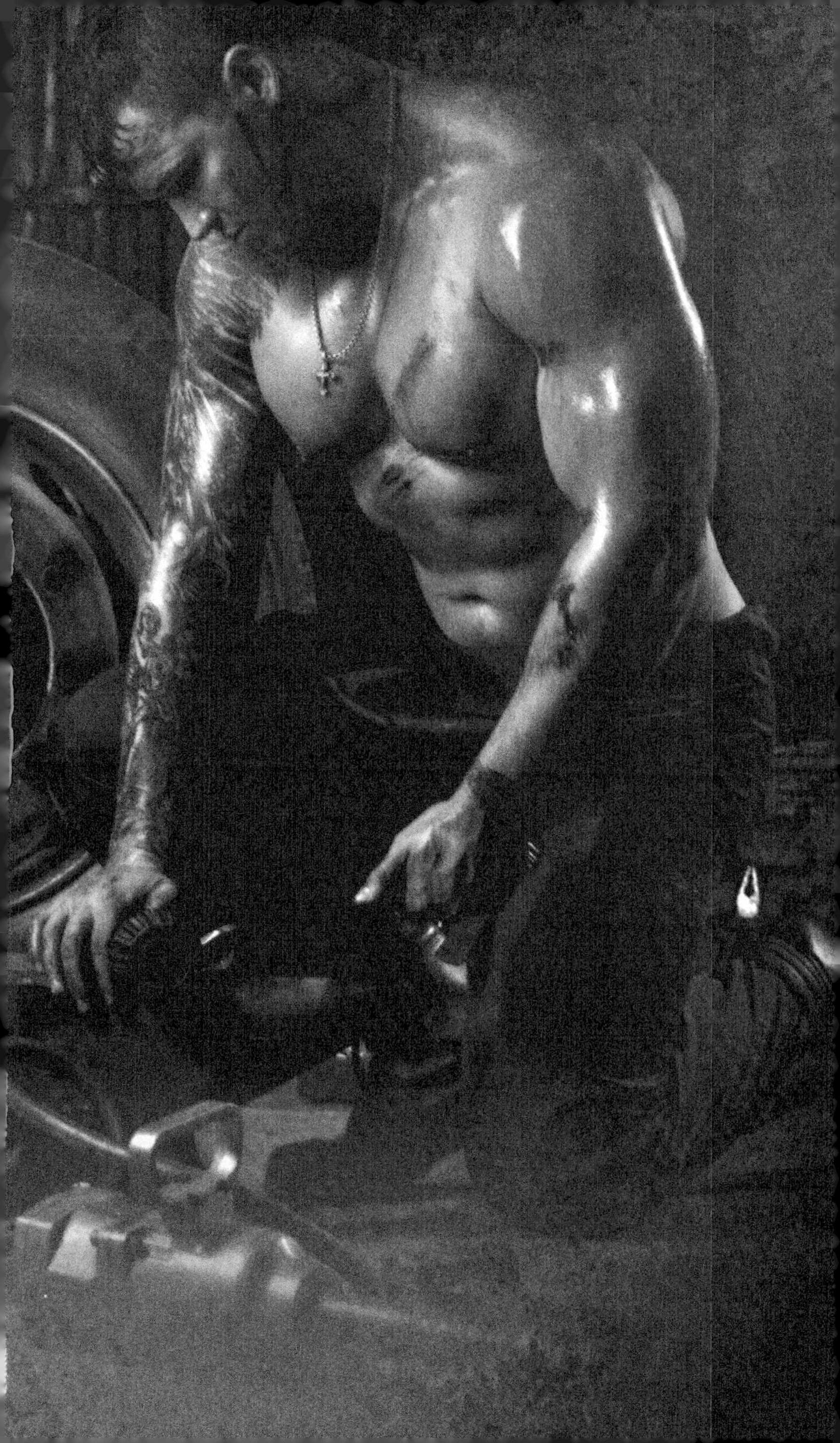

Copyright © 2025
Atlas
The Chaos Demons MC

By
Nicola Jane

All rights are reserved.

No part of this book may be used or reproduced in any manner without written permission from the author,
except in the case of brief quotations used in articles or reviews.
For information, contact Nicola Jane.

This book is a work of fiction. The names, characters, places, and incidents are all products of the author's imagination and are not to be construed as real. Any similarities are entirely coincidental.

No AI has been used in creating the cover or contents of this book.

Cover Designer: Wingfield Designs
Editor: Rebecca Vazquez, Dark Syde Books
Formatting: V.R. Formatting

Trigger Warning

This book contains triggers for violence, explicit scenes, and some dirty talking bikers. If any of this offends you, put your concerns in writing to Axel, he'll get back to you . . . maybe.

Spelling Note

Please note, this author resides in the United Kingdom and is using British English. Therefore, some words may be viewed as incorrect or spelled incorrectly, however, they are not.

Playlist:

happier – Olivia Rodrigo

Reckless – Madison Beer
The Way I Loved You – Taylor Swift
Dandelions – Ruth B.
traitor – Olivia Rodrigo
Ocean – Calvin Harris ft. Jessie Reyez
Damage Control – Elmiene
I'm your first – flowerovlove
this is how you fall in love – Jeremy Zucker ft. Chelsea Cutler
better with you – Virginia To Vegas
Can I Kiss You? – Dahl
It's Always Been You– Phil Wickham
Love Someone – Lukas Graham
Hold You 'Til We're Old – Jamie Miller
we made it. – david hugo
I'm Yours – Alessia Cara

CHAPTER 1

ATLAS

I sigh heavily and roll onto my side, watching as Nita dresses. "Are you coming back later?" I ask.

"What for?" She straightens the skirt I'd pushed up round her waist.

"Axel's barbecue," I remind her, though I know she knows. It's all the old ladies have talked about all week.

"It's a club thing," she says with a shrug as she slips her suit jacket on.

I eye her as she picks up her handbag and searches through it. "You're part of this club."

She smirks, arching a brow in my direction. "We've talked about this." She holds up a small mirror from her bag and reapplies her lipstick.

"I hate that colour on you," I mutter, and she laughs.

"You think I don't know that?" She rubs her lips together

and drops the stick back into her bag, clipping it closed. "I wear it for that reason."

"The other old ladies will want you there," I try. Rolling onto my back, I place my hands behind my head. "You're practically one of them."

"Atlas," she says on a sigh, "do we have to do this every time we hook up?" She rounds the bed to where I lay and stares down at me. "It works like this. Why change what works?"

"It'll still work when you're my old lady."

She grins, leaning down so her lips are almost touching mine. "I have to get to work."

"What's new?" I mutter, staring up at the ceiling.

"Don't be like that." Her lips brush mine. "I had a great lunch," she whispers, smiling.

I will myself to stay strong, but when her tongue sweeps into my mouth, I groan out loud and pull her down over me. She laughs harder as I roll and brace myself above her. "You're impossible," I murmur, slamming my mouth over hers in a bruising kiss. My cock instantly reacts to her . . . again. She sighs softly, running her fingers through my hair.

"I'd love to stay for another round, but I really need to go."

I could keep her here, she's usually easily swayed, but her work is important to her, and I know she'll be pissed if I keep her any longer. I drop face down beside her and rest my head on my arms. "Fine. Go."

"Enjoy the barbecue." I want to retort that it's impossible because she won't be there, but I remain quiet. The pushier I get, the further she runs. "And go for Cali. I think she likes you."

I bristle at her encouragement to fuck a club whore. I can never work out if she's being serious, in which case, it means she doesn't give a shit about me *or us*. Or if she says this crap to guard her heart. Maybe reassuring me it's okay to fuck around means she'll handle it better if I do. But it doesn't matter how much I prove myself—she still keeps me at arm's length, like she's just waiting for me to prove her right.

"I'm not gonna go," I say, pushing up from the bed.

She pauses in the doorway, chewing on the inside of her cheek thoughtfully as her eyes run over my naked body. "Why?"

"I'm gonna grab some food and chill up here."

"It's your President's birthday, you have to be there."

I grab a shirt and pull it on. "All Axel will be thinking about is getting Lexi alone," I say with a smirk. "Have a good afternoon at work." I pull my jeans on. "Text me when you get home tonight." It's the same request I always make because she refuses to let me take her home. *An independent pain in my ass.*

"It'll be a late one," she says casually.

It has the desired effect because I immediately look her in the eye. "Oh yeah?" I ask, my mind racing with thoughts about what she might be doing to keep her out late. "Well, I can always swing by and pick you up?"

"I'm a big girl." And she spins on her heel and heads out.

I groan out loud in frustration. We've been doing this hook-up dance for almost a year, and I'm as close now as the day I first put my dick in her. She tells me fuck all about her life, her past, even her family remain a mystery.

I put my boots on and head downstairs. Axel glances up from his desk. "Was that Anita I saw leaving?" I nod, stuffing my hands in my pockets and leaning in the doorway. "You good?" he adds, frowning.

"You ready for your party?" I ask, ignoring his question.

He rolls his eyes. "About as ready as a lamb is to slaughter."

I grin. "It won't be so bad."

"Lexi is currently hanging banners out there."

I laugh out loud, knowing how much he hates a fuss. "It makes her happy."

"That's the only reason I'm going along with this bullshit."

Grizz heads over. "Is he still complaining?"

"Nah, he's secretly excited."

"If she pulls out a birthday cake with candles, I'm done," Axel says firmly.

"Shit, Pres, she put loads of effort into that cake," Grizz whispers with a smirk. "She had a job getting all those candles on it though."

"Clearly, you two have nothing better to do," he states, pushing a piece of paper across his desk towards us. "Go and check out this place. It's a potential for more storage."

I grab it, glancing at the address. "We need more?"

"I'll explain in church tomorrow," he replies, going back to his laptop. "Get out of here before the old ladies sniff you out and force you to blow up balloons or some shit."

∼

I GET OFF MY BIKE AND STARE AT THE OLD WAREHOUSE. Grizz joins me, lifting his sunglasses. "Not very discreet," he comments. "And anyone driving past will see the entrance."

I glance around, nodding in agreement. "But hiding in plain sight sometimes works."

"I don't think we can afford to take that risk. Gemma reckons we're being watched by a task force."

"When are we not being watched by the police?" I ask, laughing.

"I saw Nita leaving earlier. Just a lunch call?" He smirks, heading towards the building.

I follow. "She's busy with work."

"She always is, brother. You just gotta pin her down and get your name on her skin."

I laugh. "I'm sure that'll go down well."

"I'm serious, brother. How long's she been dragging you along for?"

I shrug. "A year or so."

"Fuck, man. You have the patience of a saint. You gotta lock that shit down."

"It's not that easy," I mutter. "She's got shit going on that she don't wanna share with me, and if I push, she locks up completely."

"So, how long are you gonna let it go on?" he asks, pushing the door.

We go inside. The place is huge but not ideal. There's another entrance at the back, but it's insecure. "As long as she needs, brother," I say confidently, because I intend to stick it out for her. She's it for me.

ANITA

"What do you mean you're not coming?" Tessa demands. I sign the document she presented me with and slide it back across the desk.

"In case you've forgotten, I'm not his old lady."

"You're practically his old lady," she scoffs, taking the document.

"Why is everyone so obsessed with me and Atlas?" I'm being defensive, but I'm so tired of everyone treating me like his wife. "We're not together. I don't know why everyone struggles with that."

"Because you're meant to be," she says with sad eyes. "He's your king, and you're his queen." I arch a brow, and she begins to back out the room. "You're his lobster."

"Get out," I say firmly, "and don't interrupt me unless it's urgent."

"This is urgent," she argues. "You realise that one day, he'll meet someone, and you'll miss your chance."

I smile wide. "I can only pray for that day to come."

"Liar," she hisses, narrowing her eyes. "Where will you get your daily dose of D from?"

I laugh. "I'm not short on offers."

She shakes her head. "Don't let him hear you say that."

"Atlas doesn't care," I cry, throwing my arms in the air. "We're both happy hooking up. Now, drop it."

～

AT FOUR EXACTLY, TESSA POPS HER HEAD BACK INTO MY office. "I'm heading off." I nod. "Are you sure I can't change your mind? The girls would love to see you."

"I have a date," I say, and she gives me that sad look again. I close my laptop as the door opens, and I stare past her to see my date. I grin, stuffing the laptop away and grabbing my bag.

"An early date," Tessa mutters as I pass her.

"You found the place okay then," I say, ignoring her.

Jonathon is exactly as he described himself on the dating app, which is a rarity. I've met so many men who have lied about their age, their body, and even their relationship status.

"I did." He smiles and his white teeth gleam. Then he

leans down to place a quick kiss on my cheek. "It's great to finally meet you."

I lock up and say goodbye to Tessa, who is judging me, but I'll address it tomorrow.

We head to a bar at the end of the road. The bar workers know me here, so I always opt for this place in case anything goes wrong. You can never be too careful with dating apps.

"You're a lawyer," he says, shrugging from his jacket and placing it on the back of the chair. "Impressive."

I scoff, waving my hand dismissively. "I hate putting it on my profile because I tend to draw out all the criminals," I say with a laugh.

"Sometimes I prefer not to know," he admits, wincing. "At the risk of sounding like a pompous prick, certain jobs put me off. Can I get you a drink?"

I nod. "Just a lemonade."

He heads over to the bar, and I use it as an excuse to check out his tight backside. He's wearing a suit, which gives me hope he's got a good career. He rejoins me, this time taking his seat as he passes me the lemonade. "What jobs put you off?" I ask.

"Dog groomer," he announces, screwing up his face as I laugh. "The hair, the smell," he shakes his head, "I can't deal with that. Also, doctor or nurse, anything medical related." I arch a brow, and he leans closer. "Too busy. I need someone who'll have time for me."

"What do you do?" I ask, sipping my drink.

"Businessman," he says with a glint in his eye.

I scoff. "That covers a variety of things."

He grins, taking another sip of his drink. "Nothing shady, if that's what you're thinking."

"I've been doing this way too long," I say, running my

finger around the rim of my glass. "And I'll be honest, I get a warning sign flashing in my head when you talk."

He laughs, nodding. "Honesty, I like that." His attention is drawn to a buzzing in his suit jacket and he sighs, retrieving it and glancing at the screen. He places it back in his pocket, letting it ring out. It immediately rings a second time, and he gives an apologetic smile.

"You can get that if it's important," I say.

"It's nothing that can't wait."

When it rings a third time, he seems agitated, and my suspicions grow. It's a sixth sense I get when it comes to men. "Take the call," I say firmly.

"Really, it can wait."

"I insist." He eyes me for a second, warring with himself before taking the phone out again and pushing to stand. "Oh, please, take it here." He gives me another unsure glance, and I smile wide, nodding . . . daring him to answer. When he continues to hesitate, I roll my eyes and push to stand. "I can only assume that your reluctance to answer is because on the other end of that call is a long-suffering girlfriend . . ." I pause, gaging his reaction, and when his eyes dart to the phone, I laugh. "Wife . . . a long-suffering wife." This time, his eyes stare at the floor, and I grab my bag. "Pathetic."

"Listen, it's not what it looks—"

"If you're about to tell me she's awful to you and doesn't understand, save it." He presses his lips closed. "If she nags . . . if she doesn't give out . . . then you're doing something wrong. *You* are the problem. Because a woman who's treated right, she takes care of her man. I suggest you go home and get to the bottom of what you're doing wrong." I take a step then turn back. "And start with taking your profile off the dating apps."

I dump my bag on the bar and slide onto the tall seat.

"Another married one?" asks Claire, the barmaid, sliding a vodka my way. I nod, knocking it back and holding it out for a refill. "Bastard."

"I'm seriously thinking of dropping out of the dating game," I mutter, tapping my debit card to the card machine.

"Or you could just give in to the biker," she suggests, wiggling her brows.

I roll my eyes. "Not you as well. Me and Atlas aren't gonna happen. It's just fun."

CHAPTER 2

ATLAS

"It was a no go," Grizz tells Axel as we step into his office. "The place is too open."

"You sure?" asks Axel. "I thought it would be ideal."

"For what exactly?" asks Grizz.

"I called church early. I'll tell you my plans in there." He stands, and we follow him from the office.

"I'm your VP, shouldn't I already know?" mutters Grizz.

We all take our seats and wait for the other members to join us. Pit fist bumps me as he lowers onto the chair beside me. "Tessa wants me to head out after this and look for Nita," he says quietly so only I can hear.

I frown. "Why?"

"Apparently, Nita hasn't responded to her texts, and she's worried."

"Maybe she's just busy." Her words from earlier come back to me. "She said she had something on."

He sighs heavily. "A date," he mutters. "She went on a date, and Tessa's got it in her head that she's now lying in a ditch somewhere." He shakes his head. "I know there's some weirdos out there, but if I had to check on Anita every single time she went on a date, I'd basically be her personal bodyguard."

I clench my jaw. I suspected as much, but shit, what's so wrong with me that she can't just take what I'm offering? "Sorry, man. Tessa asked me not to tell you, but I'm sick of this bullshit every time she goes off radar. I don't get why Tessa feels so responsible for her."

I stand. "She's a good friend." I turn to Axel. "Pres, I gotta go. I'll catch up with shit later?"

He gives a nod, knowing I wouldn't walk out of church without good reason.

∼

MINUTES LATER, I'M TURNING MY BIKE INTO THE CAR PARK of Angelo's Bar. It's her favourite place to come because the staff know her.

The second I push the door open, I wince at the sound of Nita's singing. And there, on the bar, is the woman I love. Luckily, the place is deserted, with only the barmaid wiping glasses and the doorman sitting on a stool, watching Nita sway with clear amusement. He spots me and stands, shaking my hand. "I was gonna call, Atlas, but she lost her mind when I mentioned you, so I figured you were the reason she's in this state again."

I shake my head. "I'll never be the reason," I say firmly.

"Always call me." And I pass him a bundle of rolled up notes.

He takes them gratefully. "Sure thing, boss."

I head over to Nita, standing before her and holding up my hand. She groans dramatically and takes it, her singing coming to an abrupt end. I reach up and grab her around the waist, lifting her off the bar top with ease and placing her on the ground. "I told you not to call," she yells to the doorman.

I take her chin in my fingers and pull her gaze to me. "He didn't. Tessa was worried when you didn't answer her texts and calls."

"I'm fine," she cries.

"Would it hurt yah to tell her that?"

She pulls her chin from my grasp and picks up her drink. She keeps her defiant eyes trained on me as she tips it back, gulping the liquid down. Then she places it on the bar. "Another," she says, arching a brow like she's waiting for me to object.

The barmaid looks at me for direction, and I nod. "Give the lady what she wants," I reply, still holding the eye contact.

"Just say what you're thinking," Nita snaps.

I smirk. "Baby, you ain't in the right headspace to hear me."

She narrows her eyes. "Try me."

The barmaid tops up the glass, and Nita finally turns away. "Yah know what, I'm not staying here with you judging me." She taps her card against the payment machine but leaves the drink where it is, gathering her things and swaying in the direction of the door.

"Thanks," I tell the barmaid, and I follow her out into the car park.

Nita rolls her eyes, dropping her bag on the ground and

trying to put her coat on. I take it, holding it for her so she can slip her arms in. "I don't need you to keep showing up for me, Atlas."

"I know." I pick up her bag.

"And Tessa has no business telling you where I am."

"She didn't."

Nita scoffs. "So, how did you find me?"

"Call me clever."

She snatches her bag from me, spinning on her heel and almost toppling over. I take her arm to steady her before letting go and marching off in front. If I tell her to get on the bike, she'll only refuse and cause a fuss. Besides, I don't think she's in a fit state to ride pillion right now.

I eventually hear the sound of her heels following and smile to myself.

Ten minutes later, I stop outside her house, and she passes me, pulling her keys from her bag. When she sees I'm not behind her, she turns. "Aren't you coming inside?" I shake my head, and she forces a smile. "Fine. See you around."

See you around. Fuck, if she doesn't press every damn button. "Goodnight."

I turn to leave, and she adds, "I was on a date." I keep my back to her, my hands clenching as a jealous rage builds inside me. "He was hot."

"Go inside," I say through gritted teeth.

"Make me."

I turn back, and she's smirking. "Anita, you're drunk."

"I could call Jonathon back if you're not up to the job."

I don't know how I suddenly get up in her face, but she wraps her arms around me and pulls me inside, kicking the door shut and pressing her lips to mine in a hungry kiss. "I'm up to the job," I hiss, holding her neck loosely as I slide my other hand up her leg and under her skirt. "And if your date went so well, why the fuck were you singing all alone in the bar?" I shove my hand into her underwear, and she grips my shoulders, gasping. "Are you wet for me or Jonathon?" I snap, running my fingers through her folds. I pull my hand out and hold it up for her to see, and when she goes to speak, I shove my fingers in her mouth. Her eyes burn with need as she licks them clean. I want her. I want her so badly, my balls ache. But I step back and release her. "Go to bed, Nita."

She narrows her eyes. "You rushing back to someone?"

I almost laugh, shaking my head in annoyance. "I'm not like you," I say. "There is no one else for me. I thought I made that clear." I leave, slamming the door behind me and marching down the path before I can change my mind.

By the time I get back to the club twenty minutes later, church is over, so I go into Axel's office. "Sorry about that, Pres," I say, and he glances up. He points to the seat in front of his desk, and I take it.

"Pit told me it was about Anita." I nod. "She okay?"

I shrug. "She's difficult," I admit, and he laughs.

"Ain't they all?"

"I told her I'd never give up on her," I continue, "but I'm close."

"We all have a limit, brother. You've put a lot of time into her. We've all noticed."

"But she don't wanna be my old lady," I tell him, the words causing an ache in my chest. "And as much as I think deep down that she does, I can't keep putting myself through this torture."

Axel nods in understanding. "I get it," he says, "and we'll back you whatever. Hell, we'll find a different lawyer for the club if we need to."

I smirk. "Thanks, Pres. What did I miss?"

"There's a new club in town," he says, and I sit up

straighter. Gangs have come and gone, we've made sure of that, but a new biker club? "Relax, they're good. The president is an old friend of mine. He's setting up and was looking for somewhere to store his shit."

"What shit?"

"Mainly drugs," he mutters, glancing away.

"And we're okay with that?"

"You know I hate that side of things," he says. "If I can pass our business their way, knowing they're keeping it good quality like we have, I'm more than happy." The only reason the club took on that side of things was to stop gangs running shit onto our streets. I nod in understanding. "It means we can concentrate on weapons. It's what we're good at."

"And this club's gonna run alongside us?"

He nods. "I put it to a vote in church. All voted in favour."

"You know you have my vote, Pres. Whatever you think is good for us."

He leans forward. "You need to lay things on the line with Anita," he tells me, "then get your head in the game. We're gonna be busy, and if I can send you on runs, it might help you get over her."

I nod, pushing to stand. "I'll talk to her."

ANITA

My head is pounding, and I groan as I feel around for my mobile phone. Once it's in my hand, I drag it closer and force one eye open. "Shit," I mumble, when I see it's gone ten in the morning. I force myself to sit, grabbing the glass of water from the bedside table and gulping it down. It's warm—fuck knows how long it's been there—but right now, I don't care.

I drag myself into the shower and then dress for cold

weather, because standing on the football lines on a Saturday is always cold, no matter what time of year it is.

By the time I get across town to the football field Damian pinged to me yesterday, I'm very late. I sip on the black coffee I grabbed on the way here and sidle up to where Damian stands. He glances at me like I'm something he stepped in. "Late as usual," he mutters.

"Sorry. I worked late."

"Worked?" he questions, smirking. "Or played?"

"How's he doing?" I ask, focussing on my thirteen-year-old son, who's currently chasing after the ball.

"He scored two in the first half, then realised you were a no show and played shit in the second."

I bite my tongue, something I often do around this man. "So, they're winning?"

"No, Anita. Look at the damn board," he snaps, nodding in the direction of the large scoreboard.

The final whistle blows a minute later, and I groan. How the hell did I sleep through my alarm?

Leo runs over panting for breath and covered in mud. He grins wide, and I high-five him because, apparently, he's too big for hugs in front of his teammates. "Well done," I say. "You did amazing."

"You only just got here," snaps Damian, rolling his eyes.

Leo's smile fades, and I force a smile. "Two goals, that's amazing."

"Where was your head in the second half?" demands Damian. "If the scouts had shown up today, they wouldn't have looked twice."

I grit my teeth and inhale sharply. "Go and change, Leo, and I'll take you for lunch."

He nods, rushing off to change. "Not a chance," snaps Damian. "Firstly, he played crap, so he's not having a treat, especially if it involves junk food. And second of all, your day is Monday. You know that."

"Don't be spiteful. He can come for lunch, and I'll drop him back."

"Take him out Monday."

"I'll be an hour, Damian. He wants to come with me."

He turns to face me, stuffing his hands in his pockets and stepping closer. I hold my stance, determined not to let him intimidate me. "You look a fucking mess, Anita. You stink of drink and last night's cheap fuck. So, do us all a favour and leave."

I fix my eyes on his. "No," I say firmly. "He can decide for himself."

His cruel eyes narrow. "It's like you want to humiliate yourself. He doesn't want to go anywhere with you looking and smelling like that. He's embarrassed, we both are, but you keep showing up here like a desperate reject and he feels sorry for you."

Leo comes over carrying his kitbag and eyeing us cautiously. I step back, forcing another smile. "Are you ready?"

He glances at his father and then bites his lower lip like he's fighting to find the right words. "It's fine, son, be honest with her," Damian encourages.

"It's just . . . I want to go home and practise," he says, shrugging. "If I played crap, I need to put more hours in." My heart sinks at the sound of Damian's words pouring from my little boy's mouth. "And I don't want to eat junk food anymore," he adds.

I nod, pressing my lips in a firm line. "That's fine, kiddo, whatever you want. I'll pick you up on Monday from school?" He nods. "Great. Love you." I turn and force myself to walk away.

ATLAS

∽

I stride through the clubhouse like I own the place, and no one bats an eyelid. The club girls are tidying up from last night's party, and there's no sign of the bikers or their women.

I take the stairs two at a time, and just as I reach Atlas's door, it swings open and a woman saunters out. I stop dead in my tracks and frown, following her with my eyes. She's stunning but has all the marks of a club girl. "What?" she asks as she fiddles with her hair, wrestling it into a ponytail.

"Who are you?"

"Who the fuck are you?" she spits and then storms off in the direction of the stairs.

I open Atlas's door to find him sprawled out on his bed. He's face down, topless but his jeans still in place. I slam the door, and he jumps up looking dazed. When his eyes find me, he relaxes. "Nita," he mutters, looking confused. "What day is it?"

"Saturday," I mutter, folding my arms over my chest. "Good night?"

He perches on the edge of the bed and reaches for his mobile, opening it and sighing heavily. "Shit, it's almost twelve."

"New club girl?" I ask, arching a brow.

His frown deepens, then realisation hits him and he nods. "Yeah, Sasha, I think her name is. She's got a twin too."

I can't be pissed at him. I gave him the go-ahead. In fact, I encourage him all the time to get with other women as I don't need him thinking we're exclusive. But he's never actually done it. At least, not that he's told me.

"Well, she was rude," I mutter, pulling my top over my head and dumping it on the floor.

"She's not a morning person."

"You've spent a few mornings with her, have you?"

He frowns again. "What are you talking about?" I slide my jeans off, kicking my trainers with them. "And what are you doing?" he adds.

I go to him, placing my hands on his shoulders and climbing over his lap. "I saw her leaving here just now, and she was rude." I rub myself against him and slide the straps from my bra, down. "I need a release," I add, cupping his head in my hands and guiding him to my breasts.

He pulls back suddenly, lifting me from him and standing. "Stop," he snaps. Grabbing his own T-shirt and pulling it on. "Let me get this straight. You think I fucked a club girl, and then you come in here to fuck anyway?" When he says it like that, it sounds bad, but I shrug, pushing down my embarrassment. "You're just gonna fuck me after I fucked someone else?"

"I can get her back if you wanna try a threesome."

He growls and balls his fists by his sides. "Get out," he spits.

"What?"

"Get the hell out," he repeats.

"Atlas, come on," I say with a small laugh. "What's wrong?"

He crowds me, and I back up to the door with him towering over me. "I am done with this bullshit," he snaps. "I'm not being your secret fuck buddy for another second."

"You're not serious."

"Deadly. I'm gonna find myself a woman who wants me for me."

"I want you for you," I argue. "Things are just weird at the moment."

"So, tell me," he snaps. "Tell me what's going on in your life right now."

I clam up. The way he's towering over me and hissing his words, it reminds me of Damian, and I immediately recoil.

"Exactly," he snaps. "You use me, and I'm done with it, so get the hell out and don't come back."

"So much for not giving up on me," I mutter, dipping under his arm and grabbing my discarded clothes. I head for the door, and he slams his hand against it.

"Get dressed," he orders.

I scoff, grabbing the door handle and ripping it open. I storm down the stairs, and London steps in my path. "Hey, slow down. Where's the fire?"

"I need to go," I snap, feeling the tears on my lash line.

"Okay, and you can, but get dressed first."

I hear his heavy boots coming up behind me and stiffen. "Nita," he murmurs.

"I'm going," I snap, moving around London.

He continues to follow me as I step outside into the open. "Get dressed," he repeats. I unlock the car and pull the door open, throwing my clothes in the back. "Nita, you can't drive half-naked."

I narrow my eyes. "You think I care if anyone sees me?" I yell.

"Calm down," he mutters.

"Don't tell me how to act," I scream.

He takes me by the arms. "I'm not," he says firmly, and I stop struggling. "You're upset, I can see that. I'm sorry if I was too harsh back there. But please don't drive out of here upset and half dressed. If something happened, I'd never forgive myself."

I scoff. "Like you give a shit what happens to me."

"Of course, I do," he mutters patiently.

"Is that why you turn up to bars to rescue me, Atlas?" My tone is condescending. "You just love being the hero?"

He steps closer, pushing me against the car. "You drive me fucking insane," he mutters, "and every time I tell myself to stop, you pull some shit and I'm back at your feet like a goddamn puppy dog."

His hand gropes my breast, and he presses his erection against my stomach. "You're like a drug," he whispers, his lips finding mine. I reach between us, unfastening his jeans and shoving them over his backside. I wrap my leg around his waist, and he lifts me against the car, pressing himself at my entrance. "One day, you'll trust me enough to know I'd never fuck a club whore or anyone else. I'm yours," he pants, sinking into me. "Sasha was asking if I wanted breakfast."

Relief floods me and I cling to his shoulders, closing my eyes as his kisses travel down my neck and over my chest. "I love you, Nita. Only you."

CHAPTER 3

ATLAS

"We got it all on CCTV," says Grizz, laughing.

I roll my eyes. "Pervs."

"Hey, if you're gonna fuck in the car park, it's gonna get shown to the guys," says Fletch.

"And you knew we were gonna see it," states Axel, shaking his head, "cos you cleverly covered every part of her body from the cameras."

"A gentleman even when he's fucking her in the car park," Fury jokes.

"All that aside," says Axel, his tone more serious, "did you talk to her and straighten shit out?"

I shake my head. "Nah, it wasn't the right time."

"Brother, I'm gonna need to send you on a run," he adds.

I shrug. "It's fine. She don't check in with me on the daily."

"Only when she needs to fuck, right?" Grizz cuts in, his expression almost pitiful.

"Just send me the details," I mutter, pushing my breakfast away. "I'll be ready."

Axel nods once and jerks his chin towards the hallway. "Come to the office. We'll talk."

I follow him, leaving the others laughing. The door clicks shut behind us, cutting off the noise. Axel sinks into his chair and eyes me for a second too long.

"What?" I ask, folding my arms.

"You look like shit."

"Feel it too."

He leans back, lacing his fingers over his stomach. "You sure you're good for this run?"

I raise a brow. "You just said you needed me. Don't start going soft."

He smirks, but it's brief. "This one's not the usual. No drop-off, no guns, no threats."

"Well, I'm already disappointed."

Axel picks up a photo from his desk and slides it across to me. A young woman stares back at me, her eyes too wide, makeup smudged like she's been crying. "Name's Kasey. Her old man's some biker trash out in East Anglia. He ain't in a club, but he's been dealing with crews we don't like. Word is, she ran off. Last ping was a petrol station off the A47. She's got a half-sister who used to work for one of our legit fronts, and she asked for our help."

I frown. "You want me to track down some runaway kid?"

"I respect her sister. She was hard working, and she wouldn't ask unless she needed help."

I stare at the picture. "You want me to bring her back?"

"To the clubhouse, yeah. Keep her safe 'til her sister figures out next steps."

I rake a hand through my hair. "And why me?"

Axel fixes me with a look. "Because I trust you to protect her and not scare her off. And because you need to get your head straight."

I scoff. "Right. Send the lovesick dumbass to babysit."

"You said it, not me."

I stand, pocket the photo, and start for the door.

"Oh, and Atlas?" I pause. "This girl's been through shit. Handle her carefully."

I nod once, jaw tight. "Always do."

Then I leave, the image of the girl still burning behind my eyes, and something turning low in my gut.

～

I SIT WITH MY FEET APART AND MY ELBOWS RESTING ON MY knees. I glance up to find Tessa still watching me through curious eyes. "What?" I demand.

She shrugs, a small smile playing on her lips. "I used to be scared of you."

Since she got with Pit, she's gotten brave, and working for Nita probably helped with her confidence because she has to handle shitheads like me on a daily basis. "Oh yeah?"

"But the way you look after Nita . . ." She sighs with a wistful look on her face.

"If Pit saw you looking at me like that," I say with a smirk, and she laughs.

"I'm serious, Atlas. You have the patience of a saint, and I know that one day, she's gonna realise just how sweet you are."

I scoff. "Sweet? I ain't been called that before."

Anita's office door swings open, and a man storms out, not bothering to look in my direction as I stand. He slams the front door as he leaves, shaking the office windows. Tessa winces. "Always a pleasure," she mutters under her breath sarcastically.

"Who was that?" I ask, glancing back to see the man getting into a BMW.

Tessa shrugs. "He drops in every now and again. Always in that mood." I step closer to the desk, looking down at the sign-in book. "Oh, he doesn't bother filling that in either," she whispers. "No appointment and no record of his name."

I give a nod and head into the office to find Nita with her head down on the desk. "You all good?" I ask, and her head whips up.

"I told Tessa to tell you I was busy," she snaps.

"I tried," Tessa calls back in reply. "He said it was important."

Nita pushes to her feet, passing me and closing her door. "What was so important you couldn't just message me?" she demands.

"Who was the guy?" I ask.

She rolls her eyes. "Why are you here?"

"Who was the guy, Nita?"

A low, frustrated growl escapes her. "A client."

"Liar."

She eyes me. "It's confidential, Atlas."

"Must be if he doesn't sign in or book an appointment. Can anyone just turn up?"

"You need to go. I have another client due any minute, and I don't have time to nurse your jealous ego right now."

"Are you fucking him?"

She tips her head back and takes a deep, calming breath. "No."

I close the gap between us, towering over her to look her in the eye. "I'm serious, Nita. Who the fuck was he?"

There's a flicker of fear, just like there always is if I get too close, but this time, I'm not sure if it's because I'm too close to her life or in her face. One thing I know for sure is that guy meant something to her.

I step back, and she relaxes slightly. "I'm outta here for a while." She remains silent, her eyes following me as I back towards the door. "I don't know when I'll be back. Axel's got me on some rescue mission." I pull the door open, our eyes still connected. "When I get back, shit's gonna be different between us, Nita. You're either gonna let me in or let me go." Her chest rises with her sharp inhale.

~

THE ENGINE'S A LOW, CONSTANT GROWL BENEATH ME. I'VE been riding for an hour, maybe more. It's hard to keep track when all I can think about is Nita.

The wind cuts across my jaw, sharp and cold even in June. Nita's blank expression haunts me along with her sharp intake when I delivered that ultimatum. And that sinking feel I have in my gut, knowing she'll never let me in, and now I'll have no choice but to walk away.

And instead of staying and making her see we could work, I'm riding out on some halfway run because I'd rather chase ghosts down the A-roads than sit at the bar pretending I'm not wrecked over a woman who won't even admit she cares.

I roll my shoulders out and glance down at the map on my burner. The petrol station is up ahead. That's where she was last seen.

A lorry overtakes me, rattling like it's gonna fall apart. I twist the throttle and pass it easy, my eyes on the road, but my heart nowhere near it.

I pull into the petrol station. It's run-down, with flickering lights and two pumps. The kind of place you only stop at if you're running out of fuel or running from something else.

I kill the engine. The silence afterwards is deafening.

Inside, a bored-looking attendant leans on the counter, scrolling his phone. I flash the photo of Kasey.

"She been through here?"

He squints. "Yeah. Yesterday. Late. Looked strung-out, bit scared. Bought a bag of crisps and a Monster. Sat outside for a while then got picked up in some clapped-out Vauxhall."

"Driver?"

"Guy in his twenties. Skinny. Looked sketchy as hell."

Of course, he did.

"You see her again, call me."

"They headed in the direction of Norwich," he adds. "There are a lot of drugs on the streets there. She seemed the type to be looking."

I leave my number and head back to the bike. If she's with someone now, that complicates things. If she's not, she's vulnerable. Either way, she's mine to find.

As I swing my leg over the bike, I feel it, that old hum under my skin. Not lust. Not rage. The mission. The chase.

Maybe it's good I'm doing this. Something real. Something that ain't about Nita.

And maybe, just maybe, I can outrun the way she makes me feel before I go back and end things.

~

THE CITY'S NOTHING LIKE LONDON. IT'S SMALLER, DIRTIER, but the streets still pulse with life—neon signs flickering, music leaking from open doors, and bodies stumbling out of bars with too much drink and not enough sense.

The perfect place to disappear.

I park the bike then zip up my jacket and start walking. The photos in my back pocket are already worn soft from the ride.

I try the first bar. It smells like piss and sticky floors, and a couple girls at the bar are half-dressed and high. The bartender clocks me the second I walk in—patches always draw attention.

"Lookin' for someone," I say, sliding the photo across the bar.

He glances at it, then at me. "Maybe I've seen her. Maybe I haven't."

I flash a tight smile. "If you're about to ask for money, don't. I'm not in the mood."

He snorts. "Calm down, Rambo. Yeah, she came in last night. Didn't drink. Looked out of place."

"She alone?"

"No. With a guy. Greasy hair, twitchy. Tried to get her to go upstairs with him. She looked like she didn't want to, but he kept pressuring. She left before it got loud."

Something shifts in my gut. "Where'd they go?"

He shrugs. "Try over on Brighton Street. Dive bar called Maddie's. Real scumhole. If she's desperate or hiding, that's where she'll be."

I nod once. "Thanks."

As I walk, I light a cigarette. There's a thought in the back of my mind, questioning what the hell I might be walking into? Some scared kid caught up with the wrong crowd? Or bait set out by someone who wants to piss us off?

But Axel asked me to protect her. And the thing is, I

know what it's like to be young and in the dark, looking for someone to *give a fuck.*

Maddie's is two streets over, wedged between a pawn shop and a tattoo place that looks like you'd leave with tetanus. I step inside, scanning the crowd.

And there, in the far corner, near the toilets, I see her.

Leaning against the wall. Arms crossed. Talking to a guy with too many rings and too much attitude.

She's smaller than I expected. Thinner. Tired.

I don't go straight in. I hang near the bar, grabbing myself a beer and taking a seat just behind a support beam so I can watch her.

She's got that look, chin tilted like she's braver than she feels, legs crossed like she's comfortable, but one hand grips the edge of the table too tight. The guy talking to her leans in close. She keeps shifting back, eyes darting to the exit every few seconds like she's planning her escape.

I've seen that look before. Girls like her, they learn to scan every room. Look for danger and for exits. She's doing both.

She tries to laugh at something he says. It's flat. He puts a hand on her knee.

She flinches.

That's enough.

I drain what's left of my beer, set the bottle down, and cross the room.

The guy doesn't even notice me until I'm right behind him.

"Move," I say, low and steady.

He turns, blinking like he's trying to figure out whether to puff his chest or piss himself. "What the fuck?"

I hold up my patch-covered cut and raise a brow. "Say that again."

His eyes scan my badge and suddenly he doesn't look as confident.

Kasey looks up at me, wide-eyed. "Who are you?"

"Someone your sister sent." I look back to the guy. "Last chance, dickhead."

He bolts. Doesn't even say a word. Just grabs his coat and slides out the side door like smoke.

Kasey stands, still holding her bag like she expects me to snatch it.

I nod towards the exit. "We should talk. Not here."

She doesn't move.

"You really from the club?" she asks, voice sharp with doubt.

I pull the photo from my jacket and hold it up.

"I've been riding half the country looking for you."

"Congrats," she mutters. "You found me. Now, what?"

I jerk my chin towards the door. "Now, I take you somewhere safe."

She hesitates then grabs her drink and downs the last of it. "Fine, but if you're planning on locking me in a basement or selling me to some creepy biker friend, I'll stab you in your sleep."

I crack the first smile I've felt all day. "You'll fit right in."

We roll into the edge of town just after midnight. I find the least flashy, least memorable bed and breakfast I can, the kind with a flickering neon 'VACANCY' sign and zero questions asked at the front desk.

The woman behind the counter gives me a once-over and doesn't bother hiding her distaste. "Just the one room?" she asks.

"Yeah, separate beds."

Kasey scoffs behind me. "How romantic."

She hands me a key, her judging eyes watching as we both head upstairs.

The room smells like old toast and cleaning spray. Two twin beds, one rattling radiator, and a suspicious stain on the curtain. I toss my bag onto the nearest bed and lock the door behind us.

She drops her jacket and flops onto the other bed like she owns the place.

"I'm not gonna run, you know," she mutters, staring at the ceiling.

"You thought about it though."

She shrugs. "I always think about it."

I don't reply. I sit down, pull off my boots, and set them neatly by the wall. My gun goes under my pillow, not because I think she's dangerous but because it's habit. She watches me the whole time.

"You always sleep with that thing?"

"Only when I'm babysitting."

She smirks. "Cool. I've been downgraded to a toddler. I don't need you looking after me," she says after a moment.

"I'm here to get you back to the clubhouse in one piece."

She rolls onto her side, facing away from me. Her voice is quieter now. "You have kids?"

I blink. That one hits deeper than I expect. "No."

"You talk like you might've."

I don't answer that.

She shifts again. "Is it true what they say? About clubs like yours?"

"What do they say?"

"That women disappear. That you sell girls, kill people, that sort of thing."

I snort. "You watch too many shit documentaries."

"But you *have* killed people," she says. Not asking. Stating.

I don't answer that either.

She finally goes quiet. Ten minutes pass. Then twenty. Her breathing slows. I think she's asleep, until she whispers, barely audible, "Thanks for coming to find me."

I stay silent. But I hear it, the crack in her voice, and for the first time since Nita slammed the door on me, something in my chest shifts. Just a little.

ANITA

I stare at the phone longer than I should.

No messages. No missed calls. No smug little text from Atlas reminding me what I'm missing.

Good.

I toss the phone onto the sofa and cross the apartment, heels echoing off marble tiles. Everything here is curated—polished, modern, detached. Just like me.

I'm dressed for dinner. My hair is pinned into a messy updo and my dress is sharp, with a neckline low enough to distract from how much I don't want to be going. *Another date.* Another man who ticks all the boxes. Educated. Safe. *Boring.*

And not him.

Atlas hasn't reached out since yesterday when he left the office. Not even a smartass comment through one of the guys. I never usually go a couple hours without him calling me or showing up. I should be pleased that he's given me an out.

So, why do I feel so empty?

The buzzer sounds, and I grab my clutch, checking my reflection one last time. Lipstick flawless. Smile locked in.

Let the performance begin.

Damian always preferred this kind of place. Elegant, expensive, cold. My date, Anthony, fits in well. He orders wine without asking and tells me about his rich family like I'm meant to be impressed.

I laugh at all the right moments. I nod when I'm supposed to. I even let him touch my hand across the table.

But the whole time, I'm wondering where Atlas is. What job Axel sent him on. Whether he's sleeping with someone else tonight. Whether she's younger. Softer. Less of a goddamn coward than I am.

"You're quiet," Anthony says, tilting his head.

"Just tired," I lie.

He smiles. "I'd love to help you unwind."

It takes everything in me not to recoil.

Instead, I offer a polite smile and excuse myself to the bathroom. I lock the door behind me and lean against the sink, heart hammering.

What the hell am I doing?

Atlas is wrong for me. He's messy, violent, reckless. My parents would faint. Damian would use it in court. Leo might hate me.

But the way he cares for me, the way he looks out for me. It's the first time I've ever felt safe. And something inside me is screaming to tell him the truth, because the finality in his eyes as he left yesterday, scares the crap out of me.

I open my clutch and pull out my phone. *Still nothing from him.*

I lean my head back and stare at the glittering lights on the ceiling. "Come on, girl. Get it together," I whisper.

I return to the table with a fresh coat of lipstick and the same frozen smile.

Anthony stands when I approach, polite, polished, completely performative. Just like this whole evening.

"You okay?" he asks as I sit down.

"Of course." I fold my napkin back across my lap like nothing's unravelling inside me.

He launches into another story about business in Dubai, something about investors and property and *maximising market volatility*. I nod along, but my brain tunes out. My gaze drifts to the couples around us—the flicker of candlelight, laughter, fingers brushing over white tablecloths.

I try to picture Atlas here.

He'd hate it. Probably insult the wine list and order a beer they don't stock. He'd sit too close, say something crude, smirk like he knew I'd soak through my knickers when he whispered what he'd do to me under the table.

And I would.

"Nita?" I blink, pulled sharply back. Anthony is watching me, head tilted. "You looked miles away."

"Sorry," I say. "Just a long day."

He smiles like he understands. He doesn't. "You know . . . I was thinking. We should go away for a weekend. Somewhere calm. Tuscany, maybe."

Tuscany.

I try to imagine it. I see the rolling hills, the wine, the silence. And me, sitting in a silk robe on a balcony with a man I don't want, wondering if Atlas will show up just to ruin it.

"I'd like that," I lie.

Because that's what I do—I choose the path with the least resistance. The one that earns the approval of people who never had to fight to be respected.

Anthony reaches over and brushes his fingers against my wrist. The gesture is meant to be romantic.

It makes my stomach turn.

He's not dangerous. He's not possessive. He's not grabbing my waist like he owns it. He's not Atlas.

And that's the *whole* fucking point.

~

ANTHONY PULLS UP OUTSIDE MY BUILDING IN A CAR SO SLEEK it looks like it doesn't touch the road. Silent. Sculpted. Soulless.

The engine hums as he cuts it. "Is this you?" he asks, glancing up at the apartment block.

I nod.

His expression doesn't shift much, but I see it—that faint wrinkle of disapproval. Like he's trying to make sense of a designer bag hanging in a discount store window.

"It's . . . modern," he says diplomatically.

"It's central," I reply.

And it is. It's expensive, minimalist, high-end by most standards. But not *his*. Not guarded-gate-and-private-lift enough.

It's only the third date and I can see it clearly, the pressure to be something else, something better. The subtle nudges, the reshaping. It took months of therapy to see the signs, the same ones I went through with Damian. And even though I see them clearly, I'm still here, smiling politely, wanting him to pick me. *Pathetic.*

He opens the door before the valet can move and walks me to the entrance like he's guiding a guest. His hand finds the small of my back again, gentle, possessive in that soft, acceptable way.

My stomach coils as we pause by the steps.

"I enjoyed tonight," he says. "I feel like we've really connected."

I smile, automatic. "Me too."

He leans in. And I let him. His lips brush mine. They're soft, dry, careful. He kisses like someone following a tutorial. Exactly the right pressure. Exactly the right pause. It doesn't make my heart race. It doesn't make my knees weak.

It doesn't make me feel anything.

When he pulls back, he's smiling like we've sealed a deal.

"I'll call you tomorrow," he says. "Maybe book something for next week?"

"Sure," I say, voice barely above a whisper.

He waits for me to go inside before returning to his car. I watch him drive away, the lights vanishing into the city.

Inside the lift, I stare at my reflection in the polished steel walls. Lipstick barely smudged. Hair still perfect.

Everything in place.

Third date, I think, *and already he's choosing restaurants, destinations, future weekends. Already he's nudging me away from my postcode and into his world. Already I'm being reshaped.*

And still, somehow, *he fits the brief.*

But all I can think about is how Atlas kisses me with his whole body. With his hands, his teeth, his damn heartbeat.

And this one barely grazed the surface.

I press the button for my floor, pulse oddly steady. Safe *is* the right choice.

So, why does it feel so damn suffocating?

CHAPTER 4

ATLAS

I wake up to the smell of burnt toast and cheap coffee drifting through the thin walls. Light filters in through the grimy curtain, casting a weird yellow hue across the room. Kasey's already up, sitting cross-legged on her bed, scrolling her phone like she didn't just spend the night in a damp room with a stranger.

"You sleep?" I ask, rubbing a hand over my face.

She shrugs. "Enough. You snore."

"You hungry?" I ask, standing and stretching. My spine cracks like a firework.

"Yeah. But if this place serves real tomatoes over tinned, I'm out."

We head down to the dining room. The wallpaper's peeling and the chairs wobble when we sit, but the coffee's strong and the toast looks edible. Kasey stabs at her breakfast with her fork like it insulted her.

"Where're we going today?" she asks, not looking up.

"Clubhouse. Straight through."

"And then what?" Her tone's light, but her grip on the fork tightens.

"You stay under protection until your sister figures out what's next. That's all I know."

She nods slowly. "You always do what you're told?"

"No," I say, sipping my coffee. "But this time, yeah."

She chews in silence, then glances over at me. "My dad used to be in some crew. Nothing official. Small-time. Then he got into the harder shit. Smack. Trafficking. All of it."

I watch her closely, letting her speak at her pace. "He used to lock me in my room when he had 'visitors.' Told me if I came out, I'd end up like my mum."

I clench my jaw. "Where's he now?"

"Don't know. Don't care. But someone's been asking for me, someone he knows. Saying I stole from them. I didn't. I swear."

"I believe you," I say, and mean it.

She picks at the crust of her toast, not meeting my eyes. "You know, I didn't think anyone would actually come. When my sister said she was sending someone, I thought maybe she was just trying to make me feel better."

"She did more than that. She sent *me*."

Kasey finally looks at me. "And you're the best of the best?"

I grin. "Do I need to be?"

She nods. "Maybe. If they find me."

"Then I'm the best of the best. No one's gonna get to you whilst you're under the Chaos Demons."

She gives a satisfied nod. "You're lucky, Atlas," she says, pushing to her feet. "I like you. There're not many men I like or trust."

"What makes me different?" I ask, chucking some cash down on the table. She eyes it, glancing around to see where the waitress is. I grab her wrist just as she's about to take it. "Don't even think about it," I warn. "If you trust me, then know you don't have to steal anymore, kid. I've got you."

She grins. "Kid?" she repeats, following me outside. "Interesting choice of words when you've spent half the time trying to avoid looking at my tits."

I keep my eyes fixed forward as she rushes to walk beside me. "You don't have to do that anymore either," I add.

"What am I doing?"

"Using sex to distract me from seeing you."

"I didn't mention sex," she says, hooking her arm through mine. "But if you wanna go there, we don't need to check out until three."

"Does all that usually work?" I ask.

"Are you asking if men usually fall at my feet?"

"I'm asking if you offer yourself so openly just to get out of embarrassing situations."

She unhooks her arm. "I wasn't embarrassed you called me out for wanting to take the money," she snaps defensively. "That waitress wouldn't have given two shits."

I stop, turning to face her. "You think?" I ask. "And what about the tenner tip I threw on top that's rightfully hers?"

"I doubt she'd miss it."

I scoff. "Cos she wants to work in a greasy spoon for minimum wage, on her feet all day, just so you can come along and rip her off."

"Relax, I didn't even take it," she hisses.

"A word of warning before we get back to the clubhouse —don't bite the hand that feeds you."

"You sure you don't have kids, cos you're acting like a dad right now."

I drop the keys in the checkout box and head for the bike with Kasey hot on my tail. "Maybe if you had someone act like a dad before now, you wouldn't be stealing money off tables." I throw my leg over and hold out a helmet for her.

She takes it with a smirk. "Can I call you daddy?"

I shake my head in irritation. "Get on the damn bike."

∽

THE ENGINE'S HOT BETWEEN MY THIGHS AS WE ROAR DOWN the final stretch of road leading to the clubhouse. The second the place comes into view with bikes lined out front, smoke curling from the firepit, and someone revving in the garage bay, something in me settles.

It's messy. Loud. And home.

Kasey shifts behind me, arms tightening around my waist. She hasn't said a word since the petrol stop an hour ago. Maybe she's tired. Maybe she's finally thinking instead of performing.

I kill the engine just outside the front doors. A few of the guys glance over, eyebrows raised when they spot the girl sliding off my bike.

"Who's the brat?" Fletch mutters under his breath, nudging Grizz beside him.

Kasey hears—of course, she does—so she straightens her jacket, tosses her hair, and gives them both a slow, sugary smile. "Hi, uncles."

Grizz nearly chokes on his smoke.

I nod towards the clubhouse doors. "Go inside. Left corridor. Find Axel. Don't touch anything on the way."

She rolls her eyes but obeys, hips swaying more than necessary. The kid's exhausting.

I turn towards the others. "She's under protection. Axel'll explain the rest."

"You sure about this?" Grizz mutters. "She looks like trouble."

"Yeah," I reply, watching her disappear through the door. "But she's our trouble now."

The guys fall silent. Because when you say that—*ours*—it means something.

Inside, the place smells like leather, beer, and testosterone. Kasey's standing in the hallway, staring at a wall covered in framed photos and yellowed newspaper clippings. Some of the headlines are flattering. Most aren't.

"Cozy," she murmurs as I lead her through the common area to Axel's office.

He's already waiting, leaning back in his chair, phone to his ear. He ends the call and tosses it onto the desk, his eyes cutting to Kasey immediately.

"You're smaller than I expected," he says.

"Thanks," she says dryly. "Most people open with *hello*."

Axel smirks. "You'll fit in just fine."

He glances at me. "Ride okay?"

"Smooth. No tails."

"Good. You've got two hours before Fury takes over. Thought you could use the rest."

I nod but don't move. "She stays in a guest room?" I ask.

Axel raises a brow. "Where else would she go?"

Kasey folds her arms. "You gonna frisk me for weapons, or do we pretend this is a sleepover?"

"She's fine," I mutter, already tired.

Axel watches her a beat longer then tosses me a key. "Room at the end of the hall on your floor. She's under lockdown, but no handcuffs . . . *unless she asks*."

Kasey grins. "Kinky."

I groan and lead her out.

~

The room's clean but bare. A twin bed, chest of drawers, a lamp with a broken shade. Nothing fancy, but it's safe. And for Kasey, that's something.

She perches on the edge of the bed, suddenly quieter. Almost . . . shy.

"Will it be like this every day?" she asks.

"What?"

"Being watched. Locked down. Treated like a liability."

I lean in the doorway. "Only until we know you're safe."

She nods, shrugging. "Still beats my old life."

I study her a moment. "You did good. Back there, on the road." Her head lifts. "I know you're scared," I add, "but you held it together."

She swallows. "Thanks." It's the first time she's not come back with her smart mouth.

I turn to leave but pause. "Kasey?"

"Yeah?"

"No more stealing. No more mouth when it's not needed. And no calling me *daddy*."

She laughs, not her fake, flirtatious one, but something real. Lopsided. Honest. "Okay, *dad*," she says under her breath.

I close the door behind me, shaking my head.

ANITA

Two days have passed. Two whole days, and I've heard nothing from Atlas at all.

Tessa barges into the office holding a pile of files. "These are all up to date," she says, dumping them on a chair. She pauses, eyeing me suspiciously. "You have that look in your eye," she says. "You're thinking about him."

"About Anthony," I say, adding a wistful smile.

She narrows her eyes further. "No, Atlas."

I scoff, trying to throw her off. "I am not. Anthony suggested we book a mini break, so I was thinking about that."

"A mini break?" she repeats. "Where to?"

"Tuscany."

Her eyes widen in surprise. "You hardly know him."

"I know," I utter, my words sounding defensive. "He's not whisking me away right now. It was just an idea."

She lowers into the seat beside the files. "Don't you think it's a bit weird? You've been on two dates—"

"Three," I correct.

"And now he's offering you weekends away."

"It's just how them sort of guys do it," I say with a shrug.

"What kind of guys?" When I don't reply, she laughs. "You mean rich guys?"

"Business types," I mutter.

"Is that why you refuse to admit how you really feel about Atlas? Because he's not running his daddy's company and handing out free mini breaks with every fuck?" I almost gasp aloud at her words. It's not like her, but she's clearly irritated, so I stay quiet. "Anita, you're my friend and my boss and I love you. But seriously, what are you doing?"

I straighten. "You're right, I am your boss," I say firmly, fixing her with a hard glare, "and you're out of line. I suggest you go back to your desk." The words hurt me as much as they do her and she instantly leaves, closing the door gently behind her. *Fuck.*

It's almost six by the time I finish up, and I'm not

shocked to see Tessa has already left without saying goodbye. I'll make it right with her tomorrow when I'm feeling less moody.

I start my car, and it stutters before jumping to life. It wants to give out on me, I know it. Then an idea forms, and instead of heading for home, I drive towards the Chaos Demons' garage, just in case it's still open.

My stomach lurches as I turn down their street to see the shutters still up and the lights on. I pull onto the forecourt and turn off the engine. The thought of seeing Atlas fills me with excitement. We've had many evenings in this garage, me bent over someone else's car, sometimes even in it.

I smirk as I climb out and head towards the office. My hand pauses on the door at the sight of a young female sitting in the office chair with her feet on the counter, and sitting on the counter facing her, with his back to me, is Atlas.

She spots me before I can turn away, so I push the door open and step inside. "Evening, welcome to Chaos Cars. How can I help you?" Her voice is syrupy sweet, and she's clearly mocking in tone as she eyes Atlas with a cheeky glint.

"I told you, kid, you don't have to overdo it," he says, his voice gravelly deep as he turns to face me. He stiffens slightly. It's subtle but I notice.

"You're back," I say, the words slipping out before I can stop them.

"I was gonna call round tonight," he mutters. His body language is off, like he doesn't want me here in his space, and I wonder if the young girl staring back and forth between us has anything to do with that.

"I have car trouble," I say, glancing behind me at my car. "It keeps making a funny noise when I start it up. I think it's going to die on me."

"We're fully booked," says the girl, tapping her pen on her chin.

My eyes meet his, and he gives a slight shrug. "I was about to close up," he says, "but I can take a quick look."

I'm already shaking my head and backing out the office. "Don't worry, I'll try another time."

"I can book you in," the girl offers, standing to grab the large book off the desk. I notice her cropped top and lack of bra immediately. *Younger. Prettier. More fun.*

"I'll call to do that," I mutter, turning on my heel and rushing out.

I breathe the fresh air in deep, as I fumble with my keys.

"Wait." His voice is deep and commanding, but I keep my back to him. "I'll look at it," he adds, stepping beside me and plucking the keys from my hand.

I watch as he climbs into my driver's seat and starts the engine. It makes the whirring sound, and I relax slightly, pleased it doesn't look like I lied to be here. He turns it off and tries again. "You been okay?" he asks, not looking at me.

"Yeah. You?"

He nods. "Busy."

"I can see."

He glances up at me, his eyes slightly narrowed like he's trying to work out the meaning behind my words. "It sounds like the starter motor," he adds, turning the engine off and stepping out. He drops the keys in my hand. "I can order the part." I nod. "And if you're free later, I can stop by."

The office girl is watching us through the window, her arms resting across the desk like she's fully invested in us. "New girl?" I state, nodding past him.

"Kasey," he says.

"Is she a club girl or . . ." I trail off.

"No," he says simply. I wait a beat, hoping he'll explain,

but when he doesn't, my stomach ties in knots. "So, later?" he asks.

"I have plans," I mutter, throwing my bag across to the passenger side.

"You came all this way with some bullshit story about your car. Don't pretend you don't wanna see me, Nita."

I bristle at his words. "I was passing and saw the light on. Thought I'd ask you to check it wasn't more serious," I say.

"Hey, Daddy, we going home or what?"

Atlas stiffens at Kasey's words, rolling his eyes and shaking his head. "Ignore her. She's trying to piss me off," he mutters.

"Enjoy your evening," I almost whisper as I slip into the car.

Atlas braces himself in the doorway, leaning down to look at me. "When can we talk, Nita?"

I start the engine. "There's nothing to say," I mutter.

"You heard me before I left, right?"

"Jesus, Atlas. Stop pushing me all the goddamn time," I snap. "Go fuck the new girl. She's got her tits out especially for you." I begin to back out, and he steps back. I slam the door and pull off at speed, instantly regretting my childish words. I groan out loud. *Fuck.*

CHAPTER 5

ATLAS

I watch her rear lights vanish down the road, the sound of her engine still echoing in my chest like the words she just threw at me.

Go fuck the new girl.

I exhale hard and rake a hand through my hair.

"She's got her tits out especially for you," I mutter, mimicking. Like I asked Kasey to show up braless and mouthy. Like I haven't spent days aching for a woman who won't let herself be wanted.

Behind me, I hear the door creak.

"You really know how to pick 'em," Kasey says, stepping into the open air and stretching like she hasn't just poured petrol on a fire.

"Don't," I warn, still facing the road.

"What? I didn't *do* anything."

I turn to her slowly. "You called me *daddy*. . . again."

She shrugs, unbothered. "Yeah, and judging by her face, that word hits different in her world."

I stare at her, jaw tight. "You wanna keep stirring shit, or you wanna stay under protection?"

Kasey doesn't flinch. "Look, I don't care who she is, but she came in here like she owned you. Didn't like what she saw, so she stormed out and tried to make you feel small."

"She didn't make me feel anything," I lie, heading back inside.

She trails behind. "That's not what your face says."

I stop short, turning just as she crosses the threshold. "You want to keep pushing, go for it. But don't mistake whatever that was for something it's not."

She lifts a brow. "Which part? The way she looked at me like I was dogshit, or the way you looked at her like your heart just fell out your ribcage?"

I stare at her a long second. "Go do something useful. Find the broom. Sweep the bay. Stay out of my business."

Kasey rolls her eyes and backs away slowly, hands in the air. "Whatever you say, boss man."

When she disappears inside, I lean against the shutter frame and drag a hand over my face. I can still smell Anita's perfume. Feel the heat in her voice when she told me she had plans. The sting in her eyes when she saw Kasey.

She thinks I want someone else?

No. She *wants* me to want someone else. It'd be easier. *Cleaner.*

I SHOULDN'T BE HERE. SHE MADE HER FEELINGS PRETTY fucking clear when she peeled off like I'd slapped her.

The concierge tries to stop me at the front desk. I stare once, say her name, and he folds like paper.

She lives on the eighth floor. Clean, glassy, sterile. The kind of building that doesn't have room for men like me. The hallway smells like lemons and expensive silence.

I knock once. Then twice, harder.

Nothing.

I'm about to turn away when the door swings open and there she is.

Barefoot. In joggers and a vest top. No makeup. Her hair scraped into a messy bun like she's halfway through a breakdown or a Netflix binge.

She freezes.

"Jesus Christ," she mutters. "What the hell are you doing here?"

I lean against the doorframe. "Checking if your starter motor's acting up again."

"Piss off."

"You gonna slam the door in my face?"

She hesitates. That's all I need. I shoulder my way past her into the flat.

"Make yourself at home," she snaps, slamming the door behind me.

"Thanks. Don't mind if I do."

The place looks like a magazine spread. Designer couch. Art she probably doesn't even like. It's her and not her, all at once. Too polished. Too cold.

She crosses her arms and glares. "Did you come here to gloat?"

"No."

"To throw the word *jealous* in my face? Cos I'm not."

"You sure about that?" I ask, turning to face her fully.

"Because you nearly took my fucking head off over a girl who wears crop tops and lives to piss me off."

"She called you *daddy*," she spits. "What was I supposed to think?"

"That she's a kid I was told to protect, not fuck." She flinches. "Or," I continue, stepping closer, "you could've trusted me. But that's never been your style, has it, Nita?"

Her chin lifts. Defensive. Proud. God, she's beautiful when she's pissed.

"I *do* trust you," she lies. "I just . . . I saw her there and it caught me off guard."

"You think I'm screwing someone else. You think I moved on. Hell, you *want* me to move on. You keep pushing me away like I'm some bad habit you're trying to quit."

"I'm trying to protect my life!" she shouts suddenly. "You don't get it, Atlas. You never did. I can't have people like you in it and expect everything to be okay."

I step in, closing the gap between us. "You mean people who make you feel something." She doesn't speak. "You'd rather marry a man who makes your parents smile at dinner than admit you love someone who'd burn the world down for you."

Her eyes flash. "You don't know what I feel."

"I know," I say quietly, "because I feel it too."

We're nose to nose now. Her breath's shaky. Mine's a wildfire.

"You were supposed to be gone longer," she says, voice cracking. "I thought I had more time."

"To do what? Replace me?"

"No. To forget."

I nod slowly, jaw clenched. "Then you're fucked. Because I'm not going anywhere."

I reach up and tuck a strand of hair behind her ear. She doesn't stop me.

"Nita," I murmur, "just let yourself want this."

"I already do," she breathes.

I close the distance and kiss her, slow at first, then deeper. All heat and heartbreak and every unsaid thing that's been building between us for months.

She grabs my shirt. I lift her onto the counter without breaking contact. Her legs wrap around my waist like they remember every second we ever spent in the dark.

She tugs at my shirt, and I make quick work of ripping it over my head and discarding it to the floor. "I should shower," I murmur between desperate kisses.

She shakes her head, tugging her own shirt off as her kisses work along my jaw. She lifts slightly, allowing me to remove her joggers, and then I loosen my belt before she takes over, fisting my cock. "Shit, I've missed this," she breathes, pumping her hand slow.

She lines me up to her entrance, bracing her hands back on the counter as I thrust into her, savouring the feel of her tightening around me. I pause, gathering myself. "I need this all the time," I mutter, gently tilting her head back so we're eye to eye. "All. The. Time."

"Just fuck me," she pants, wriggling against me.

I hiss, unable to control myself as I grip her hips and fuck her. Hard and fast. Exactly how she likes it.

She comes, crying against my chest as her body shudders involuntarily. It's seconds before I follow her over the edge, filling her. I thrust one last time and still, resting my forehead against her shoulder whilst we both catch our breath.

She's still trembling, arms around my neck, breath hot against my throat. Her skin smells like sweat and something sweeter, something that's *hers*. I brush her hair back, press a kiss to her temple, and let myself believe for one stupid second that this is what normal could feel like.

"I should clean up," she murmurs after a moment, voice hoarse.

I nod, slipping out of her. "You want me to run you a bath?"

Her eyes flick to mine, surprised, like the idea of someone looking after her short-circuits something in her brain. "No. I'll just jump in the shower."

She slides off the counter, legs shaky, grabbing her shirt from the floor and disappearing into the bathroom.

I breathe in, out. Heart still thudding. I rest my hands on the counter where her body just was, trying to ground myself. Trying not to think about what the hell this means, or if she'll even let it mean something tomorrow.

The door buzzer sounds, and I frown, wondering who would be calling after seven. I pace to the intercom screen. The guy looking around, waiting, looks damn near picture perfect, like a preppy dream straight out of a romance novel. Smart suit. Hair that probably hasn't moved all day. And in his hand is a bouquet of pale pink roses, the kind florists charge triple for just because they're *imported.*

I stare at the screen. My pulse kicks up for a whole different reason now.

Another buzz.

I glance back towards the bathroom. The shower is still running, meaning she hasn't heard.

He buzzes again, insistent now.

I hit the button.

"Yeah?"

He straightens, clearly not expecting *me* to answer. "Um, sorry, I must have the wrong apartment. I'm looking for Anita?"

"She's busy," I say, my voice low and flat.

"I'm sorry, who is this?"

I grin, even though he can't see it. "The guy she was underneath five minutes ago."

Silence.

Then, a clipped, "Tell her I dropped by."

"Will do."

I end the call.

The bathroom door opens behind me, steam rolling out, and Anita steps into the hall, towel wrapped tight, her hair damp and curling at the edges.

She freezes when she sees my face.

"What?"

"Your little boyfriend just came by. Brought you flowers."

Her eyes widen, panic flickering. "*What?*"

"Roses. Expensive ones. Pale pink. He buzzed the door like he's done it a hundred times."

"Oh my god." She scrambles to the intercom. "What did you say?"

"I told him the truth."

She turns slowly, eyes wide with disbelief. "You didn't."

"I said you were busy. And then I might've added that you were under me about five minutes ago."

"Atlas," she snaps, flustered now, pacing towards the window like she can still catch a glimpse of him, but he's long gone. "Why would you *do* that?"

"Because he doesn't belong in your fucking doorway, Nita. You had my cum dripping down your legs, and he shows up playing Romeo?"

"That's *not* the point," she hisses. "This is messy enough already!" She storms to her bedroom, and I follow, leaning in the doorway to watch her as she rushes to dress.

"Tell me who he is," I say. "Tell me why you won't just be with me."

"It's complicated," she cries.

"Tell me and I'll uncomplicate it for you."

She stops, her eyes full of pain. "If it was that simple, don't you think I'd have told you everything by now?"

She shoves her feet into her trainers. "Where are you going?" I follow her to the door.

"To sort out the mess you just made."

I glare. "You're going after him?" She doesn't answer, just looks down at the floor with one hand on the door. "If you walk out of here, we're done," I say, my heart slamming against my chest. "I mean it."

She waits a beat, then pulls the door open and rushes out, letting it slam closed behind her. I stare at it, willing it to open, willing her to come back and tell me she picks me. But when she doesn't, I take a breath, shake out my shoulders and release it slowly. "It's done now," I mutter to myself. "Let her go."

ANITA

I hate this part of London. I mean, it's beautiful to look at and growing up here I was the envy of my friends, but there's something about the white buildings with their posh gold door knockers and black gated fencing that makes me feel uncomfortable. Like I'm no longer good enough to be here.

Anthony never gave me his address, so I don't know how he'll react to me just showing up, but I did my research and realised he lived just two streets away from my childhood Kensington home.

I raise my hand and grip the lion shaped knocker, gently tapping it a few times before crossing my arms and looking around the area, praying Atlas hasn't followed me. The door opens and Anthony takes a surprised step back. "Anita," he murmurs, clearly confused by my dripping wet hair.

I'm suddenly self-conscious, running my hand over the tangled locks. "I'm so sorry. I came to explain," I rush to say.

He glances around the street, probably hoping the neighbours haven't spotted me, before taking my arm and guiding me inside. He turns on the lamp by the door and takes a second to scan me with curious eyes. "Are you okay?"

"Yes . . . no . . . I'm not sure."

His frown deepens. "Take your shoes off and come through," he mutters.

I kick off my trainers and follow him through the large hall to a kitchen that mirrors the one I grew up in. "You have a beautiful home," I compliment. "Have you lived here long?" I spot the discarded bunch of roses on the side, and he follows my eyeline.

"I wanted to surprise you, only you beat me to it," he says dryly.

"About that," I mutter, avoiding his eye. "Atlas is a friend. He was just messing around."

"Atlas?" he repeats. "A curious name."

"It's not his real name," I say absentmindedly.

"Have you slept with this friend?"

I bite my lower lip, the lie almost choking me. "No."

"Ever?"

"He called by to check my car. It's been making crazy noises," I say with a slight laugh, trying to lighten the mood.

"So. he's your mechanic?"

I nod. "Sort of."

"Well. which is it, Anita, a friend or your mechanic?" he snaps.

"He's both. His boss is my client," I say, wincing at how

complicated I'm making this, "and sometimes they fix my car for me as a favour."

"Is that the only favours they give out complimentary?"

I nod, feeling my cheeks colour slightly. "He was just messing around, I'm really sorry."

He steps closer and I try not to stiffen as he reaches a hand to my face and gently tucks some hair behind my ear. "To make it up to me, I think you should have dinner with me," he says, placing a gentle kiss on the tip of my nose. "And I can show you holiday destinations." I find myself nodding. "Can you cook?" he asks, and I laugh, waiting for him to follow. When he doesn't, I clear my throat to hide my surprise. "Erm, sort of."

"Great. There's some chicken in the fridge, also some noodles and vegetables. Whip up a stir-fry and I'll quickly go shower."

I glance towards the fridge. "You want me to cook dinner?"

He nods, cupping my cheeks a little too hard and pressing a firm kiss to my lips. "Then we'll call it quits on the entire embarrassing situation."

I force a smile as he steps back. "Oh, and I'll have your car looked at tomorrow, the garage I use is reputable." And he heads off, leaving me to cook.

CHAPTER 6

ATLAS

I've spent the last two days elbow-deep in oil, noise, and distraction.

I haven't checked my phone once. Haven't walked past her street. Haven't replayed the look on her face when she shoved me off the pedestal I never even asked to stand on.

She ran.

Not just from me but from the truth.

She ran back to the guy with the flowers.

So, yeah . . . *fuck her.*

I'm underneath a van when Fury calls my name.

"Someone's here for Kasey," he grunts. "Sister. Thought you'd wanna handle it cos Axel ain't around."

I slide out from under the car, wipe the grease off my hands, and shove the wrench into the toolbox. "On it."

When I step into the main room, she's standing near the

bar, looking wildly out of place. Not because she doesn't belong, but because she's so clearly trying *not* to be noticed.

She's dressed in skinny jeans, a navy cardigan, and there's a satchel hanging from her shoulder like she just stepped out of a bookshop. Her hair is in some kind of bun with dark curls escaping like they gave up trying to behave. Her glasses slide down her nose as she nervously tucks a strand behind her ear.

She's not Anita. She's not anything like Anita.

And I can't stop staring.

She spots me and straightens, hitching the strap of her bag higher on her shoulder.

"You're Atlas?" she asks, voice soft but steady.

"That's me."

"I'm Rue. Kasey's sister."

She offers her hand. Not the flirty kind but a proper handshake, like I'm a business partner and not a biker who once buried a body in the woods. The gesture brings a smile to my face.

I take it.

Her hand's small. Warm. She holds my gaze even though I can see she's intimidated.

"Thanks," she says. "For everything you've done. I didn't think anyone would get to her in time, but she told me what happened. That you didn't leave her side."

"She needed someone," I say, shrugging like it's no big deal. "Did what I was asked to do."

Her eyes shine a little. "Still. You didn't have to be so kind."

Kind.

That's not a word I hear often. Especially not from women. Especially not when my knuckles are still stained with blood from being exactly the opposite.

She glances around the room, uncertain. "She said this place was loud."

I smirk. "That's putting it lightly. You want to wait outside? The prospect has gone to find her."

"Is that okay?" she asks, relief in her voice. "I think I'd just get in the way in here."

She steps towards the front door, and I fall into step beside her, holding it open.

Once we're outside, she turns towards the sun, tipping her face back slightly like she's enjoying the warmth on her skin. I watch her more intently than I should.

"She doing okay?" she asks after a beat. "Really?"

I nod. "Better than when I found her. She's mouthy but strong."

"She always has been," Rue says softly, a smile playing at her lips. "Even when everything else fell apart."

I'm too lost in her to hear whatever she says next. She's not dressed to impress. No heels, no perfume, no plumped lips or power moves. But she glows, quiet, grateful, *grounded.*

The complete opposite of what I'm used to.

And for the first time in days, I don't think about Anita. Because this woman in front of me, this sweet, geeky, graceful girl, is something else entirely.

"Rue," I say, testing her name again. It fits her. "That short for something?"

She glances up, smiling slightly. "Ruby. But no one calls me that. Not even Kasey."

"Why Rue, then?"

She shrugs, the motion delicate. "She started calling me that when we were kids. Said I looked like the girl in some film she watched, one with a tragic ending, obviously."

I huff a laugh. "Sounds about right for your sister."

"She's got a flair for the dramatic," Rue agrees. "Always has."

A breeze picks up, and she pushes her glasses up her nose again. It's such a soft, habitual gesture that I find myself watching it like it means something.

"You in school or working?" I ask.

She blinks, surprised. "I teach. Year six. English and art."

I grin. "Let me guess . . . bookworm."

Her smile grows, a little bashful. "Guilty. I read everything. It drives Kasey mad."

"She said something about a sister who never leaves the library," I murmur. "Didn't expect her to look like you, though."

Rue's eyebrows rise. "Like me?"

"Yeah. Was expecting . . . older. Stricter. Less," I wave a hand vaguely, "you."

That earns a laugh. It's light, genuine, spilling out of her. "I'll take that as a compliment, I think."

I lean back against the wall beside the door, arms crossed. "So, how'd a quiet girl like you end up with a sister knee-deep in biker drama?"

She looks down, her expression softening. "She's like a magnet for trouble."

"She get that from your dad?"

"Most likely. Although her mum was the queen of trouble. Before she ran off, that is. She never really bonded with Kasey. I spent my teens raising her the best I could." She sighs. "When Dad called to say she'd ran again, only this time he was done with her, I panicked. He said she was in all kinds of trouble and men were going after her. Of course, he's distanced himself. He wouldn't want to put himself in the firing line." She shrugs. "I'm not street-smart, but she is. I'm more the write-a-letter, call-a-hotline type."

"So, you called the club."

Her eyes meet mine. "I didn't know what else to do."

"You did the right thing," I say. "You trusted the right people."

She nods slowly, chewing the inside of her cheek. "I'm trying to find out how to get her out of this mess. Dad isn't returning my calls."

"She's safe. No one is coming for her here."

"But this can't be forever, right? I'm working on getting some money together so we can leave London, maybe even the UK."

I don't like the thought of them out there unprotected. "She's under our roof now. That means she's one of ours."

Rue studies me—not like I'm a threat, but like I'm a puzzle she wants to understand. "You sound like you take that seriously."

"I do."

She brushes a loose curl off her cheek and gives me a shy smile. "You're not what I expected, either."

"Oh?"

"I thought you'd be scary, dangerous."

"I am."

She tilts her head, considering. "Maybe. But there's more to you, isn't there?"

I look at her a long moment, and for once, I don't feel the need to hide it. "Yeah," I say finally, "there is."

And right then, Kasey barrels out the door like a hurricane, snapping the spell.

"Ugh, finally," she groans. "You two having a moment or what?"

Rue rolls her eyes but laughs, and I find myself watching her again, loving the way she lights up around her sister.

Kasey throws her arms around Rue in that clumsy way

she hugs, more like a shove with affection hidden inside it. Rue just laughs and hugs her back properly, like she means it.

"You look tired," Rue says, pulling back slightly.

"You look like a librarian," Kasey shoots back with a grin. "Glad to see we're both thriving."

"You're an idiot," Rue mutters affectionately, brushing a thumb over a small scrape on Kasey's cheek. "You okay?"

Kasey nods, but there's a flicker of something raw in her eyes. "Getting there."

She says it so casually, like *getting there* doesn't mean recovering from the kind of trauma that leaves marks you can't see.

I step back a little, ready to give them space, turning towards the clubhouse door.

"Hey," Rue calls gently, and I glance back. She's still got one arm looped around Kasey's shoulder, but her gaze is on me. "You don't have to go."

I hesitate.

Kasey smirks, catching the shift in the air between us. "Oh god. Don't flirt with my sister, please. I'm begging."

Rue flushes instantly. "I wasn't." There's a softness in her face that wasn't there when she arrived, like she's easing into something without even realising it. "Why don't we walk a bit?" she suggests. "It's stuffy in there."

Kasey arches a brow at her. "Wow. First you hug me, and now, you're going on a romantic stroll with my babysitter?"

"I'm not your babysitter," I mutter.

"Sure, you're not, Daddy," she throws back, and Rue chokes on a laugh.

I shake my head, smirking despite myself. "Come on, before she says something else I can't unhear."

Rue falls into step beside me, her arm brushing mine lightly, like she's still not sure how close is too close.

"You fancy my sister," Kasey states, walking backwards so her eyes can flit between us.

"I didn't say anything," I reply.

"I mean, look at her," Kasey continues. "What's not to fancy, right?"

"Jesus, Kase, stop," hisses Rue, her cheeks burning brightly.

I laugh, enjoying the flow of the conversation. "Right," I agree.

"Then ask her out," Kasey pushes.

"Did I tell you she has some kind of autism?" Rue cuts in. "She says things as she sees them. And I'm certain there's some ADHD there too."

I give a nod. "I noticed that."

"Which is why I can see how well you go with my sister, especially over that suited-up posh bird."

"There's a posh bird?" asks Rue, her eyes finding mine.

I groan.

"Don't mention her. He gets really moody," Kasey warns.

Pit's two dogs are running free on the field behind the club and Kasey jumps with excitement, rushing towards them.

"I am so sorry about her," Rue says with a small, shy smile.

"I'm kind of used to her already."

"She has no tact."

"Maybe she's right," I say, glancing her way to check her expression. She catches me and blushes further. "I mean, if you'd like to grab a drink sometime . . ." Fuck, why do I sound like a pussy?

"Oh, I don't drink alcohol."

It's not a no, so I smile. "Coffee?"

She nods. "I'm a coffee addict." Then she stuffs her hands

in her pockets, watching Kasey roll around with the dogs. "Although, if there's someone else . . ."

"There isn't," I say firmly, the lie falling from my lips too easily.

"That's settled then."

ANITA

It's nearly six and the office is silent. Tessa's long gone for the day, leaving her desk unnervingly neat and my inbox annoyingly full.

I'm halfway through reading over some case notes when the familiar low rumble of a bike engine vibrates through the window.

My stomach drops.

Before I even stand, there's a sharp knock at the door, and then Atlas steps in, filling the doorway with his huge frame.

He doesn't smile as I approach my office door, just crosses his arms over his chest and stares me down before saying, "I came to get the car. Your part's in."

Right. The starter motor. *Shit.*

"Oh, crap. I forgot to tell you, I've sorted it already."

His eyes narrow. "Sorted it?"

"Yeah. Sorry, I was meant to text you, but I've been so busy all day—"

"I told you I'd order the part. The job wasn't urgent, Nita."

"I can pay for the part if it's put you out."

He scoffs. "I don't need your money." He glances out the window to where my car usually sits. "Which garage did you take it to?"

I rack my brain trying to think of a nearby one but come

up with nothing, so I shrug. And then, as if he realises, he rolls his eyes. "You got your man to sort it."

His words cause an ache in my heart. "He's not my man," I mutter.

"Does posh boy know a good mechanic who'll charge you triple?"

"He offered," I say with a shrug. "He was quite insistent."

"Of course, he was."

We fall silent and then my office phone shrills, and I glance back at it like it's about to explode. "I should get that," I utter, rushing to grab it. If anything, it gives me a chance to regain my nerve.

It's routine. A client follow-up. I jot down notes on a Post-it while nodding and humming politely.

When I return to the reception desk, Atlas is looking down at some paperwork on top of Tessa's filing pile.

"Did you need something else?" I ask. He's so very still which sets alarm bells ringing. "Atlas?"

He holds up a sheet of paper, it's white, official, and instantly recognisable.

My stomach lurches.

The court letterhead is glaring at me, mocking me with its bold, black font and fancy logo.

I snatch it from him, my heart pounding. "That stuff is private," I spit, holding it to my chest.

"What is it?" he asks, his voice low.

"Nothing," I say quickly. "It's just work."

"Anita."

I squeeze the document tight, hating how my fingers tremble. "It's a review hearing. For custody."

Atlas exhales slowly, like someone just punched the breath out of him. "But your name is at the top."

"Yes."

"So, that means Leo Carpenter is—"

"My son," I snap, "yes."

"And you don't have custody."

I shake my head, not quite meeting his eyes. "I haven't for a long time."

"Jesus Christ," he mutters, dragging a hand over his jaw. "Why didn't you tell me?"

"Because it's not relevant to us."

"The hell it's not."

My voice cracks, the pain spilling out. "I told you I couldn't give you more, Atlas. You wanted reasons, well, there's your fucking reason."

"You've got a fucking kid," he utters like he can't quite believe it.

"You should go."

"Not until you explain," he says firmly.

"There's nothing to explain," I yell. "It's no big deal."

"No big deal? We've been sleeping together for over a year, and I knew nothing about this. Do you see him?"

"When Damien allows it."

"Allows it?" he repeats, his expression still full of confusion.

"He's . . . difficult. The situation is messy and complicated."

"He's the reason," he almost whispers and I can see him connect the dots in his head. "You can't settle for me because it'll make this harder," he says, pointing to the letter in my hand.

"Lord knows he uses anything and everything against me."

"You could've told me," he mutters. "I would've understood."

"It's not just about Leo," I snap. "It's everything. You're a biker," I almost yell. "And I'm a . . ."

He's already nodding with anger pulsing through him when he cuts me off. "A stuck-up bitch."

Tears fill my eyes. "Yeah, that," I whisper, crossing my arms over my chest like that will somehow stop his words cutting me deep.

"I will never be good enough for you, will I?"

I remain silent and he turns, heading for the door. I want to scream, tell him that it's me that's not good enough. It's me that doesn't deserve him. Just like I don't deserve Leo. Instead, I let him go. *Again.*

∼

THERE'S SOMETHING ABOUT A RESTAURANT THAT MAKES ME feel uneasy. Especially when it's times like this, times I want to spend alone with my son. Instead, I have to follow orders from Damien, which is why today, I'm sitting in a top end place waiting patiently for my parents to arrive.

Of course, he organises this sort of thing on purpose, trying to derail me. He knows things are strained between my parents and I, but I think he gets a kick out of knowing it'll hurt me.

I spot my father first. George's large frame barrels towards me as the maître-de tries to take his coat. My mother, Carol, is behind him, dressed in a powerful suit with oversized pearls hanging around her neck. *God, how I wish they'd choke her.*

I stand, smiling. "It's great to see you," I lie.

"You reserved a window seat?" It's the first thing my father says as he arches a brow.

"Yes. Leo prefers to sit by the window," I tell him.

"So, he can daydream," he snaps, thrusting his coat at the maître-de. "Move us to a central table," he tells him firmly and the man nods, leading my parents to a new table. I sigh heavily, gathering my things and following.

"Your hair needs a colour," Mother mentions as she takes her seat.

"I know, I've been too busy."

"Criminal law will keep you busy," Father snaps. "London is full of them."

"And how is your work going, Father?" I ask with a forced smile. He was bitterly disappointed when I refused a job in his corporate law firm.

"You've seen last year's turnover," he states with a boastful grin, "and I still get to play golf on Fridays."

I spot Damien heading our way and inwardly groan. Usually, he sends Leo in to me, choosing to wait in the car so we don't have to interact. Father stands, shaking his hand, and Mother turns her cheek so he can kiss it in greeting. He ignores me, *standard*.

Leo smiles awkwardly, the way teenagers do when they're forced to attend things they don't want to. I don't blame him, eating out in a place like this is ridiculous when all he wants to do is go to the cinema and eat junk. Our visits used to be like that, cinema, skate park, pizza and swimming. But Damien realised he was having too much fun, which meant I was too, and he hated it. Now he restricts visitation and dictates where we go.

"George, Carol, it's great to see you again. We didn't get chance to talk at last week's gala."

I roll my eyes at the way he plays them. His act is perfect.

"You were busy," says Mother, her cheeks the perfect shade of pink as she flutters her lashes.

"Are you going on Friday?" Father asks.

"Yes. I'll look out for you. Anyway, I came in to apologise. Leo won't be able to join you this afternoon. My fault entirely, I double booked us."

"No," I cry, pushing to my feet and they all turn to stare at me. I gather myself, lowering back into my seat. "Damien, surely the other thing can be rearranged," I say, my voice lower.

Leo gives me a sympathetic smile, and I know he feels the pain just as much as me.

"Unfortunately, not. He's got extra practise for piano so he's ready for his final exam next week."

"Piano," I practically scoff. Leo hates it, it's just another thing Damien forces him to do. "I think seeing his mother is more important than piano practise."

"Anita, get a hold of yourself," Father hisses.

"But you enjoy your meal," Damien says, ignoring me and staring at my parents. "I'll pay the bill to compensate for the inconvenience."

"That's very kind," Father tells him, shaking his hand.

"And I know how you all love to get together. It's not often your schedules align." He gives me one last smirk before looking down at Leo. "Say goodbye." Leo turns to me, but Damien cuts in sharply, adding, "To your grandparents."

I stand abruptly. "Can we talk?" I ask Damien.

He eyes me reluctantly. "If we must, but you know we should do it through our solicitors."

"Fuck the solicitors," I snap, grabbing my things and marching out the restaurant. I wait for him to follow, and when he steps out, he looks calm, even though deep down I know he's angry. He hands Leo the car keys and tells him to get in the car, which he does.

"You went to all this trouble so I could have lunch with my parents," I snap.

"I don't have time for your childish accusations."

"When can I see him?" I ask.

"You just saw him."

"You know what I mean. I want quality time with my son."

"Did you get the court date?" I nod. "Then let's wait to see the outcome of that before we fix any more dates."

I narrow my eyes. "Damien, that's weeks away."

"I'll see you in court," he mutters, heading to the driver's side of the car.

I growl in frustration and before I can stop myself, I rip open the passenger door, taking Leo by surprise. "I love you," I tell him.

"Anita, close the door," Damien snaps.

"And I will get you back so we can do all the things we used to do." Leo's eyes soften. "Do you remember them?" I ask, smiling with tears in my eyes.

"Anita, I'm warning you," Damien hisses, getting back out the car.

"Ice cream Sundays," I continue, keeping my eyes on Leo. "Trips to the beach. Film nights way past bedtime." Leo nods, his eyes also filling with tears.

Damien rounds the car quickly, gripping my arm until it's painful but I refuse to let Leo see. "You just have to be honest, Leo," I whisper, wincing as he twists it up my back. "And we can be together again." I'm hauled back, and Damien slams the door closed, spinning me and pushing me against the car. I smirk, unaffected by his face so close to mine, because for the first time since this all began, Leo acknowledged our time together, and I know he misses it too.

"You try a stunt like that again and I'll have a restraining order slapped on you," he sneers, gripping my arm tighter.

"Careful, Damien," I whisper. "We both know how you

get when you're feeling violent." His nostrils flare. "Pinning me down was your speciality," I add.

"Everything that happened between us," he whispers, pushing his forehead against my own roughly, "was because you deserved it."

A smile plays on my lips. "No, Damien," I whisper back. "Everything that happened between us was abuse. Now, get the fuck off me." I shove him back, and he releases me, his hair falling out of place. It satisfies me to see him dishevelled for once, and I laugh as he rounds the car and gets back into the driver's seat, speeding off.

CHAPTER 7

ATLAS

"It's just coffee," I tell Fletch, grabbing my keys off the table.

He leans against the doorframe, arms folded, smirking. "Sure, it is."

"She's not like that."

I say it too fast, too defensive, and I know I've given myself away.

Fletch raises a brow. "Didn't say she was. But if your game's good, she'll be whatever you want her to be."

I shoot him a glare and spritz on some aftershave, hoping it masks how wound-up I suddenly feel. "Can't you go bug Gemma?"

"She's busy," he mutters, pushing off the frame with a dramatic sigh. "And now, you're ditching me to have coffee with a librarian."

That one lands wrong. I turn to him slowly, feeling the

shift in my mood settle across my shoulders. He must see it because his smirk fades.

"Joking," he says quickly. "Shit, Atlas, don't look at me like that."

I don't respond, just grab my kutte from the back of the chair. "Keep an eye on Kasey," I say instead, my tone sharp enough to cut. "She's not to leave this place."

"Got it," Fletch replies, more serious now.

Kasey's been itching to get out, pacing the walls like a caged animal. I can't blame her, not really, but I can't let her go either. Not until we figure out what the hell we're doing with her.

I shrug on my kutte, take one last look at myself in the mirror, and try to shake off the feeling that I'm heading into something I'm not ready for.

Just coffee.

But nothing about Rue feels casual.

~

THE CAFÉ SHE PICKED ISN'T LIKE THE ONES I'D USUALLY STEP into. Too many fairy lights strung across the ceiling, weird, mismatched mugs on every table, and a chalkboard menu with terrible handwriting.

But then I spot her.

She's already at a table by the window, legs crossed, a book open in her lap, and her glasses sliding down her nose. Her hair is up in some messy twist, and there's a coffee cup in front of her with something pink and foamy on top. Of course, she ordered something with foam art.

She hasn't seen me yet, so I pause for a second and just watch her.

She licks her finger and turns a page, eyebrows

scrunching like whatever she's reading is serious business. I'm halfway across the room before she looks up, and when she does, she startles so hard, she nearly knocks her drink over.

"Sorry," she blurts, scrambling to close the book and bumping the table in the process. "I was . . . reading, *obviously*. Hi."

"Hi." I bite down a smile and slide into the seat across from her. "Didn't mean to scare you."

"You didn't . . . well, you did, but it's fine." She tucks a loose strand of hair behind her ear and won't quite meet my eyes. "You're, uh, early."

"You're adorable when you panic," I say without thinking.

Her eyes snap to mine, wide, and then her cheeks colour. "Can I get you a coffee?"

"Can I get you one?" I counter, nodding at her half-drunk cup. "A fresh one."

She glances at it. "This one has gone a little cold," she admits. "I got so lost in the book . . ."

"What are you reading?"

She hesitates. "A fantasy novel."

"And that's about . . .?"

Her eyes are suddenly alight with passion. "There's a necromancer, and a banshee prince, and a haunted carriage that eats people . . ." She trails off, clearly realising how that sounds. "Sorry, that's weird, isn't it?"

I shrug. "Sounds better than real life."

She nods with enthusiasm. "That's why I love to read so much. My dad hated my books," she tells me, almost like she couldn't stop the words even if she wanted to. "So, I'd sneak them in and read under the covers at night."

I grin. "I bet you spent most of your teenage years tired."

She giggles and the sound stirs something inside of me. "I did."

"Which explains your addiction to coffee."

She bites her lower lip to stop her smile getting wider, but her eyes shine under the twinkling lights, letting me know she likes our conversation. "I do have an obsession."

"Yeah, me too," I say, "but it's not for coffee."

Her eyes flick to mine, shy and unsure, and fuck I have to force myself to stand and turn towards the counter and pretend to scan the menu just so I don't kiss her right here in the middle of this little coffee shop.

The barista smiles. "What can I get you?"

"I'll take a double espresso." I turn back to Rue who's watching me. "And the lady will have . . ."

She blinks, seemingly pulling herself back from wherever her mind had taken her. "Erm, a pistachio latte, please."

"Tap your card to the machine and I'll bring them over," she tells me.

Once I'm sat down again, I relax back into the chair. "Do you read here often?"

She giggles again. "Most nights. I love it here, and it's quiet."

"Do you live far?"

She shakes her head but doesn't comment further. It pleases me to know she doesn't just blurt her address out. "How's Kasey?"

I nod. "A royal pain in my arse, but she's all good."

She grins. "I swear I'm trying my best to get the money together, so she'll be out of your hair for good."

"Is that the plan?"

Her smile fades and she stares out the window for a moment before replying, "I don't know what else to do."

"Have you asked Kasey what happened?"

She nods. "She just said it was to do with Dad, and she'd speak to him."

"Will he help?"

"I doubt it, but she seems to think he will."

"Do you want me to talk to her?"

"Do you think she'd tell you anything?"

I shrug. We've spent the last week together. She follows me to the garage and insists I teach her shit, and she takes it all in, like she's some kind of fucking genius. "She might. I think she trusts me now."

"After I left, I didn't realise things were that bad. I mean, Dad's always been a lost cause, but he's never gotten us involved. And Kasey, well, if Dad tells her to keep things from me, she does."

"We need a plan that doesn't involve you running out on me," I say with a small smile.

"So, who's the posh woman Kasey mentioned?" She blushes before quickly adding, "You don't have to tell me."

Our coffees arrive and I take a moment to gather my words. "Apparently, it wasn't serious."

She eyes me over her cup, poised to take a sip. Instead, she asks, "You thought it was more?"

"I thought it was heading that way, yeah."

"I'm so sorry it didn't work out for you," she says, placing her cup down. "Love can be brutal."

"Lucky for me, I've had your sister around to distract me, and she doesn't do sympathy in any shape or form."

Rue laughs. "Yeah, emotions aren't one of her strong points."

"I'm glad about that. And it's worked because I feel much better already." I hold eye contact for a second longer than needed. "I'm over her."

She arches a brow. "How long were you . . . not a thing for?"

I shrug. "A few months."

"How many exactly?"

I take a sip of the coffee. "Almost a year . . . maybe."

Her eyes widen. "A year. That's a relationship."

I give a humourless laugh. "Some would agree."

"Wait, you stuck around for an entire year and she broke up with you?"

"She didn't break up with me. Technically, it was never a thing."

She slumps back in her chair and pushes her glasses farther up her nose again. "Wow."

"See, now, I feel like you're judging me," I say, my tone teasing. "Like you're wondering what I did to scare her away."

She smirks, shrugging. "Did you do anything?"

I think on her words. "I don't think so."

"Um, that usually means you did do something, but you don't want to say."

I laugh, letting the smile fade as I think over how things were between the two of us. "I love too hard," I admit, suddenly feeling like I need to be honest with her and give her a chance to see the real me so she can run now. "I care too much. And I let myself fall too hard. I'm an all-in kind of guy."

I catch her expression soften. "That doesn't sound like something a woman would run away from."

I huff out a small laugh. "They do if they're scared of love."

RUE

He loves too hard. He's an all-in kind of guy. What the hell is wrong with his ex? This guy is every woman's dream, surely.

I mean, he's easy on the eye with broad shoulders and tattoos begging me to trace with my fingers. He's got a mean, angry kind of scowl which sits permanently on his face, but for some reason, it doesn't scare me, it intrigues me. His eyes are dark green, and they're forever darting around like he can't truly relax . . . like he's looking for danger. It makes me wonder what he's seen, what he's looking out for.

"Anyway," he says, resting his elbows on his knees and staring me in the eye. "What about your past relationships."

I give a nervous laugh. "I'm pretty sure I read somewhere that you should never talk about exes on a first date." The words tumble out before I realise what I've said, and Atlas gives me a wide grin.

"A date?"

"I mean . . . not a date . . . it's a—"

"No, no, you can't take it back now. You said it was our first date."

"Oh God," I mutter, burying my burning face in my hands. "I want the ground to swallow me whole."

"If this is a date, you must be single." I want to laugh. Is he serious? He thinks anyone would want to date me! He's staring at me now, waiting for a response. "Unless you're with someone?"

I shake my head. "No, I'm not with anyone."

"Good," he says, his smile returning. He finishes his coffee. "Cos I didn't want to beat anyone to death and ruin my good mood." My eyes widen and he laughs. *"Kidding."*

But I'm not shocked at what he said, I'm shocked at how

excited it made me feel. My Dad was right; I read way too much romance.

God help me, I like him. Not just in a *he's hot and makes my insides fizz* kind of way. But in a *I want to keep talking to him until the café closes, until the sun comes up, until I've accidentally told him all my secrets* kind of way. And that's terrifying.

"You didn't answer my question," he says after a beat.

"What question?"

"Your past relationships."

Ah, yes. That fun topic. I stir the cold remains of my pistachio latte like the froth might suddenly offer wisdom. "There's not much to say," I admit. "A few dates. One almost-relationship. Nothing worth putting in a scrapbook."

"Why?" he asks, not cruel, just curious.

I sigh, giving a half-shrug. "I used to think it was me. Like maybe I wasn't enough. Not pretty enough or interesting enough or . . . whatever enough." He frowns, and suddenly his whole-body changes, like I've triggered something in him, something protective. "But then I realised," I go on, trying to play it cool, "I just hadn't met someone who made me want to stay around long enough to show them the real me."

His gaze sharpens. "You've been waiting for the wrong people."

I smile, soft and a little sad. "Story of my life."

He stretches, muscles shifting under the sleeves of his t-shirt. His knuckles are rough. His nails are short. He looks like someone who's built things, broken things, fought for things. He looks like someone who feels too much and hides it behind smirks and sarcasm.

I'm in trouble.

"So," I say, desperate to shift the conversation before I

spontaneously combust, "if this was a date, hypothetically, what would happen next?"

He leans forward again, slow and deliberate. "Easy," he says. "I'd walk you home."

I snort. "Wow. Living on the edge."

"Oh, don't worry." He grins. "I'm thinking very inappropriate things while doing it."

I nearly choke on my latte.

Yeah. I'm *definitely* in trouble.

ANITA

I drop into the seat opposite Tessa and release a breath that feels like it's been stuck in my chest for days.

She glances up from her laptop. "You okay?"

I give a shrug that I hope reads as *not now*, but she doesn't buy it.

"Okay," she says, snapping the laptop shut, "out with it."

I stare at the table for a beat, gathering the chaos into something I can say out loud. "It's just been a rough couple days. Damien won't let me see Leo, I walked out on dinner with my parents, and Atlas isn't speaking to me."

Tessa sits up straighter, her expression shifting like I've just given her a test she wasn't prepared for. "How come?"

She says it casually, but there's something off in her tone —a little too light, a little too rehearsed.

I narrow my eyes. "What?"

"Nothing," she replies far too quickly.

"Tessa." She won't meet my eyes now. "Has Atlas said something?" She shakes her head, but it's too fast, too forced. "Tessa," I repeat, firmer this time. "What do you know?"

She groans and leans back. "Okay, but don't kill the messenger. He went on a date the other night."

The words hit harder than I expect. I inhale sharply and try not to let it show. "Oh."

"I don't know if I should be telling you," she adds, guilt creeping into her voice. "He never said not to, but . . ."

"It's fine," I cut in, waving a hand like it's no big deal. "I've been telling him to go on dates for months." She gives me a look—it's soft, pitying even, like she sees right through me. "As long as he's happy," I add.

"He seems happy," she murmurs, and my heart gives a sharp, traitorous twist.

The silence stretches between us before she changes the subject. "And you're seeing Anthony now. How's that going?"

I force a smile. "Good."

A lie.

"He's so nice," I continue, like I'm reading off a list of things I should want. "In fact, he's asked me to go to a ball this weekend."

Tessa perks up. "A ball? As in big dresses and cute hair?"

I nod. "Yeah, it's a business thing, but he needed a plus-one."

"Great." Then, without missing a beat, "And has he booked that weekend away he promised?"

I lift a shoulder. "I'm not sure."

She frowns. "The girls will be disappointed you're not coming to the club on Saturday. They were complaining last night about how they hardly see you anymore."

My stomach sinks. I used to go all the time. Before everything got messy with Atlas. Before I stopped feeling like I belonged.

"What's happening on Saturday?" I ask, though I already know it's something I'll probably regret missing.

"Axel's throwing a barbeque. Reckons we all need cheering up."

∼

THE BALLROOM IS EXACTLY THE KIND OF PLACE YOU'D expect Anthony to belong to with chandeliers that drip crystal, a string quartet in the corner, and waiters who somehow manage to glide rather than walk. Everyone here seems polished, filtered, filtered again.

Including me.

Or at least, I tried. It wasn't an easy task after years of snubbing this kind of event.

I smooth down the front of my dress and take a breath as Anthony returns with two glasses of champagne.

He hands me one with a smile that doesn't quite reach his eyes. "You look beautiful tonight," he says, then adds, "though you really should've worn your hair up. It elongates your neck."

I nod, swallowing the sting. "Next time."

He clinks his glass to mine. "To us."

I echo the words, but they taste flat in my mouth. We sip. He immediately starts scanning the room, already more interested in who's watching us than in me.

"Remember, that's Harrow from the board," he murmurs as we start to walk through the crowd. "And that's his wife. She runs a charity or something. Smile."

I smile.

We stop in front of a couple, and Anthony slides straight into charming mode, introducing me with the kind of rehearsed warmth that makes me feel like I'm part of a presentation. I laugh at the right moments, nod when expected, and try not to fidget under the weight of polite, slightly condescending small talk.

Eventually, the couple are swept away by someone shinier, and we move to the edge of the room. Anthony's hand rests lightly on my lower back, a constant reminder of his presence . . . or his control. I haven't quite worked out which.

"You did well," he says, brushing a speck of lint from my shoulder. "I mean, a little less nervous energy would be good next time, but still. Proud of you."

I nod again. That word, *proud*, always lands strangely when he says it. Like I'm a student, not a partner.

"Thanks," I say quietly.

We dance for a little while, or rather, he dances, and I try to follow. He's good at leading. Of course he is. He's good at being in charge of things. People. *Me.*

At one point, when I catch sight of myself in one of the wall mirrors, I barely recognise the woman staring back. Perfect posture. Perfect makeup. Perfect dress. But there's something vacant in her eyes, like she's not sure how she got here again, in this world.

Later, we're seated at a long table covered in gold-dipped menus and floral arrangements. The conversations swell and fade like tides, and I try to join in where I can. Anthony's hand rests casually on my thigh under the table, but it's not intimate. It's possessive.

When dessert arrives, he leans in close, his voice low. "You hardly touched your main. Are you feeling alright?"

"Just not that hungry," I whisper.

"You have to be careful," he says, eyes still on the table. "You're naturally slim, which is lovely, but skipping meals can make you look drawn. Especially under lights like these."

I nod and stab at my dessert, even though I feel sick now.

Compliment, correction. Compliment, correction. That's how he does it.

I don't know when I started noticing it—the way every kind word is a velvet-wrapped critique. The way he shapes me, or tries to. It's happened much faster this time. Damien was slower, building me up over a year or so before showing his true colours.

Maybe I'm imagining it. Maybe I'm being dramatic. But deep down, I know I'm not, because I've seen it all before. First with my parents, then with Damien, and now, I'm here again.

We've just finished dessert when I spot them.

My mother's dress is ivory with silver beading that probably cost more than this entire ball, and my father is in his usual uniform—black tux, tight smile, eyes that sweep the room like everyone's beneath him. I feel my spine stiffen.

"Everything okay?" Anthony asks.

I nod, trying to keep my head to the side, praying they don't spot me.

"Anita?"

I briefly close my eyes at the sound of my mother's voice, turning in her direction and forcing a smile. "Mother, what a wonderful surprise."

"What are you doing here?" she asks as I stand and lean over to kiss her cheek.

"I was invited," I say, glancing to Anthony, who also stands, straightening his jacket.

"Anthony Carlisle," he says, holding out his hand to my father, who grabs it firmly and shakes.

"George Jenson, and this is my wife, Carol."

"Lovely to meet you," Anthony says, his arm snaking around my waist. "At last."

I want to point out that we've only been on a few dates,

five max, so meeting my parents wasn't really on the agenda for at least another few months.

Anthony continues, "I've heard a lot about you both. It's great to finally meet the people responsible for raising such a remarkable woman."

I should call him out on his lie. I haven't told him a single thing about my parents, but I remain silent, knowing somewhere in the back of my mind that correcting him in front of them will piss him off.

"I'm sorry to say Anita hasn't told us a thing about you," my father replies, shooting me an irritated look. "And she ran out on our dinner plans the other day, so we didn't get to catch up."

"I apologise for that," I mutter. "I had an emergency come up."

"Maybe we can rearrange and all four of us can go for dinner," Anthony suggests. "I'd love to hear more about your work," he says, looking at my father.

"I didn't know you were interested in law," I say, the words practised.

He side-eyes me, waits a beat, then says, "Corporate law is different to criminal law."

I almost scoff, but my father jumps in, delighted with the comparison. He slaps Anthony on the back, and they begin to walk towards the bar. "I tried my best to have her work for me," he says. "She was determined to set up herself in criminal law. If she'd have stuck with me, she'd be partner by now."

"And it wouldn't be on my own merit," I say, but neither hear me as they get lost in business talk, leaving me to make conversation with my mother about her book club.

CHAPTER 8

ATLAS

I'm nervous.

I hate that I am, but it's there, buzzing under my skin, making my leg bounce and my fingers drum impatiently against the bar top. I can't stop glancing towards the gates like some lovesick idiot.

"Can you stop tapping?" Kasey snaps, clearly fed up with the soundtrack of my anxiety. "What's gotten into you?"

"He's nervous," Grizz says before I can answer, his tone far too casual for the chaos in my chest. "Doesn't want your sister to meet us all."

"Why?" Kasey asks, turning to me with narrowed eyes.

"In case she decides one of us is better looking," Kade throws in with a grin.

I don't take the bait. My gaze is locked on the gate and then I see her.

I'm already halfway across the yard before I've registered

moving. I hear Kasey calling something behind me, probably teasing, but I don't care.

Because Rue's here.

She spots me approaching and offers a shy little wave, the kind that barely lifts her hand, like she's still not sure she belongs here.

She does. She always will, even if she doesn't know it yet.

"Hey," I say, trying to play it cool even though my heart's beating like I've just come off a job. "You made it."

"I did," she says, tucking a strand of hair behind her ear. "I almost turned around twice."

I smirk. "Why?"

"I don't know. I pulled up outside and thought, 'This is a bad idea'."

"It's not."

She eyes the bikes, the noise, the general chaos of barbeques and beer and men in black leaning against railings like they're in a gang recruitment poster. "I feel like I walked into *Sons of Anarchy*."

"You kinda did, only we're much scarier."

That earns a smile. I let it settle between us for a second before I reach out and take the bag from her shoulder without asking. She stiffens for a beat but doesn't stop me.

"Come on," I say. "You're meeting the family."

"Oh god," she mutters. "That sounds terrifying."

"Yeah, well, they are." She gives me a look. "Okay, fine, *some* of them are. Don't let Kade offer you tequila and don't, under any circumstances, believe a word Grizz says."

We reach the others, and I can feel the way Rue pulls herself tighter, like she's bracing for impact. I rest my hand lightly on the small of her back. Not possessive, just steadying.

"Everyone, this is Rue."

Kade's the first to react. Of course, he is. "So, you're the mystery girl."

Rue blinks. "I didn't realise I was a mystery."

"Hey, if you're quieter than your sister, it's good to meet you," says Grizz, holding out a hand. "I'm Grizz."

She takes it, shaking it. "Hi."

"She's real cute," Kade says, and I shoot him a look that has him raising both hands. "What? I'm being supportive."

Kasey hooks her arm through Rue's. "Let's grab some food before this lot eat it all. Seriously, they get through tonnes of meat every day."

Rue glances up at me like she's checking if that's okay. "Go on," I say, brushing my knuckles lightly against hers. "Make yourself at home."

She heads off with Kasey, and I stay back, watching them.

"She's sweet," Grizz says beside me. "You like her."

"I do," I admit.

"She won't last in this world," says Kade.

I glance sideways. "You don't think so?"

He shrugs. "Girls like that don't usually stick around. But maybe she's not like the rest."

I look back at Rue, sitting with Kasey, laughing at something, completely out of place and somehow fitting in anyway.

"She's not."

Axel joins us. "Damn she's grown since I last saw her." he says, watching them too.

"Rue?" I ask.

"She was a kid when she crunched some numbers for the club. She's a bloody genius."

"Really? She teaches English now."

He grins. "Yeah, figures. Accounting would have made her big money, but for some shady people."

"Pres, what the fuck we gonna do with Kasey?"

"He's got some mystery biker club on speed dial," says Grizz. "He's gonna ask around and find out who's looking for her."

"The same one we were checking that warehouse out for?" I ask.

Axel grins at Grizz. "Are you jealous?" he asks in a teasing tone. "Cos you'll always be my favourite VP."

"Shut up," says Grizz, laughing. "I just don't know why we haven't met them yet?"

"There's no big mystery," he replies. "Once they're up and running, I'll make the introductions."

"I just can't settle," Grizz admits. "This is the quietist we've been in months, and it doesn't feel right."

Axel slaps him on the back, "Brother, this is how it should be. Calm. Quiet. Easy."

"The calm before the storm more like," says Fletch.

"See, there you go again," snaps Axel. "Negativity. Just enjoy it."

"I plan to," I say, pushing off the bar and heading towards Rue. We've been apart long enough.

RUE

This is a terrible idea.

I knew it when I turned into the car park and saw the row of gleaming bikes, all lined up like metal animals. I knew it when I heard the bass of someone's music vibrating the walls from the inside. And I definitely knew it when Atlas walked towards me with that crooked smile that made my stomach twist like it didn't know what side it was on.

Now, I'm sitting beside Kasey with a paper plate of barbequed chicken and trying very hard not to look like a lost child at someone else's family reunion.

They're not what I expected. They're louder. Rougher. But there's something easy about them, too. Like they've all known each other for decades and the world outside doesn't matter unless it tries to get in.

Kasey's mid-rant about someone named Kade and a truly horrifying tequila incident when I glance up and find he's watching me.

Atlas.

Leaning against the bar, arms folded, talking to a few of the guys, but still looking like his attention's stuck on me. When our eyes meet, something shifts in the air, in my chest, and I have to force myself to look away before I melt into the plastic chair.

"You okay?" Kasey asks.

"Huh? Yeah, sorry. What were you saying?"

She grins. "You're so gone for him."

I laugh, but it's nervous. "Is it that obvious?"

"Only to everyone."

I take a sip of whatever's in my cup, it's sweet and fizzy and I don't recognise it, but I'm too flustered to care. "He's different," I admit.

She snorts. "Yeah. He is. But he's also steady. The kind of guy who fixes things instead of walking away."

"Sounds nice."

"It's rare," she says, eyes softening just a little.

I glance her way, seeing her eyes fixed on him. "You like him," I gasp.

She scoffs. "Not in the same way you do," she shrugs. "But yeah, he's alright for a man."

I nod, even though my insides feel tangled. "Yeah, he is."

A shadow falls over us, and I look up to find Atlas standing there, plate in one hand, drink in the other. "Hope you're hungry," he says, offering the plate to me like he's been watching how slowly I've been picking at mine.

I smile up at him, stupidly grateful. "Thanks."

He shrugs like it's nothing, then sits beside me, not across, not away, but close, thigh brushing mine like he needs the contact.

And suddenly, I don't feel so out of place.

After another hour of loud laughter, dodging Kade's flirtations, and watching someone try to shotgun a beer and fail spectacularly, I lean towards Atlas and murmur, "Is there somewhere quieter?"

He looks at me, and I know he gets it—the noise, the eyes, the unfamiliar terrain.

"Come on," he says, pushing up from his chair and offering me his hand like it's the most natural thing in the world.

I hesitate for half a second, then slide my hand into his. The contact sends a thrill through me, lighting up my insides.

He leads me around the back of the building, down a gravel path, and through a gate that opens to a side yard lit only by a single flickering bulb. It's quieter here, just the faint hum of music and the occasional burst of laughter from the other side of the fence.

There's a bench against the wall. He gestures to it.

"Did you bring me out here to murder me?" I tease, sitting.

He grins. "Not tonight."

He lowers himself beside me, elbows on his knees, head

tipped back to look at the stars barely visible through the glow of the club's lights.

"It's a lot," I say quietly, picking at the edge of my sleeve. "All of it. The people. The noise. The way they look at me like I don't belong."

"You belong," he says firmly.

I glance at him. "You sound so sure."

He thinks for a minute. "It takes them time to accept someone that doesn't know our world. But once they see what I see, they'll accept you and you'll find it hard to leave."

"You make it sound so easy."

He turns to face me, his voice lower now, almost gentle. "It's not. But I don't want you to feel like you have to fit into their world overnight. Or even at all. Just be in mine."

Something tightens in my chest. "And what is your world, exactly?"

He's quiet for a moment, then says, "Right now? It's you."

I blink, stunned. We went on one date, and we've text a few flirty texts back and forth, but he's talking like we're about to marry. As if he senses my panic, he gives me an easy smile. "I'm sorry. I'm doing it again, aren't I?"

I chew on my lower lip. "The all-in thing?" I ask, then nod. "Yeah, you are."

We both laugh but it breaks the heaviness of the conversation, and I relax a little.

"I just don't want you to see all this and run a mile," he adds. "Because I know it's a lot, but they're my family. I won't ever leave them, but I'd like you to stick around and give them a chance."

I nod, rubbing my hands over my jeans. "I wasn't planning on running anywhere."

He reaches out and tucks a loose strand of hair behind my

ear. His knuckles graze my skin, and I swear the world shifts slightly.

"Good."

My heart's hammering. The kind of beat I usually only feel when I finish a really good book. Or start a really dangerous one.

And without thinking, I lean in closer, our eyes connected in something deep, wanting. I inhale, holding my breath, praying he reads the signs, and almost crying in relief when he does, inching closer until we're just a breath apart. "Stop me now if I'm going too fast," he murmurs. When I don't move, his hand cups my jaw, his thumb brushing over my cheek, and then he kisses me. It's soft at first, nothing like I imagined. But as our lips brush together, and his hands slip to cradle the back of my head, he takes it deeper, sweeping his tongue into my mouth and groaning in the back of his throat like it's everything he's ever dreamed of. The fluttering in my stomach intensifies and just as my hands twist in his t-shirt, he pulls back, panting and breathless as his eyes trace my swollen lips.

ANITA

I pace outside, checking my watch for the tenth time. "Are you sure I can't drive you home?" Anthony asks.

"Tessa is right around the corner," I tell him. "Please stay and enjoy the rest of the evening."

I lasted all of two hours before I faked a migraine and made my excuses to leave. This sort of thing isn't for me. It wasn't then and it isn't now. Nothing's changed. Apart from the fact I have friends I can call upon these days that'll giggle when I call them desperately from the bathroom and ask them to come and get me because I'm in hell.

When her car slows to a stop right beside me, I sag in relief. I glance back to where Anthony is watching me and give a quick wave before opening the door and sliding into the passenger seat. I stare straight ahead. "Please get me out of here," I mutter, hardly moving my lips.

"It looks swanky," says Tessa as she puts the car into drive and wheelspins out of the carpark. She laughs to herself. "But boring as fuck."

"You're not wrong," I say, flipping down the mirror and checking my makeup. "How's the barbeque?"

"Lively," she replies with another laugh. "Fletch is playing guitar by the fire, and some of the guys are trying to sing, if that's what you can call it. You called me just as shots were being poured."

"How come you haven't drunk?"

"I will when we get back. Day drinking isn't for me. My hangover comes early and I end up in bed before the party's really begun, so I thought I'd pace myself."

"I'm glad you did."

"Do you want to come back for a bit?"

I nod, stifling a yawn. I haven't seen Atlas all week, and it would be good to try and clear the air.

Minutes later, we turn into the club's car park. Off to the left, there's a group of bikers sat around a fire. Atlas isn't one of them, and I fight the urge to ask Tessa if he's even here.

I follow her over to where some of the old ladies are sitting, and they get up to greet me with hugs. It feels good to be back here, I've missed it.

I'm handed a drink before I even sit down, and someone tucks a throw blanket over my legs like I'm visiting royalty. It's warm, comforting. Familiar in a way I forgot I needed.

"So, how was your *other* party?" Luna asks, raising an eyebrow.

"Stuffy," I say, then lower my voice with a little smirk. "I forgot how much I hate those things. It's like a male pissing contest, strutting around trying to impress one another."

The women laugh, and I sip the drink, letting the taste of something sweet and spiced take the edge off my mood.

I don't mean to look for him, but my eyes wander anyway, skimming past leather jackets and laughter, searching for a shadow I've missed more than I'll admit. And then I see him.

Atlas.

He's across the firepit, standing near the bar setup, holding a beer. He looks good, too good, and I ache to rush over and tell him how much I miss him. His sleeves are pushed up, ink on show, flexing as he gestures to someone beside him. His head tilts slightly, that crooked grin forming on his face, and something sharp twists in my gut.

I take another sip. A bigger one this time. Then my gaze shifts to the girl he's smiling at.

Petite. Pretty. Cute in that art-student-who-doesn't-know-she's-hot kind of way. She laughs at something he says and nudges his arm with hers. They look comfortable together.

My stomach drops.

"Oh," I say, the word barely audible.

Tessa leans in. "What?"

I blink, trying to school my features into something neutral. "Nothing. Just spotted Atlas."

She follows my gaze, and I can tell the second she sees Rue too. She goes unnaturally still.

I turn to her slowly. "He's bringing her to the club barbeque," I say, like it's a stray thought, but there's a hint of pain in my tone. If she's here, he's serious.

She hesitates. "Maybe Kasey asked her to come."

Something tightens inside me. "Kasey?" I repeat, not dragging my eyes from the pair.

"They're sisters. Kasey is the one the club's helping, and the woman talking to Atlas is Rue."

It clicks then. "Oh, I met Kasey at the garage."

"Yeah, she loves it there. Apparently, she's picking up some stuff from the guys and she's really good at it."

"And Rue is the one you told me about. The one he took out?"

"Yeah," she whispers, her voice barely audible. "I'm sorry, Nita. I didn't realise she was here."

Atlas is laughing now, and the girl, Rue, tucks a piece of hair behind her ear, looking up at him like he's the only one here.

I feel something fizz in my chest. Not jealousy, not quite. Just that familiar ache that comes from realising someone you wanted to believe was still yours has already moved on.

"I'm going to get another drink," I mutter, rising from my seat before anyone can stop me.

Because if I'm going to be here, I'm not going to be *that* woman who's quiet in the shadows while another girl takes centre stage.

I fix my shoulders, smooth my expression, and head towards the bar.

I weave through the bodies with my chin high and my expression smooth, the kind of expression I've perfected after years of pretending I wasn't quietly breaking. The laughter and music buzz around me like static, but my focus is sharp. Singular.

He hasn't seen me yet.

Atlas is leaned against the makeshift bar, his beer dangling from his fingers, his smile easy and unbothered. Rue is still beside him. I clock the way she's angled towards him like gravity's pulling her in without permission. It's subtle, but obvious once you know what to look for. I used to stand like that too.

I step up to the bar and reach for a bottle of water, twisting off the cap slowly. It takes him a second to notice. But when he does, he stills.

His eyes lock onto me, and the change is immediate. The smile fades. His spine straightens. That beer freezes halfway to his mouth.

I take a few long pulls; my eyes fixed on his. And when I come up for air, I force a tight smile. "Hi."

"Anita," he utters, and I still see it there in his eyes, that possessive glint. That burning heat for me.

Rue follows his gaze, maybe she can see it too. I don't look at her, so she takes her gaze to the ground, shifting uncomfortably between us.

"I didn't think you were talking to me," I state.

His brows pinch together. "What?"

I let out a breathy laugh, shaking my head. "You haven't been in touch. Not even a message."

He shifts awkwardly, rubbing the back of his neck like he's a teenage boy who got caught skipping school. "I've been busy. Club stuff. Work."

"Right," I say, drawing the word out just enough to make my point as my eyes flick to her. "Of course."

There's a beat of silence, heavy and uncomfortable. Rue quietly excuses herself, mumbling something about needing the bathroom, but I don't look at her. I keep my gaze on Atlas, steady and calm, even as my heart hammers in protest.

"Anyway," I say, finishing the rest of my water and setting the bottle down, "I didn't come over here to start anything. Just thought I'd say hi. Didn't realise you had company."

"Are you okay?" he asks.

"Is it a thing?" I counter.

He looks past me in the direction Rue went. "Yes."

I didn't expect it. That single word to break my heart, but it does, and I gently rub my hand over my chest to try and somehow ease it.

"Well," I say, smoothing a hand down my jacket. "Enjoy the rest of your evening."

I walk away before he can say anything else. Before I let my expression crack. Before I can break.

CHAPTER 9

ATLAS

"Everything okay?" Rue asks.

I've been quiet since out little encounter with Anita. I didn't expect her to be here. Seeing her again is hard. It's much easier when I'm with Rue and I can pretend Anita doesn't exist. But now, faced with her, everything feels messy and painful.

"Yeah, fine."

She bites on her lower lip for a second, like she's finding the right words. "That was her, the posh woman Kasey told me about?"

"I didn't know she'd be here," I mutter, rubbing the back of my neck.

"If you want to go and talk to her, go," she says. "I can find Kasey to keep me company."

I shake my head. The last thing I want to do is send her off to Kasey who's chatting with the guys. I don't need to be getting into fights with my brothers if they try it on with Rue. "I don't need to talk to her. I've said everything I need to." And my words are true, there is nothing else to say.

"You sure?" she asks. "Because she keeps looking over here."

"Ignore her." Her eyes go back to where the old ladies are sitting. "Ignore her," I repeat, a little too firmly. Rue blinks, surprised, and I exhale to soften the edge in my tone. "Sorry. It's just . . . complicated."

She nods slowly, the firelight catching the flecks of gold in her eyes. "I figured."

I hate the way one look from Anita can yank me back in, and now, she consumes my thoughts again. She's a hard habit to break, but one I have to if I want to keep seeing Rue.

She takes a sip of her drink and fiddles with the hem of her sleeve. "She's really pretty."

Her words surprise me, her tone is soft and unsure, like she's comparing herself to Anita. I glance at her. "So are you."

Her lips part slightly, like she wasn't expecting that. She gives me a shy smile, but I can tell she's still unsure. I'm not used to women like her. Women who doubt their beauty.

I lean against the side of the bar, turning slightly towards her. "Anita and I . . . we ended things badly. There's a lot of history there, but it's history for a reason."

Rue studies me, like she's trying to read between the lines. "Do you still love her?"

The question hits me in the chest. Not because I don't have an answer, because I do. It just doesn't fit into anything neat.

"I don't know what I feel," I admit, my voice low. "I thought I could put it all in a box and move on. But seeing her again . . ." I trail off, clenching my jaw. "It's hard."

Rue nods, looking down to the floor. "Thanks for being honest."

I reach out, fingers brushing hers where they rest on the edge of the bar. "I'm glad you came."

Her eyes lift to mine. "So am I."

But there's still that shadow between us, Anita's presence, looming like smoke from the firepit. I can feel her gaze burning into my side.

I turn back towards the crowd. She's still there, drink in hand, laughing at something one of the old ladies says. And yet, her eyes flick to me the second she thinks I'm not looking.

Rue follows my gaze. "You're not as done as you think."

"I don't want her back," I say quietly. I say the words with a confidence I don't feel, but it's not because I want Anita—*I don't think*—more that she's a habit I'm still trying to break.

"That doesn't mean you're over her."

I sigh. Rue doesn't say it like an accusation. More like a truth I haven't wanted to face. She finishes her drink and offers me a half-smile that doesn't reach her eyes. "I'm gonna use the bathroom," she says, stepping away before I can respond.

And I'm left standing there, the weight of two women and all the silence between us pressing against my chest.

RUE

I knew she'd follow. Maybe that's why I came in here. She clearly has things to get off her chest and although I hate confrontation, I'd rather she just say what she needs to instead of staring at me.

I run my fingers through my hair, staring at my reflection

whilst she drops her bag on the sink unit and rummages through. She pulls out a lipstick and glances at me through the mirror. "I'm glad he's found someone," she eventually says.

Her words surprise me. She doesn't look glad at all. "It's barely even begun," I reply.

"But you like him?"

"So do you," I state.

She smirks, applying the lipstick. "We just hook up from time to time."

"It's just you're watching him like he's yours."

"I'm surprised is all," she says, putting the lipstick away and turning to me. "One minute he's asking me to be his old lady and the next he's with you."

"He told me you were hooking up for a year. And when it came to it, you didn't want to commit."

Her eyes narrow slightly. "Seems he's quite the open book with you."

"Look, I'm not here for any trouble. He told me you and him were done. If that's not the case, just tell me and I'll leave."

The door opens and Atlas fills it; his arms folded across his chest. "Well," he says, his eyes fixed on Anita. "Tell her the truth."

Her smirk is back. "And what's that, Atlas?"

"That we're done. That you've moved on. That you're not interested in anything serious with me because I'm not good enough for you."

Her smirk soon fades. "That's not it," she almost whispers. "You are more than good enough."

I step towards the door. "I'll let you two talk."

Atlas doesn't budge. "No," he says firmly. "There's nothing left to say. Anita doesn't want me."

I press my lips together in a fine line. "But you want her," I say, the words almost choking me. "I can see it in your eyes. Anyone with half a brain can see it."

His brows furrow like he's trying to make sense of the words. As if I've just told him something he doesn't already know. And then he shakes his head. "I don't."

Anita scoffs but I keep my back to her, my eyes fixed on his. He gently places his hands on my shoulders. "We're over. I don't want her," he adds.

ANITA

I owe it to him to be honest, to tell him I love him more than I've ever loved anyone. But I can never be with him, not really, not if I want my son back. So, I force a smile. "He's right," I say, and Rue turns to look at me. Her eyes are innocent, unsuspecting, like she'll believe whatever I say but still deep down know the real truth. "We were just sex, nothing more." I take a step towards the door, feeling the way Atlas glares at me. I give a small laugh. "And he's good at it." I pat him on the shoulder, and he steps to the side so I can leave.

"When was the last time?" Rue's question stops me.

I exchange a glance with Atlas. "Ages ago," he says. "Way before us." Her eyes train on me, and I shift uncomfortably. "Nita," Atlas barks, making us both jump with fright, "fucking tell her."

I nod in agreement. "A few weeks ago," I admit.

I give Atlas one last lingering look before stepping out and heading back to the old ladies.

Gemma pats the empty space beside her, and I lower to the blanket. "You okay?" she asks.

I nod. "I think so."

"And you and Atlas are . . ."

"Done," I confirm with a nod. "He really likes her. I can see it in his eyes."

"You did go on dates with other guys," Tessa points out.

"I know."

"He was gonna get sick of waiting eventually," she continues.

"I know, Tess," I say a little more sharply.

"Doesn't hurt any less though," Gemma cuts in, knocking her shoulder gently against mine.

My phone buzzes, and I glance at Anthony's name on the screen. "Is this the new guy?" asks Gemma, also looking at the screen.

I nod, cancelling the call, but when he calls straight back, I stand and step away from everyone to answer the call. "Hi?"

"Hey, I just wanted to check you're okay?"

I smile to myself, because even though I see the warning signs in almost everything he does and says, there are sweet moments like this that still make my heart stutter. "I'm okay."

"How's the migraine?"

"A little better," I reply, glancing out towards where the bikers are gathered. My eyes seek Atlas out without permission, watching as he chugs a beer. Rue isn't beside him and I wonder if she left upset or happy.

"I could come by your place if you like. I'm just about to leave."

"No, I'm not much company right now. I'll call you tomorrow?"

"Okay. And it was great meeting your parents, Anita. I think they loved me."

"I'm sure they did," I say with as much enthusiasm as I can muster. "Goodnight."

I disconnect and tuck my phone away, looking up as Atlas steps into my space with a fresh beer in his hand. "You happy with yourself?" he asks, arching a brow. "You don't want me, but you don't want me to be happy either?"

I shake my head. "That's not true. I want you to be happy."

"So, what the fuck was tonight about?"

"Tessa invited—"

"I don't care," he snaps, cutting me off. "I don't give a shit who invited you, Anita. You're not a part of this club anymore. You chose not to be."

His words hurt way more than I want them too. "I work for the club," I remind him.

"But being a part of the old ladies, was because you were with me."

"We weren't actually together."

"Fuck you," he yells, running his hand through his hair in irritation. "You keep playing it down, but you were in my bed most fucking nights."

"We should go somewhere and talk," I suggest, looking past him to where some of the brothers are watching us. "I'll explain everything."

"You had your chance," he mutters, shaking his head. He turns and marches away in the direction of the club.

CHAPTER 10

ATLAS

I down my drink, throwing the empty bottle in the bin as I head inside the club. I take the stairs two at a time and I'm about to go into my room when I hear her call my name. I spin to see Anita rushing after me. "Just wait," she cries. "Please."

Seeing her upset still twists something in my heart so I wait for her to join me. "There's nothing to say."

"I want Leo back," she says firmly. "I can't do that without the help of my parents."

"So?"

"For that, I need to be accepted back into the fold."

"What does this have to do with me?" I snap, pushing my door open and going inside. She follows.

"They'll approve of Anthony."

Her words finally make sense and I scoff in disbelief. "So you don't wanna be with me because they won't approve."

She nods. "But it's not because I don't love you, Atlas."

I hold a hand up and she stops talking. "Don't say another word."

"But it's true."

"If you loved me, none of that would matter."

"I will never get him back if I stay with you," she cries, tears suddenly slipping from the corners of her eyes. "Don't you think I've thought about it, how that would work? Damien would lap it up and use it in court. He'd tell the judge every piece of shit he could find on this club and ensure I never got to see my son again." Her words sink in as I take a seat on the bed. "He will do anything to stop me having contact, Atlas, and I couldn't stand to never see my boy again." I watch her, noting the seriousness in her expression. "He's my world, and as much as I love you, I can't choose you."

My heart cracks a little, and I hold out my hand. She takes it, and I tug her closer. "Why didn't you just tell me everything from the start?" I wrap my arms around her, resting my forehead against her stomach. "We could've worked something out together."

She runs her fingers through my hair, gently grazing my scalp with her nails, and I close my eyes, enjoying the stillness of the moment. "Because you can't kill him," she whispers with a hint of humour in her tone.

I grin. "That was a last option."

"He's a judge," she almost whispers. "Anthony. I arranged to bump into him on purpose because I'm hoping he'll help me with Leo."

"Does he know your plan?"

She shakes her head. "No, I'll pretend it's a coincidence." She cups my face in her hands and tilts my head back so we're staring into one another's eyes. "I love you so much," she whispers. "And I knew I could never keep you, so I tried to keep you at arms-length . . . and now, seeing the way you look at her," she takes a shuddering breath, "I realise exactly what I'm giving up."

I allow myself to get caught up, the words soothing the ache I've felt for so long. And when she lowers, bringing her lips closer, I don't pull away like I should. When she crawls onto my lap, placing her legs either side of mine and wrapping her arms around my neck, I kiss her. It's hungry and heated, like we've both been starved of the moment for too long. Her fingers are in my hair, and my hands are around her waist. She's rubbing against me, knowing exactly how to get me hard.

And then I think about Rue. Her innocent eyes, the way I just promised her I was done with this, with Anita. And here I am again, lost to her. *Fuck.*

I pull back, panting for breath, and I lift her from me. "No," I say, shaking my head. "I can't."

She runs her fingers through her hair and wipes her mouth on the back of her hand. "Right," she mutters, the pain etched on her face. "Of course."

She pushes to her feet. "It's not that I don't want to," I admit. "But if I keep doing this dance with you, I'll be the one hurting. Your situation won't change. I'm always gonna be the biker you can't take home to meet the family."

She heads for the door, looking defeated. "And Anita . . ." She looks back. "Can we keep this between us? If Rue was to find out—"

"You should be honest, Atlas. Nothing good ever came from lies."

∼

"So," says Kasey, leaning against the bonnet I currently have my head under, "what happened with you and my sister last night?"

I give her a sideways glance. "Huh?"

"Well, one minute, she was happy, and the next, she was leaving."

"I don't know what you mean." I go back to tightening the bolts and thinking about Rue. She was fine when she left but refused to let me walk her home or even arrange a cab. But she insisted she was okay, that she understood the Anita shit. I groan, throwing my spanner back into the toolbox. "Has she said anything to you?"

Kasey gives a satisfied smile. "So, you did upset her?"

"I didn't say that."

"Your face did." She crosses her arms over her chest. "It was the posh bird, right?"

"Her name is Anita," I snap, wiping my hands on a rag. "And I didn't know she'd be there yesterday."

She shrugs. "It's not like you and Rue are together. I don't think she'll be upset over it. She's not the jealous type."

"No?" I ask, unable to hide the hope in my tone.

"Go and see her. She's not working today." She snatches the rag from me and whips my leg with it. "I can't stand to look at that miserable face any longer."

"Actually," I say, leaning against the car. "I wanted to talk to you."

"Sounds serious."

"About your dad and the shit he's got you involved in."

She groans and begins to walk away. I grab her wrist and pull her back. "Kasey, this ain't going away. Your sister is talking about getting cash together and leaving the country with you. She can't uproot her life like that. And if you tell me what's going on, I might be able to help you."

She eyes me for a second. "You're panicking she might leave."

I sigh. "No, Kasey. We've been on a couple dates. What she does is her business. I'm just saying it could be avoided."

"You can't help me."

"Until you tell me, how will you know?"

"The men after me, or the man, is powerful."

I frown. "What does he want with you?"

She stares at the ground. It's the most unsure she's looked since I found her. "He thinks I stole money from him."

"Did you?"

Her head whips up. "No."

"Tell me everything, from the start."

"I was sleeping with him," she announces, almost looking apologetic.

"How old is he?" I ask, my frown deepening.

She shrugs. "I didn't ask. It was business . . . yah know, as in, he paid me for sex."

I rub a hand over my brow. "Right."

"And this one time, he called me over and after we did it, he accused me of taking some cash from his safe."

"Why did he think it was you?"

"Cos he said he'd left it unlocked and I was the only one who could've taken it." She takes a breath. "But that's not true. His kid was in the house too."

"Now you're accusing his kid?"

"It wasn't me, Atlas. I swear."

"So just tell him. I don't understand why he's coming for you. Why didn't he just call the police?"

She shrugs. "I don't know where the cash came from. It was probably dodgy."

"Who is this guy?"

"A lawyer by day, but who knows what he does in the evenings. He always had dodgy people coming and going."

"And he didn't think they would take his money?"

She shakes her head again. "I think they worked for him."

"In law?"

"No," she says with a laugh. "With whatever extracurricular activities he does."

I sigh heavily. "Fine, give me his name and I'll see if I can find out some more."

"I don't know it."

"What do you mean you don't know his name. You were sleeping with him."

"He never gave a real name. Just Mr. D."

I laugh. "Right. Well, give me his mobile number and I'll get Axel to put a trace on it." She pulls out her mobile and turns it to me so I can snap a picture of the number. "Until then, stay low."

RUE

It was in his eyes. So blaringly obvious that I'd be an idiot to pretend Atlas wasn't crazy in love with Anita.

I'm so lost in thought, I don't see him until it's too late, and I crash into Atlas's hard chest. He steadies me with his hands on my shoulders, and I ignore the warm feeling his touch sends through me. I look up into his amused eyes. "Steady."

His voice is deep, rumbling in a sexy sort of way and I shiver involuntary. "Sorry, I was . . ." I trail off because I can't exactly tell him I was lost in thought to him . . . again. "What are you doing here?"

He looks past me to the coffee shop where we had our first 'date'. "I could lie and say I was passing and fancied an over-priced shot of coffee, but we both know I'm here hoping to find you."

My stomach does a somersault. "Oh?"

His grin reaches his eyes. "Are you busy?"

"Not really."

"Good." He turns me around and guides me back inside the coffee house.

Jen looks up from the counter and frowns when she sees me. It soon fades when she realises I'm with 'the biker' again. She's spent the entire morning giving me shit about him and encouraging me to go for it, and forget about his ex. "Ha, you're back," she says, eyeing me with a mischievous glint. "With company."

Atlas reaches out a hand, and she takes it. "Atlas," he introduces.

"Jen."

"I'll take a double espresso, Jen, and whatever Rue wants."

"Just a water, please," I mutter feebly.

I'm glad the place is empty as we take a seat. Things already feel awkward without a crowded, noisy café adding into the mix. I shift uncomfortably. He's staring intently, like he's searching my soul. "Is everything okay with Kasey?" I ask.

"You're pissed at me," he states.

I shake my head, my words failing me. I am pissed but I can't admit that. We've literally been on two dates—if they were even dates—but I've spent so much time avoiding men, especially ones like Atlas, that he caught me off guard, and for a second there, I thought he might be different . . . nicer. "I'm really not."

"You're looking at me differently."

I shake my head a second time. "I'm not."

"I spoke to Kasey. We're gonna run a trace on the man looking for her."

"Okay. Then what?"

He shrugs. "The club will sort it."

"No," I blurt a little too quickly. "It's fine. If you go after him, I'll owe the club, and I can't get caught up in that life again."

"You weren't too concerned about that when you called Axel for help."

"He owed me then. It was one favour." I stand. "Thanks for everything. I'll have Kasey cut your hair soon, I promise."

He stands too. "I kissed Anita," he blurts, and I inhale sharply. "Or she kissed me," he mutters, with a shrug, "I'm not sure."

I recover quickly and laugh. "So?"

"I wanted to be honest."

"There really is no need." I take a breath. "Look, maybe I let myself get carried away for a minute and—"

"It felt right, didn't it?" he asks, cutting me off.

"What did?"

His finger hooks around mine, and he steps closer. "The other night . . . that kiss."

My mouth opens and closes, lost for words again. "You've just come out of a relationship," I try.

"Just give us a chance."

"I think you need to work out whatever unfinished busin —" He kisses me, cutting off my words and stealing my breath as his hands cup either side of my head and his lips caress my own.

He pulls back. "Me and Anita are finished. It's you I'm interested in."

"Awww." We both look to find Jen staring at us with a smile. "You guys are too sweet."

He throws a twenty on the counter and slips his hand in mine before leading me from the shop and back out into the street. "Say you'll go on a third date with me?" he asks.

"I don't know."

"You want me to beg?" he asks, glancing around and starting to bend at one knee.

I laugh, shaking my head. "Okay, okay, I'll go on another date with you."

He grins. "That's all I'm asking for . . . for now."

ANITA

Rejection feels like a slap to the face, but the kind you didn't see coming. It's the sudden realisation that the person you thought was a sure thing, your safe place, your answer, isn't even looking in your direction anymore. It hits hard, deep in your chest, a stinging ache that spreads outward. There's a hollow emptiness that settles in your stomach, like you've been knocked out of orbit and you weren't prepared for the fall.

I rub my temples, pushing the thought of Atlas aside, desperate to focus on the task at hand. As much as I want to avoid it, the custody battle looms, and I need to find a way to fight.

A soft tap on the courtroom door breaks my concentration. Before I can respond, it swings open and Tom's head pops in, eyes locking with mine.

"What are you still doing here?" he asks, his tone more teasing than concerned.

I force a smile, gathering the scattered papers in front of me and folding them neatly. "I have to get these to the clerk before five."

He steps inside, confident, leaning casually against the

wall. I can't help but notice how effortlessly he exudes authority. He might be a lawyer, but he could easily be mistaken for a mafia boss in that tailored suit.

"Y'know, I've branched out into family law," he says, flashing a grin that's crooked enough to suggest trouble.

I glance up, raising an eyebrow. "I didn't know that."

He shrugs, unbothered by the casual dismissal. "And a little birdie told me you're . . . in a bit of a situation."

I freeze for a moment, suddenly hyper-aware of the stack of legal documents between us. The papers, usually so professional and cold, now feel like a weight on my shoulders. I glance up at him, my gaze lingering just a second too long. "Oh?"

Tom's smile deepens, knowing he has my attention. "So, if you're looking for someone—"

"I'm not," I say, my voice sharp as I stand, cutting him off.

He doesn't flinch. In fact, he steps closer, his presence filling the room, and the air between us thickens. His voice drops, more serious now. "Relax, Nita," he says, shoving his hands in his pockets. His stance widens, authoritative, commanding, the kind of thing that makes most people fold. "It's no secret I don't like your ex." He smirks. "And if I can crush him in court, it'll be the highlight of my career."

I narrow my eyes at him, trying to keep my cool. "I'm not interested in being part of your pissing contest."

"You sure about that?" He takes a step forward, challenging me. "You're going to let Dopey Dennis handle this for you, and you'll lose. I've seen how your ex operates. Dennis is too nice to handle someone like him."

"Dennis is a good lawyer," I say, my tone clipped. I want to defend Dennis, but my words feel weak in the face of Tom's piercing gaze. I shift uncomfortably.

"I'm better," Tom shoots back, his voice low but certain. His eyes are no longer playful—they're laser-focused. "And I'd do it without the ego trip. It's not just about the win for me, Nita. It's about making sure you don't lose."

I stand there for a moment, caught between pride and practicality. Tom's right. Dennis is good, too good, in fact, which sometimes works against him. But Tom . . . he's relentless, and that could make all the difference in a case this high-staked.

But then I think about the last thing I need right now: someone else trying to take control of my life. Someone who doesn't understand what this means, who's just trying to prove something.

"I don't need your help," I say firmly, though my stomach tightens at the lie. "I can handle this."

Tom doesn't back off. Instead, he steps even closer, his voice dropping to a softer, more intimate register. "Are you sure, Nita? Because this fight isn't just about custody. This is about your and Leo's life, your future together. A son needs to be with his mother. We both know that. I can win this."

The sincerity in his tone is . . . unsettling. I don't know what to make of it. He's right about one thing—this isn't just some battle over Leo. It's a fight for our future. It's a fight for our freedom. And most of all, it'll break the cycle of abuse. The cycle I know Damien is already trying to instil in our son.

I take a deep breath, meeting his gaze with more resolve than I feel. "Okay. I'll give you a chance to look over the case files and see what your angle is. Then we can discuss."

CHAPTER 11

ATLAS

"You're telling me that sweet, crazy chick out there is a prostitute?" asks Grizz, his brows raised in surprise.

"We know what women will do to survive," Axel reminds him. "And no one chooses that life, it's something they have to do for whatever reason."

"Hey, I'm not judging," he replies, holding his hands up. "I just can't see it. For a start, she never shuts the fuck up."

I laugh. "He's got a point. I imagine Kasey talks through sex."

"She could definitely talk with a cock in her mouth," laughs Pit.

"I have her dad's address," Axel says, looking at me as he slides a piece of paper towards me. "Take whoever you need."

"Hold on, I thought Rue asked you not to get involved?" asks Grizz.

"She did."

"Yet here you are, getting involved."

I grin. "I'm just making enquiries to check they're both safe." I stand. "Who wants a ride out?"

Fletch stands, along with Pit and we head out.

∽

THE HOUSE ISN'T AS RUN-DOWN AS I'D PICTURED. FROM THE outside, you'd think a respectable family lived here. I knock once, but I know he's already seen me from the Ring doorbell attached to the door. After a minute, it swings open, and a young boy looks up at us through his floppy fringe.

"Adam, what have I said to you about opening the damn door?" snaps a woman as she bustles towards us, grabbing the child by the upper arm and dragging him back behind her. "What?" she asks, glancing to my patch.

"We're looking for Frank."

"Well, good luck finding him. Tell him he owes me a shit tonne of child maintenance when you see him."

I look past her and notice a shadow lingering in the kitchen doorway. "You sure that ain't him hiding?" I ask, nodding in that direction.

She rolls her eyes. "If he owes you money, we don't have it."

I shove past her and head inside. Frank backs into the kitchen the second he spots me. His eyes dart around nervously. "I don't have anything."

"What do you think I'm looking for?" I ask.

Fletch picks up a stack of unopened mail and flicks through it. He holds up a letter for Kasey with an arched brow. "You looking for Kasey?" Frank asks. "She ain't here, man. She did a runner ages ago."

"I know," I say. "I found her."

"So, what do you want with me?"

"Who's looking for her?" I ask, stepping closer.

He falls back onto a chair. "Some guy she was fucking."

"What guy?" asks Pit, impatiently.

"He's a suit from the city. I don't know his name. She was always getting mixed up in some shit."

"Not good enough," Pit growls, landing a fist to his stomach. He coughs violently. "You know way more than that, so get talking."

"She's always bringing trouble back here," the woman yells from the doorway. "That's why we kicked her out."

I turn to her. "I hear your man's been good at that too." Her eyes flit to him. "Maybe if he was a proper father figure."

"She was selling herself from a young age," she spits with disgust. "He tried to help her."

"Now that's a load of bullshit." We all turn to the sound of Kasey's voice as she enters the room looking smug. Adam is tapping her leg for attention and she ruffles his hair affectionately.

"What the fuck are you doing here?" I snap.

"I heard you were heading here so thought I'd tag along."

I grab her upper arm and back her from the room. "You're not meant to leave the club," I whisper hiss.

"I'm a big girl," she says, pulling free.

"How dare you bring bikers to my door?" the woman yells. "It's always something with you, Kasey."

"Oh, boo-hoo, step-monster. And why you always yelling?"

Kasey heads back to the kitchen with me hot on her tail. "We all know who stole that money, daddy dearest," she says, stabbing a finger in her dad's chest. "I told you not to. I warned you he was dangerous."

"What are you talking about?" asks Pit.

"He was always setting men up," she tells us. "He'd arrange the meet, I'd go into the bedroom to do the deed, and he would have someone rob the punter."

"Why didn't you just tell me this before?" I demand.

"It wasn't your business," she says with an arched brow. "And then you went and made it your business. Anyway, Mr. D was different. I met him by accident, and we got talking. He offered me money for sex and taking care of his kid sometimes. Dad found out I was onto a good thing and had to ruin it."

"Shut your mouth," Frank roars, jumping out the chair. Pit is between them in a flash, shoving him back down and hitting him a second time.

"Stay in the chair," he warns.

"Kasey, I need this guy's name," I say.

"I don't know it. But I can take you to his place."

~

I knock gently on Rue's apartment door. She opens it a second later looking flustered. She smiles, blowing a few strands of hair from her face. "Hey." She opens the door wider for me to go inside.

The apartment is small, but she's made it into a cosy living space with fancy cushions and fairy lights. "Nice place."

"It's not much but it's all mine and I love it."

She points to a door, and we head through into a small kitchen where a table is set up in the centre. I take a seat, and she goes to the cooker and stirs something in a pan on the hob. "You can cook," I state with a smile.

"My mum was a good teacher."

"You and Kasey have different mums?" I ask.

She nods. "Same dad, unfortunately. I was the result of a brief relationship between Mum and Kasey's dad, Frank. Kasey came a few years after."

"Do you still see him?" I ask.

"Not if I can help it," she says, offering a small smile. "He was different when Mum first met him. Worked in a decent job and was generally a functioning adult. He started doing extra shifts to support her, even though they weren't together. To get through the late nights he started taking cocaine. After that he went downhill. Lost his jobs, couldn't pay Mum any money. He went off radar for a long time, and when he popped back up, he had Kasey. Her mum had done a runner and left him with the two-year-old. He couldn't cope."

"So, your mum stepped in?"

"She helped where she could, but she was barely getting by. She passed when I was thirteen. I went to live with him for a few years and helped raise Kasey."

"I'm sorry," I almost whisper. "That must have been tough."

"My mum was my world," she admits. "I don't know how many times I prayed to God to take my dad instead and bring her back to me."

"It's a cruel world."

"Anyway, as soon as I had enough money, I left. He wouldn't let me take Kase, by then he was using her to make his own cash. But she came to stay regularly."

"How did you get involved with the club?" I ask.

She smiles, lifting the pan from the hob and placing it in the centre of the table. "I'm a math whizz," she says with a hint of pride. "I was fourteen and did the books for a few of the businesses."

"Fourteen!"

She laughs. "Tank, Axel's dad, was good to me. He gave me cash in hand and knew I needed it to get away from my dad. He never asked too many questions."

"I've been in this club for years and I don't remember you."

"You think he was stupid enough to let me round his men?"

I laugh. "Good point."

She takes my bowl and begins to ladle a chunky soup into it. "What about you?"

"Me?"

She replaces my bowl and fills her own. "Family?"

"The club is my family. I don't have blood relatives."

"None?"

I shake my head. "But I'm good with that. I have all I need at the club."

She sits and picks up her spoon. "I hope you like it," she says, nodding to my bowl.

I scoop some and place it in my mouth. The mixture of beef and vegetables warms me instantly and I groan in delight. I don't remember the last home cooked meal we had. "It's delicious."

She smiles wide under the praise and tucks in.

"Didn't the posh bird cook?"

I swallow a mouthful and meet her eyes. "Can we just call her Anita?"

Rue gives a small shrug. "Sure."

"And no, she didn't."

She tilts her head. "What about others?"

"Others?"

"Women. Old ladies?"

I grin. "There weren't any... old ladies, I mean. When I take one, I want her to be forever."

Her smile falters just slightly, like she's not sure how to take that. Then she murmurs, "Anita said you asked her."

I set my spoon down with a little more force than I mean to. "Do you really want to talk about Anita?"

Rue blinks, caught between curiosity and regret. After a second, she gives a slight shake of the head.

"Good," I say, softer this time, "cos neither do I."

We finish the rest of the meal in relaxed silence.

Afterwards, I help her clear up, even though she insists she can manage. The kitchen's so small that every time we turn, we brush against one another. First our arms, then the small of her back against my front. She laughs the first time, but it's breathy, a little too light. The next time, she doesn't laugh at all, feeling the sexual tension buzzing around us.

Her body's warm, and she smells like whatever lotion she wore last—vanilla maybe, or almond—and something sweet from her shampoo.

I hand her a plate, our fingers grazing. She doesn't pull away.

"You do this for everyone?" I murmur.

She glances up, cheeks pink. "What, cook them dinner?"

"No," I say, "let them in here." I nod at the cramped space between us. "This close."

Her eyes drop to my chest, then flick back up. "Not really."

"That a no, then?"

Rue smiles again, slow, shy, almost dangerous. "Guess you're special."

I step in closer. Not touching, not quite, but her breath hitches anyway.

She leans against the counter, palms behind her, grounding herself. It forces her chest forward slightly, and I notice, of course I do, but I keep my eyes on hers.

"Careful," I say low. "Might start thinking you like me."

Her lips part like she's going to say something smart, to tease me back, but no sound comes.

God, she's cute like this. Slightly overwhelmed, trying to play it cool, knowing damn well she's not.

"You're not what I expected," she says finally.

"And what did you expect?"

She shrugs. "Someone rougher. Scarier." Her voice softens. "Less kind."

I take the plate from her hands and set it down on the counter beside her. "You think I'm kind, Rue?"

Her lashes lower. "I think you're trying to be."

I lean in just a little. "Only with you."

She exhales shakily, and I swear, if I moved an inch, we'd be kissing. But I don't. Not yet.

"I should, uh, get dessert," she says, slipping to the side, brushing against me again as she heads for the fridge.

She opens the door and pulls out a large glass dish containing some kind of chocolate thing, topped with whipped cream and raspberries.

She turns. "It's just store-bought. I didn't have time to—"

I kiss her.

There's no warning, no slow lean-in, no testing the waters. Just the thud of need in my chest and her scent in the air and the way her lips part in surprise, like she's been holding her breath for me this whole damn time.

The dessert shakes slightly in her hand, cream tipping at the edge of the dish, but she doesn't drop it.

I cup her face with one hand, the other settling on her

waist as I deepen the kiss — slow but claiming. She tastes like strawberries or chocolate and something uniquely *her*.

Rue breathes into my mouth, her free hand curling into my shirt. I feel her fingers tighten, like she's anchoring herself. Like she doesn't trust her legs to hold her steady.

When I finally pull back, her lashes flutter open. Her cheeks are flushed. Her chest rises and falls like she's just run a mile.

I glance down at the dessert between us. "You didn't drop it."

She looks too dazed to speak at first. Then she swallows and mutters, "I like chocolate."

I smile. "Noted."

She stares at me for a second longer, then turns abruptly, setting the dessert down on the table.

Her voice is a little shaky when she speaks again. "You want coffee, or . . .?"

"Rue."

She pauses.

I step behind her, close enough that my chest nearly brushes her back. I lower my mouth to her ear.

"I want you."

She shivers.

Then, she slowly turns to face me, cheeks still flushed and lips swollen, and says, "I thought you might."

RUE

I shut my eyes. My throat works on a swallow. My body says yes. God, it screams it. But there's this old fear lodged inside my chest, tangled up with nerves and memories I wish I could forget.

I turn slowly, heart pounding like it's about to rip from my chest.

When I look up at him, I say it before I can lose the nerve. "I've only done this once."

Atlas stills. His eyes scan mine, but not in a predatory way. It's soft. Focused. Careful.

I keep going, because I need to. "And it wasn't . . . good. It wasn't bad, but it just . . . it felt like something I was supposed to get over with. And I did, but I didn't feel anything."

His hand brushes a piece of hair from my cheek. "You felt that kiss we just shared?"

"Yes," I whisper.

"Everything else will feel a million times . . . more."

And then he kisses me again, slower this time. Deeper. Like he heard every word and is trying to rewrite the bad memories.

His fingers curl into the curve of my hip as he backs me up gently, guiding me until I feel the edge of the table behind my thighs. When he pulls away, I can barely breathe.

"I'm not gonna rush you," he says, voice rough. "I just want to touch you. You good with that?"

I nod, fast.

But he stays right where he is.

"Rue. Tell me yes."

I look up at him, everything in me trembling, but not with fear. With want. *Need.*

"Yes," I say. "Touch me."

He doesn't move fast. His hand settles on my waist again, warm and steady, thumb brushing slow circles that make me shiver. He watches me like I might break – not fragile, but precious and for some reason that undoing starts in my chest.

"I've been thinking about this since the café," he

murmurs, his mouth near mine. "The way you looked at me with that sweet, nervous energy."

I breathe out a shaky laugh, and he kisses me again. Slower this time. Lazier. Like we've got all the time in the world.

My hands find his shoulders. I feel the tension there, the restraint. He could pin me to the table, kiss me breathless, ruin me in every possible way. But he doesn't, like he senses this is important to me.

Instead, his mouth trails from mine to my jaw, down to the soft skin below my ear, and I swear I feel it everywhere.

"You smell so sweet," he murmurs, lips against my neck. "You always smell sweet."

I tip my head to give him more, because his mouth on my skin makes my knees weak. "It's just lotion."

"No, it's you."

His hands move to my hips and lift me, like I weigh nothing. I gasp softly as he sets me on the edge of the table. The cold wood against the backs of my thighs sends a shiver up my spine.

Then he steps between my legs, crowding me just enough that I feel the pressure of his body, but still . . . he's holding back.

His hands skim the hem of my dress, teasing just above the knee, fingers warm on my skin.

"If you change your mind, just say the words . . . at any point."

My voice is barely a whisper. "Okay."

He leans in again, mouth brushing mine. "You sure about this, Rue?"

I look at him and I know he means it. He'd stop if I blinked the wrong way. I reach for his hand, guide it higher. "I'm sure."

That's when something shifts.

His mouth claims mine with more urgency, tongue brushing against mine in a kiss that steals the air from my lungs. One hand slides up to cradle the back of my neck while the other keeps hold of my thigh, fingers curling tight like he's been holding back for too long.

I feel his body pressing into mine, hard where I'm soft, and my whole-body lights up like a switch has been flipped.

Still kissing me, he slips one hand up between my thighs, not inside, just exploring. And I realise I'm shaking.

He pulls back an inch. "Too much?"

"No," I whisper. "I just . . . I've never felt like this before."

His forehead rests against mine. "Good. I want to ruin you for every other man."

I laugh, breathless, nervous, and wrap my arms around his neck to pull him closer. "You already have."

His mouth is back on mine in seconds, and this time, there's nothing held back. The kiss is messy, open-mouthed, all heat and wanting, and I match it, surprising myself. Surprising *him*, too, judging by the low sound he makes in his throat when I tug his shirt higher.

His hands roam, rough and warm and reverent. Up my legs. Under my dress. Across my thighs. It's like he's memorising the shape of me.

"You're still shaking," he says against my lips.

"I know."

His thumb brushes the inside of my thigh, just shy of where I need it. "Do you want me to stop?"

"No."

His hand stills. "Then tell me what you *do* want."

"I want you to keep touching me," I whisper, every nerve ending sparking. "But I don't know how to ask for it right."

"You just did," he says, his voice a low rumble vibrating through me.

He slides my underwear down slowly, like he's unwrapping something fragile. I lift my hips to help him, my cheeks flushing as the cool air kisses my skin. But he doesn't laugh, doesn't stare.

He groans.

Like seeing me is a relief. A reward.

"You're soaked," he murmurs. "Fucking beautiful."

I shiver, my legs falling wider without meaning to. He takes the cue, trailing his fingertips along my opening, feather-light at first. I inhale sharply, my head falling back.

He watches me. Every reaction. Every tiny gasp.

And when he finally slides one finger inside, my body clenches around it like it's been waiting for him, like it *knows* him.

"God, Rue . . ."

He kisses me while he moves his hand in slow, steady strokes that build heat in my belly. And when his thumb finds that sweet, aching spot at the top, I jolt, clutching at his arms like I'm falling.

He doesn't stop, adjusting until he has me squirming, gasping, panting into his mouth.

When I come, it's not quiet. It's full-body. Overwhelming. I cry out against his throat, and he holds me through it, murmuring, "That's it, baby. That's my girl."

When I open my eyes, he's looking at me like I just did something impossible.

I reach for him. "Don't stop."

"You don't have to—"

"I want to."

He curses softly and kisses me hard. He steps back only

long enough to shove his jeans down to his thighs, and my breath catches when I see him.

Big. Hard. And way more intimidating than I remember from my one awkward, forgettable first time.

He notices the shift in my face. "Hey," he says gently, stepping between my legs again. "We go slow. We stop if you need."

"Okay."

I watch as he reaches into his back pocket and pulls out his wallet. He retrieves a condom, something I hadn't even thought about until now. *Fuck.* I can't think straight around him.

He leans his forehead to mine as he rolls the condom over his thick length. "You trust me?"

I nod. "Yeah."

He guides himself to me with one hand and cups the back of my neck with the other, kissing me as he pushes in slow and careful. I gasp at the stretch, my body tensing.

He pauses, breathing hard. "You okay?"

"Yeah. Just . . . give me a second."

He waits, not moving. He just kisses me again and again until I melt around him, my body relaxing enough to take more.

Then he starts to move again.

And it's *nothing* like last time.

This isn't fumbling or rushed or selfish. This is Atlas groaning my name in my ear, his hands gripping my hips, our bodies moving in sync like we were always meant to fit this way.

My fingers dig into his back. His thrusts are slow and deep, hitting something inside me that makes me tremble all over again.

"Look at me," he says, and I do—I *can't not*—and he kisses me like he's starving. "You feel so fucking good, Rue."

I hold his face, fingers in his hair, and that pressure builds again, faster this time, sharper.

"I think . . . I think I'm . . ."

"I've got you."

And I fall apart around him, again. Completely.

He follows a moment later with a curse and a shudder, burying his face in my neck as he comes, his whole body trembling against mine.

The only sound in the room is our breathing. Sharp. Rapid.

He kisses my temple, my cheek, the corner of my mouth.

Then he rests his forehead against mine and says softly, "If that was your second time ever, I'm terrified for what your third is gonna do to me."

I laugh, breathless. "You planning ahead?"

He grins. "Damn right I am."

CHAPTER 12

ANITA

> Anthony: You're not home again?? Where are you???

My fingers curl tighter around the stem of my wine glass. I take a slow sip, just to busy my hands, then tap out a reply.

> Me: Dinner with Tessa. She's been nagging me to catch up.

> Anthony: You work with her all day. Evenings should be for me, Anita. We discussed this.

> Me: Sorry. I won't be out long. I'll call at yours after?

Three dots appear then disappear. Then, nothing.

A chill slides through me, settling low in my stomach. I tuck my phone face-down on the table and scan the bar again. Tom's late. I shouldn't care, but I do. I shouldn't be here at all, if I'm honest. I should've met him in his office, kept it professional.

But I said yes because something in his voice made me believe he could do this. That maybe, for the first time in a long time, I wasn't completely screwed.

When the door swings open, I spot him instantly. He doesn't walk in like he owns the place, but people notice him anyway. There's something in the set of his jaw, the way his eyes take everything in. He's not handsome in a polished way —he's too blunt around the edges for that—but he's magnetic.

And he looks like someone who doesn't lose.

Tom spots me and gives a nod. No smile, just calm, unflinching focus as he strides towards me and shrugs off his coat.

"You alright?" he asks before he's even fully sat down.

I nod too quickly. "Fine."

"You don't look it."

I open my mouth to respond, but the words catch. My usual mask, smoothed out and fixed tight, is slipping. Anthony's message still echoes in the back of my head, the way it always does. Every compliment laced with suspicion. Every silence sharp enough to draw blood.

Tom watches me. Not the way other men do. Not like he's weighing me up or peeling me apart. He just . . . waits.

I glance at the menu, just for something to do. "Thanks for meeting like this. I didn't want to bring the notes to your office. It felt too formal."

He doesn't buy it. "You get spooked easily?"

I meet his eyes. "Not usually."

He leans forward slightly, resting his arms on the table. "But tonight, you are."

The honesty hangs between us. Thick. Undeniable. I press my lips together and shake my head. "I don't talk about my personal life."

"Isn't that why we're here?"

A smile pulls at my lips. "Yes."

He takes the folder from his bag and taps it. "Your ex, Damien, I've come up against him before. Smart, sure, but cruel. Petty. He wins because he knows how to tear people down before they even step foot in the courtroom."

I nod once, trying to swallow past the lump rising in my throat. "I'm not scared of him," I say, my voice too tight to be convincing.

Tom just watches me. "You should be. That's what makes men like him dangerous."

I look away. My chest aches, not from what he's said, but from how true it all is.

"I can't lose my son," I whisper. It's the smallest I've ever felt. "Leo deserves better than Damien. He'll mess him up, make him a carbon copy. I can't let that happen."

Tom's jaw ticks. "We're not going to let it."

I breathe in deeply, steadying myself. "Anthony—" I stop, biting back the name before I can explain.

"The judge you're dating?" I glance at him sharply. "Rumours," he says with a shrug. "The court clerks love to gossip."

Heat floods my cheeks. "It's not like that."

The silence that follows is heavier than before. Then Tom leans back in his chair and says simply, "You don't need him." I look up, startled. "You think you do because the system is stacked and you're tired and you think he holds more power than Damien. He doesn't. He can't help you. Don't waste your time."

For a second, I just sit there, stunned. No one talks to me like that, not even Tessa. No one cuts through the bullshit. No one sees what I don't say.

I clear my throat, blink hard, and reach for my wine again.

Tom offers me a small smile, real this time. "Let's talk strategy."

And for the first time in months, maybe years, I feel something I'd almost forgotten.

Hope.

∼

THE BUZZ FROM THE WINE HAS LONG FADED, LEAVING ONLY nerves humming low in my stomach. I grip the steering wheel tighter as the sharp-edged glass and steel box Anthony calls home comes into view. I've already practised the lie in my head a million times—Tessa needed cheering up, nothing serious, just girl talk and wine.

I pull into the underground car park, kill the engine, and check my reflection in the rearview mirror. I smooth my lipstick, finger-comb my hair, then pause.

Is that . . .

I lean closer.

A faint scent clings to my jacket. Something woody. Masculine. *Tom.*

I exhale sharply through my nose. *It's nothing.* Just a brief hug goodbye, two professionals, one human moment. Still, I slip out of the jacket before I reach the lift.

When I knock on Anthony's door, he opens it almost

instantly. He's still in work attire, his shirt sleeves rolled up and a drink already in hand.

"You're late," he says. Not playful. Not teasing. Just flat, cold.

"I got caught up," I say, stepping inside. "Tessa was venting about her guy. You know how she gets."

He closes the door behind me. It clicks with a sound that feels louder than it should.

"Didn't realise venting involves cologne," he mutters.

I stop mid-step. "What?"

Anthony takes a slow sip of his drink, eyes narrowing. "You smell like another man."

Heat creeps up my neck. "I don't know what you're talking about."

His voice is calm, but his jaw ticks. "Don't lie to me."

"I'm not . . . Anthony, seriously. It must've rubbed off when I hugged someone goodbye. One of Tessa's friends stopped by for a bit." The lie slides off my tongue too easily. I've had practice.

He steps closer. "Do you think I'm stupid?"

"No," I say softly, "but I think you're being paranoid."

His eyes darken. He steps even closer, too close. I try not to shift back, but something in me coils tight.

"You go swanning off dressed like *that* to meet Tessa," he says, voice low, dangerous, "and come here smelling like a man I don't know, and I'm supposed to believe nothing happened?"

I shake my head. "You're being ridiculous."

He slams his glass down on the sideboard, the sharp clink making me flinch.

For a moment, there's nothing but the sound of his breathing. Then, quieter, too quiet, he says, "Don't make me feel like I can't trust you."

My throat is dry. "There's nothing to feel that way about."

He exhales, forces a smile, and reaches to tuck a strand of hair behind my ear. The gesture makes my skin crawl. "You know I hate when I feel like you're hiding something."

I nod, mute.

Because I *am* hiding something. A case file. A son. A war I'm quietly waging without his knowledge. And a man, Tom, who saw straight through me and didn't flinch. And I . . . liked it.

Anthony brushes a hand down my arm, lingering for a second too long.

"You're lucky I'm an understanding man."

The words steal the breath from my lungs.

Because they sound like a threat.

Because I can feel the steel cage forming again, only now, it's not Damien's name on the lock.

ATLAS

It's just past noon when I hear the sound of heels on concrete. Not the kind that belong here. Not boots. Not the clunky stomp of club life.

She always walks like she knows where she's going, even when she doesn't.

I look up from the engine I'm elbow-deep in, grease on my forearms and sweat sticking to the back of my neck. And there she is.

Anita.

Black trousers, tucked white shirt, sunglasses perched high. Her hair's scraped back, sleek as ever. But her shoulders look tight, like the weight she's carrying today is heavier than usual.

She doesn't see me right away. She's talking to Nyx, who

nods and gestures towards the office. Paperwork for Kade, no doubt. He's coming out on licence next week after a brief stint inside for assault.

She steps into the office without a glance in my direction, and I tell myself to leave it. To stay in the garage, finish what I'm doing, let her handle the job and go.

But my feet don't listen.

I wipe my hands and follow, pausing in the doorway like I've done a hundred times before.

She's standing at the desk, flicking through a document, frowning down at it like the words are trying to escape her.

"You always did hate paperwork," I say softly.

She startles, just a flicker, then looks up. There's a pause. It's long enough to be awkward. Long enough to feel like the past few months are thick between us, taking up all the air.

"I didn't know you were here," she says.

I shrug. "Didn't know *you* were coming."

"I'm just sorting Kade's release conditions," she says, lifting the sheet in her hand. "Axel needs to sign. I won't stay long."

"You can." I lean against the doorframe. "You used to."

She looks at me, and her expression softens just a touch. "That was before."

"Before what?"

She doesn't answer.

I nod and glance down at my boots, then back up. "You look tired."

She laughs under her breath, but it's hollow. "It's been a long year."

"I noticed." I step farther inside, giving her space to leave if she wants. "You alright?"

She hesitates. Her mask flickers for a second, just enough for me to see what's behind it. Worn edges. Fragile corners.

The way she bites the inside of her cheek when she's trying not to cry.

"I'm fine," she says, but it doesn't land the way it used to.

"Anita—"

She cuts me off with a soft voice. "Don't, Atlas."

I nod slowly. "Right."

She places the document on the desk, fingers brushing over the surface like she's grounding herself. "I miss this," she says, almost too quietly to hear.

"Miss what?"

"This." Her gaze flits up to mine. "Us. The friendship. The . . . safety of it. You were the only person I didn't have to fight around."

My chest tightens. "You had to do what was right for you."

She swallows. "I know."

For a second, we just stand there, the silence thick with everything we never said. Everything we can't say now.

"Well, isn't this cosy?"

I almost groan out loud at the sound of Kasey's voice. "Posh and . . ." She laughs, stopping beside me. "I can't exactly call you Becks."

"Not now, Kase, hey," I mutter.

"You got a car you need to be under," she says bluntly.

I arch a brow. "Now, you're the boss?"

"Someone needs to be." She gives me a pointed stare. "I was just speaking to Rue on the phone. She sounds happy."

My eyes flit to where Anita stiffens. "Seriously, Kasey, get the fuck out," I snap.

She rolls her eyes but heads out, slamming the office door.

"I should go. Ask Axel to sign this and get it back to me," says Anita.

"We can still be friends," I blurt. "Can't we?"

She stares for a moment. "I don't know, can we?"

I nod. "We can at least try."

A small smile pulls at the corners of her mouth, and I relax a little. I prefer it when she's happier. "Okay, that sounds good."

"If you need anything, with your son or whatever, you only have to ask." Tears fill her eyes, and I panic. "Shit, sorry, I don't want to upset you."

"It's all just . . . hard."

The tears roll down her cheeks. I've never really seen her cry and it breaks me. I tug her to me and wrap my arms around her, automatically burying my nose in her hair and inhaling her familiar scent. It feels grounding, safe. "Don't cry," I whisper.

I feel her shoulders shake as she sobs against my chest. Her arms wrap tighter around me, and I know without a doubt she needs a friend right now. "Shall we get some lunch?" I offer.

She takes a shuddering breath. "If you're busy, it doesn't matter."

"I'm never too busy for you, Nita."

RUE

Kasey is usually singing or talking or just generally bouncing around like a puppy. But this evening, she's quiet. It's worrying.

"Out with it," I say, flopping onto my back and staring up at her bedroom ceiling. The club gave her a basic bedroom but every time I see her, I bring something to make it homely. Today's gift was a fake plant, because she'd kill a real one. "You're unusually quiet, and I hate it."

"You tried to have me medicated in school because I drove you mad," she reminds me. "You said I talked way too much."

I smile at the memory. "You were exhausting."

"Are you and Atlas serious?" She picks at her fingernails, keeping her eyes fixed on them like they're suddenly the most interesting thing in the world.

"It's been a few dates," I say with a laugh. I'm playing it down. She doesn't need to get attached in case it doesn't work out, and that's one of her downfalls, she gets attached so easily. And truthfully, I have no idea what's going on with me and Atlas. He's great, too great if I'm honest, and I keep waiting for the flaws to show.

After we slept together, I thought that would be the downfall, he'd suddenly ghost me and I'd be embarrassed and have to stay away from the club, from Kasey. But he was attentive after, sticking around until late when I couldn't hide my yawns. He texted the second he got back to the club and video called me the following day to wish me good morning. The truth is, he's a dream and I have to keep pinching myself to check he's real.

"Do you like him?" she asks.

"Yeah, he's a nice guy so far."

"So, you think it could get serious?"

I frown. "What's going on, Kase?"

She bites the corner of her lip, dragging it through her teeth, whilst she gathers her words. "His ex came by yesterday."

I bristle at her words but try to hide it. "Okay. So?"

"They went to lunch together."

"It's not a crime," I say with a shrug that I hope passes off as easy.

"Did he tell you about it?" she asks, eyeing me closely.

I shrug it off, shaking my head. "He doesn't need to. I'm not his owner."

"But if he's with you then—"

"I never said he was," I snap, instantly regretting it. "Sorry. It's just, you're reading into it too much. Me and Atlas . . . we're, friends and—"

I glance up as he fills the doorway with a pissed expression. He arches a brow. "A word, Rue," he states.

"I'm a little busy," I mutter, unsure if I'm ready for him to confess all about him and Anita.

"Now," he adds, turning in the direction of his own room and disappearing down the hall.

"Great," I mutter, pushing to my feet.

"He looked annoyed," Kasey points out.

I shoot her a glare. "Yes, I noticed."

"Maybe he thought you were more?" she asks hopefully.

"I doubt it, if he was with his ex yesterday. He's probably about to tell me he's getting back with her."

She sits up. "Shit. Do you want me to come with?"

I scoff. "And watch me get dumped? No thanks."

"I thought you said you weren't together."

I groan as I head out, ignoring her.

I find Atlas pacing. The second I step into the room, I'm swept off my feet and pressed to the wall, where he wraps my legs around his waist and presses his forehead against mine. "Friends?" he asks, and there's a glimmer of hurt in his eyes.

"I didn't know what to tell her," I say, avoiding his glare.

"You tell her we're a thing," he growls. "You tell her we're the step between fucking and forever." My eyes shoot to his. "But don't tell anyone we're *just friends*, Rue. We're way past that."

His hand runs through my hair, gripping it at the roots and gently tugging my head back so he has access to my throat.

His beard rubs against my skin roughly as he presses his nose there and inhales deeply. "That smell," he murmurs, his eyes filling with heat. "I'm addicted."

I should ask him about Anita. I should tell him the context of mine and Kasey's conversation, but I don't. I'm too focussed on the way his erection is pressed between my legs.

"I've missed you," he whispers, nipping at my neck. His mouth finds mine, and when he kisses me, it's like the first time all over again.

"It's been a couple days," I say with a laugh.

"Far too long. Shouldn't you be naked?"

I laugh again as he slides me down his body and takes a step back. He lifts his shirt over his head, dropping it to the floor. Then he waits, watching me until I do the same. He keeps staring, nodding at my bra, so I remove it and add it to the pile. He hasn't seen me naked, but under his intense stare, I don't feel worried or self-conscious. I feel sexy and wanted.

Atlas unfastens his jeans and shoves them down his legs, stepping out of them, then looking at me to do the same. I make quick work of the loose fitted cotton trousers, kicking them to the pile. I hook my thumbs in my knickers, but he shakes his head and takes a seat on the edge of the bed. "Leave them on."

CHAPTER 13

ANITA

I take a bite of the sandwich Tessa grabbed me and screw my nose up. Cheese. I hate plain cheese, but she swore it's all the local deli had left. I drop it on the packaging and turn back to my emails.

The door opens and I glance up as Tom enters. My heart stutters in my chest. I've been waiting to hear from him since I left him with my case notes a few days ago. I didn't want to seem too keen by hassling him, so I lean back in my chair and watch as he saunters towards me with all the stealth of a black panther. He passes Tessa's empty desk. I gave her the afternoon off.

"Hope you don't mind," he says, sitting in the chair opposite. "I came right from court so was passing."

"No, it's fine."

He dumps some files on my desk, then reaches into his bag and pulls out a paper bag. "I skipped lunch and I'm starv ing," he says, opening the bag. He glances at my sandwich. "Not a fan?"

I look at it and shake my head. "It's cheese."

"Ah, sweaty cheese sandwiches remind me of packed lunch as a kid."

I laugh. "Yes."

He stuffs the paper bag back. "How about we go for a late lunch or early dinner?"

I hesitate. Anthony would go mad, and I don't have it in me to keep creating stories to keep him calm. As if Tom senses, he shrugs. "Or not. I can make this quick and leave you to it."

His words stir something in me. I don't want him to leave. Right now, he's the only man who knows it all. *Everything*. And I want to talk about it.

I stand, smiling. "No, it's a great idea. I know a wonderful place a few streets away."

I lock up and lead the way to a quiet little French place I sometimes go to when I need a quiet lunch alone.

It's practically empty to my relief and we're seated straight away.

The waitress asks if we'd like a drink and I stare at Tom who stares back at me. "Ladies first," he says.

I'm so used to men ordering for me, I'm almost lost for words. "Erm, I'll take a small glass of house red."

"I'll have the same," Tom adds.

The waitress leaves us to look at the menu. "What would you recommend?" he asks.

I chew nervously on my lip. "I always have the steak," I tell him. "They cook it to perfection."

He closes his menu. "Steak it is."

I close mine as the waitress brings our drinks. "Are you ready to order?" she asks.

Again, Tom waits for me to order first before adding his own. For the first time ever, I feel respected. I'm still marvelling at that revelation, when he leans closer and says, "I read the case notes."

I come back to earth with a crash. "Right."

"The shit that bastard has put you through."

I stare down at the table, focussing on the patterned tablecloth. "Hey," he says in a sharper tone. I look up. "It's not your fault. None of it." I want to believe him. But my mother's words echo in my ear. *You wanted him to be like this and now he is, you want to leave. Well suck it up because marriage is hard and you owe it to Leo to stick at it.*

It wasn't true of course. I never asked for Damien to switch the way he did. I felt betrayed, like he'd reeled me in with dreams of a better life, only to crush them the second I got pregnant.

"And I know there's more," he continues, bringing me back from my thoughts. "Stuff you're keeping in there," he says, gently tapping my head. "I need it all, Anita. Even the ugly stuff you're ashamed of."

"It won't help," I mutter. "I told my solicitor the first time, when Damien got custody. He said the judge wouldn't take it into account because I didn't report it to the police."

"Can I ask why you didn't?" More shame washes over me and I fidget uncomfortably. "I'm not judging," he adds. "It's a genuine question."

"At first because I wanted it to work and was terrified of him being arrested, losing his job. Then it was because my parents shamed me into staying. And eventually, it just became a way of life. Until I left."

"And you chose to leave?"

I shrug. "I'm not sure."

"What does that mean?"

I allow my mind to go back to that time. "I wanted to leave, for a long time. But I was scared for Leo. I think Damien knew I wanted to go so eventually he forced me out."

"How?"

"Affairs. Violence. His treatment towards me was getting worse and worse. He'd do things to embarrass me, and when I was at my lowest, he'd convinced me to go on antidepressants."

"And he used that against you in court."

I nod. "He said I'd had a break down but refused help. He made out it was untreated post-natal depression. He even told the judge he'd caught me screaming at Leo." I give my head a shake, like that will somehow dispel the bad images. "I ended up agreeing to the deal because I couldn't fight anymore."

He nods in understanding. "So what's changed, Anita?" I look up. "Things have changed, right, in you?" I remain silent. "You're stronger this time. Freer." He clasps his hands together on the table. "I know you're stronger, Anita, I've seen the way you handle your clients. Even the biggest fuckers are scared of you."

I offer a weak smile. "It's a show."

"It's not. It's you. And I need you to bring that to the court room. That judge needs to look at you and see exactly what I see." His eyes linger a little too long, but before he can elaborate, our food is placed in front of us.

I take the first bite of steak, and as I look around, my eyes land on my father who's walking in with Damien. Tom sees my panic and frowns before turning around to see what the problem is. He gives an easy grin and sits straight. "Are you ready?" he asks.

"Ready for what?" I whisper hiss, panic taking over.

"That show we just spoke about." He takes a sip of wine. "You need to put it on right now."

I shake my head frantically. "No. I can't be seen here with you. You have to leave."

He laughs. "Take a breath, Anita." His eyes pierce mine and I find myself following his instruction. "That's my girl," he whispers, his words surprise me, sending a fluttering through my stomach.

"Anita," my eyes snap to my fathers as he assesses me, then Tom, who pushes to his feet and straightens his suit jacket.

"George," he greets, holding out his hand.

My father reluctantly shakes it. "Tom. I didn't realise sharks ate out in nice places like this."

Tom laughs, releasing my father and turning to Damien. He gives a slight nod and lowers back to his seat without acknowledging him properly.

"Is there a reason you two are here . . . together?" Damien asks stiffly.

"Client confidentiality, Damien," says Tom sternly.

He scowls. "You're acting for Anita?" he snaps, glaring at me.

"I haven't fully decided," I mutter feebly.

"Yes," says Tom, staring him down.

"Last week you were with the other fella," scoffs Father and I feel my cheeks redden.

"There's more?" asks Damien, suddenly interested.

"I don't mean to be rude," says Tom firmly. "But this is a business dinner."

My father looks amused as he steps back. "Enjoy."

I stare in horror as they head away to be seated across the restaurant. I bury my face in my hands. "Hey," says Tom, gently pulling my wrists apart. "Let's not look any other way than confident."

"He's going to ruin my life," I mutter.

"Hasn't he already?" I stare wide eyed. "You don't have Leo. You're trying to date a judge to impress them all in the hope they'll support you. Anita, you're already leading a miserable life, you're exactly where Damien wants you to be. So take control."

"I'm not using Anthony," I lie.

He gives me a look that tells me he isn't buying my bullshit. "We both know the truth."

"He doesn't even know about Leo," I snap defensively.

"But that's your plan, right. Tell him and hope he'll somehow pull strings." I look away and he leans closer. "He's not a good man, Anita. You need to stay clear of him."

"Surely with both of you, I'm more likely to win."

"To what cost?"

ATLAS

Rue stares at the bike with wide eyes. "I've never . . ." she trails off, lost for words.

"It's part of dating a biker," I say with a laugh. "Kind of a deal breaker if you can't get on the back," I add with a teasing tone.

"Isn't this a big deal for you?" she asks, still keeping her feet firmly on the pavement. "I mean, not just anyone can be on the back of a club members bike, right?"

"You been researching, Rue?"

She shrugs her slender shoulders, and folds her arms over her chest, still eyeing the bike with curiosity.

"Will you go slow?"

I shake my head. "No."

"But it's my first time."

I grin, grabbing her around the waist and tugging her closer. She let's out a yelp, laughing as her hands land against my chest. "You usually like it when I go fast," I murmur in her ear before nipping along her jaw.

Her cheeks go pink, but she doesn't pull away. Her fingers curl into my shirt the way they always do when I hold her to me. Like it's the only place she wants to be and she's clinging on for dear life.

"You're such an arse," she mutters, but her mouth is twitching like she's fighting a smile.

"Maybe," I say, brushing my nose along her temple, "but I'm *your* arse. Now come on, Rue. Live a little."

She exhales hard, scanning the bike like it might bite her. "What if I fall off?"

"You won't."

"Easy for you to say. You're not the one trusting your life to this small thing."

I gasp in mock horror. "Don't ever call my beast small again." I hand her the spare helmet, watching as she hesitates. I take it back. "Let me," I say, gently pushing it on her head and fastening the chin strap.

"Okay," she says, drawing in a breath like she's about to jump out of a plane. "But I swear to God, Atlas, if you go too fast, I will scream."

I slide her visor closed. "I'm counting on it, baby." Then, I swing my leg over the seat, fire the engine to life, and grin up at her. "Now get on."

She hesitates for just a beat more, then climbs on behind me, legs awkward, body stiff. I feel her arms wrap around my waist, tentative at first, then tighter when I rev the engine. I reach back, my fingers sliding behind her knees as I drag her closer. "Hold on tight."

And then we're off.

The bike roars beneath us, and I can feel every inch of her pressed to my back. She's tense at first. But as we roll through the streets, I feel the shift in her. The way her grip loosens, just a little. The way her body starts to move with the curves, instead of bracing against them.

I don't take her far. Just enough to give her the thrill without pushing it. I keep it smooth, easy. Not because I'm soft, but because it's *her*. And somehow, that changes everything.

When we slow to a stop overlooking the edge of the city, I kill the engine and glance over my shoulder. Rue's eyes are wide, as she pushes her visor up.

I take off my helmet and hook it on the handlebars. "Well?" I ask.

She takes off the helmet, blinking like she can't quite believe it. "Well I didn't die."

I laugh, twisting round and lifting her around the waist, placing her on my lap so she's straddling me. I hang her legs over my thighs. "That's usually how it goes." I take her helmet and hook it on the other side.

"It was . . . thrilling," she says on a breathy sigh. "Freeing."

"Careful," I murmur, cupping her jaw. "You're sounding dangerously close to a biker's girl."

She scoffs, but she's smiling now. Bright and full and just for me. "Don't get ahead of yourself."

"Too late," I whisper, before claiming her mouth. I'm already gone for her.

"I want to go again," she whispers, a little breathless, her smile addictive.

Fuck. She liked it and it's making me hard for her.

"You sure?" I murmur, curling my hand around her waist. My thumb slips under the hem of her tee, finding the warmth of her bare skin. "You looked pretty terrified back there."

"I was." She leans in closer. "And I enjoyed it."

Jesus. Her voice is low, almost teasing, and I don't think she has a clue what she's doing to me. Or maybe she does.

"You feel that?" I ask, pressing her tighter to me. There's no hiding the hard line of my cock through my jeans. "That's what you do to me, Rue."

Her breath catches, but she doesn't pull away. Her hips shift slightly, enough to make my jaw clench.

She dips her head and presses her lips to mine, soft, then firmer. I grip her hips and hold her there, her body flush to mine, the heat between us like a lit fuse.

The kiss turns messy, deeper. Her fingers twist into my kutte, anchoring herself as she moves against me, and I can feel her heart pounding in sync with mine. Everything else disappears, the road, the noise, the club, *Anita*. It's just her. Just *us*.

"You're dangerous," she breathes, her lips brushing my jaw as she kisses down my neck.

I grip her tighter, dragging her against my hard length. "You have no idea."

Her laugh is soft, and fuck, it's the best sound I've ever heard. Then she rocks her hips again, and I swear I nearly lose it right there.

"Rue," I growl, my fingers digging into her thighs. "We keep doing this, I'm gonna take you right here on this damn bike."

She nips my bottom lip, eyes blazing. "Please."

Holy *fuck*.

I don't know if she's teasing or testing me, but it doesn't matter. I'm two seconds from lifting her tee and finding out just how far she wants to go.

I press my forehead to hers, forcing myself to breathe. "You keep making moves like that, baby, and you're not gonna be able to walk."

Her mouth curves, wicked and sweet all at once. "Good thing I like the bike, then."

She leans her hands back behind her, watching, waiting. I bite on my lower lip, taking in her beauty as I trail my fingers over her stomach. Her t-shirt lifts with the movement until my fingers graze under her breasts. No bra. My cock twitches and she smirks, knowing she's got me right where she wants me. I lift it higher, and her nipples pucker as the evening air surrounds us. Her eyes are burning with heat as I lower my mouth to her nipple, gasping as I graze it with my teeth then suck it into my mouth. I swirl my tongue around the sensitive bud before moving to the other. She's panting now, her head relaxed back and her body squirming with anticipation.

I run my hands up her thighs, her skirt giving me easy access. I hook my fingers in her thong and drag it down her legs. She lifts her hips so I can strip it off, and I stuff the lace into my pocket with a smirk.

She plants her feet on my knees and parts her legs, grinning.

Fuck, I love how confident she's become with me.

I drag my thumb through her slick folds, and she bucks against the touch, a moan breaking from her throat. I press to her swollen clit, rubbing slow, teasing circles. Her hand cups my cheek, then slides behind my head, tugging me down to her nipple.

My phone rings, sharp and unwelcome. I glance towards the sound, but Rue shakes her head, breathless.

"If you stop now, I might combust."

I laugh, sucking her nipple into my mouth as I work her faster. Her body arches, trembling. I pop the button on my jeans, freeing my cock. She's already reaching into my back pocket, pulling out my wallet and handing me a condom without breaking eye contact.

I sheath myself and pull her closer. She lifts her hips, and I guide myself to her entrance, her thighs trembling against mine.

My phone rings again, right as she pushes down on me, slow and tight. I groan, gripping her hips as she rocks against me. *Fuck.* She feels better every time.

I straighten the bike, knocking our helmets to the floor, but I don't give a shit.

"Let's try something," I say on a groan, starting the engine. The bike roars to life beneath us, a sharp jolt of power thrumming through her.

"Sit on the seat," I tell her, shuffling back and guiding her off me. She does, settling onto the leather, her eyes wide, cheeks flushed.

I rev the engine. She gasps, eyes fluttering closed as the vibration pulses through her.

I rev again, watching as she begins to rock, grinding against the seat, shameless and fucking beautiful.

I reach for her breast, tugging her nipple as I hold the revs longer. She shudders, chin dropping to her chest, her movements uncoordinated and raw as she chases the high.

I watch her come apart, her slick smeared on the seat, on *my* bike, and it's the hottest thing I've ever seen.

I kill the engine and pull her back onto my lap, guiding myself back inside her. She cries out, hands clinging to my shoulders as she rides me hard.

I stand, keeping her wrapped around me as I swing my leg off the bike. I glance back at the mark she's left on the seat.

Mine.

I pull out and turn her around to face the bike. She braces herself on the leather, backside high, waiting for me. I bend her over, line myself up, and before I thrust in, I murmur, "Taste yourself."

She bites her lower lip, throwing a dark look over her shoulder. Then she lowers herself, tongue darting out as she licks her own wetness from the seat.

I growl, deep and guttural, and slam into her, gripping her hips, fucking her hard, claiming her all over again.

RUE

My legs are jelly, my body is humming, and my cheeks ache from smiling.

Atlas wraps me up in his arms, pulling me against his chest as we sit together on the bike, looking out over the glittering skyline. It's quiet now, except for the distant hum of city life and the steady beat of his heart beneath my cheek.

His hand strokes slow circles on my bare thigh, and I melt into him. *Safe.* Completely undone and somehow more whole at the same time.

I love this version of me, brave, bike riding, daring and chasing pleasure like it's something I'm owed. He brings out something in me without even trying.

"I'm not scared of the bike anymore," I murmur, tilting my face up towards his.

He chuckles, pressing a kiss to the top of my head. "You shouldn't be. You were made for it."

I smile, eyes flicking to the skyline, the deep inky blue of night hugging the city lights, the hazy gold glow stretching towards forever. I wish I could bottle this moment and keep it.

Then his phone rings again.

The sound slices through the silence, and I feel him tense behind me. His arms don't loosen, but they still. My gaze drops to the phone on the ground near the helmets, screen glowing.

Anita.

And five missed calls.

My stomach twists, not sharp, not painful, but enough to make my skin prickle. He doesn't move to pick it up, but I can feel the way his body reacts. Like he *wants* to.

He's torn.

I don't want to ruin this. I don't want to be *that* girl, the jealous one, the insecure one. She meant something to him, hell, I think she still does. And being jealous and pissed won't change that.

"It's okay," I say quietly, trying to keep my voice even. "You can answer it."

He doesn't speak for a second. Just breathes, slow and heavy, like the weight of the moment's shifted. Then he kisses my temple, lips lingering.

"She can wait," he says finally.

But the way he says it, it's like he's restrained and holding something back.

I nod, forcing a small smile, but the warmth between us has shifted. It's still there, flickering but edged now. Lined with questions I'm too afraid to ask.

He sits a little straighter. "We should head back," he says gently, his eyes flicking to his mobile again.

"Right," I say with a nod.

"Don't do that," he says quickly, almost pleading. His thumb brushes across my lower lip, slow and soft, his eyes locked on mine. "It's nothing."

A small, unsure smile tugs at my mouth. "Then why is she calling you?"

He shrugs. "Maybe she's chasing something for the club."

"Then why isn't she calling Axel?"

His hand drops, and something shifts in his expression, his stare hardens, jaw tight. He doesn't want me digging.

"It's fine," I say again, this time sharper. "Phone calls. Lunch. It's what friends do."

I slide off the bike, still bare beneath my skirt, and bend to pick up his phone. I hold it out, but he stares straight ahead like the weight of my words are too heavy.

Eventually, he takes it and tucks it into his pocket.

I pass him his helmet and tug on my own, fingers fumbling. I think about asking for my underwear back, but the words stick. I'm irritated . . . at him, at myself, at the sudden shift in his mood that's left me feeling exposed and cold.

I climb back on behind him.

A second later, his hands reach for my thighs, gently tugging my skirt down and tucking the hem beneath my legs. It's a small thing, but it makes my throat pinch and my heart ache.

I say nothing.

We speed off, both silent, both lost in thoughts we're not ready to share.

Then my helmet fills with the sound of ringing. I frown, confused, until I hear Atlas's voice.

"Anita?"

My blood goes cold.

"Where the hell are you?" she demands. Her voice breaks, like she's been crying.

Atlas tenses beneath my touch. "What's wrong?"

"I needed you and you didn't answer," she almost whispers.

"I'm sorry," he mutters. "I was dealing with club stuff."

He doesn't know I can hear him. His words hit like a slap, sharp and unexpected. I force my body to stay still, my breath to stay even.

"I thought maybe you were with Rue," Anita says, her voice trembling. "But I need you."

There's a beat of silence, and then Atlas replies, low and tight. "I'm on my way. I just need to drop something for Axel. I'll be ten minutes."

The call disconnects.

He speeds up, weaving through traffic like something's chasing him. My arms stay wrapped around his waist, but it doesn't feel the same. I feel cold again. Hollow.

A minute later, he turns onto my road, slowing outside my place. I climb off, unfastening the helmet and handing it to him. I wait patiently while he sticks it in the saddlebag then turns to me. "Axel just called me," he says, not meeting my eyes. "You okay if I shoot off?"

I can't hide the pain in my eyes, my heart screams with it. "You didn't ask me," I say, keeping my voice calm.

"About?" he asks, his eyes flitting to his watch impatiently.

"How I knew about your lunch with Anita."

He bristles at my words. "Like you said, she's a friend."

"Just a friend?"

"What is this?" he snaps. "Will I get the Spanish Inquisition every time she calls me? I didn't even answer it."

I offer a sad smile, clutching my hands together. "But you did, Atlas. You did." I turn on my heel and take a few steps towards my apartment.

"What are you talking about?" he calls after me, but I don't respond because the tears have already started to fall and I'm too proud to let him see.

"And there it is," I whisper to myself as I head up the steps. "His flaw."

CHAPTER 14

ANITA

I yank open the door the second I hear his boots on the stairs.

Atlas.

My chest caves with relief. I don't think, I just throw myself into his arms.

His warmth, his solid presence, the familiar scent of leather and smoke and something distinctly *him* . . . it all hits me at once, and I break. My arms wrap tight around his neck, and I bury my face there like I've done a hundred times before.

Only this time, I'm shaking.

"I've got you," he murmurs, low and steady. His arms lock around me, lifting me off the ground like I weigh nothing. He carries me inside, kicking the door shut behind us with one heavy boot.

And then he sees it.

The mess.

My apartment is trashed. The coffee table smashed. The lamp on the floor. My bookshelf tipped, pages torn like confetti across the rug. My photo frame cracked. Kitchen drawers open, contents scattered like someone was looking for something, anything, to destroy.

Atlas stops walking, and his jaw tightens. I feel it under my cheek.

"What the fuck happened?" he asks, his voice low, *dangerous.*

I pull back just enough to look at him. "I told him it was over." He stares at me like he doesn't quite understand. "Anthony," I clarify. "I told him I was done, that I didn't want to see him again. He lost it, started screaming. Threw a glass at the wall. I think he was trying to scare me."

Atlas's grip on me shifts, tighter. Protective. His nostrils flare, and his eyes scan the damage like it's a crime scene.

"He hurt you?" he growls.

I shake my head quickly. "No. He didn't touch me. He just lost control. Said I'd ruined his life. That no one else would put up with me. That I was lucky to have him." I don't mean to tear up, but the adrenaline is crashing now, and they sting hot behind my eyes. "Then he left. I locked the door and called you. You didn't answer."

I feel his chest rise and fall beneath me, like he's trying to stay calm. "I was—" He stops, jaw twitching. "I was busy."

I pull back farther to look at him properly. His face is stormy, unreadable. "Yeah, you said," I reply. "Club stuff, right?" I ask, trying not to sound like I'm digging for more.

He doesn't answer right away. Just sets me down gently, like I'm fragile now. Like I might break. "I didn't think things were that serious between you and Anthony."

"You didn't ask," I say quietly. "We don't really talk about my life anymore."

His eyes flick to mine, and something passes between us —old history, old hurt.

He runs a hand through his hair and turns away, pacing once before he kicks a broken chair leg aside and mutters under his breath. "I should've fucking known. Should've kept an eye on you."

"I didn't need you to watch me," I say, softer now. "I just needed you to *answer*."

His shoulders tense, his hands flex like he's holding back from punching something. He leans against the wall, breathing hard. And then, softer: "I was with Rue."

Ah.

Right.

Of course he was.

"I figured," I say, keeping my voice steady, even though my stomach twists. "She makes you happy?"

He doesn't answer right away. Just rubs a hand across his jaw like he's trying to scrub the guilt off his skin. "She does," he finally says. But he doesn't sound sure.

And maybe that's the problem.

He crosses the room again and crouches in front of me, taking my hands in his. His thumbs brush across my knuckles, gentle like I'm something he still wants to protect. "You scared the shit out of me tonight," he says.

"You took your time," I whisper, not accusing, just honest.

"I told her I was on club business," he admits, voice low. "I lied. I didn't know why at the time . . . I just . . . didn't want her to know I came running to you."

I nod slowly, my voice barely above a whisper. "Because if she knew, she'd wonder why."

He looks at me like he doesn't have the answer either. Like maybe he doesn't want to admit that some part of him still belongs here. *With me.* Even if he's already falling for her.

I should be stronger than this. I should push him away. But the second his eyes meet mine, I know he's not here just out of duty. I know the truth buried under his silence.

I lean in slowly, brushing my lips over his.

Soft. Lingering. Familiar. Cautious, waiting for him to reject me again.

He doesn't kiss me back immediately, but he doesn't pull away either. He just stays frozen, his grip on my hands tightening, like he's fighting a war inside himself.

When I finally pull back, I whisper against his lips, "You lied because you still love me."

His jaw clenches. His eyes close. Still no words. But silence can be louder than the truth. And it's all I need.

I reach for the front of my dress, fingers trembling slightly, and tug the zipper down. The fabric parts, slow and deliberate, exposing the top of my lace bra and the bare skin of my chest.

His eyes snap open, and he looks wrecked. *Torn.* I should stop, put an end to his misery. But a sick part of me needs to see if he's still mine, even a little. And fuck knows I need to feel something other than the drowning I currently feel.

"Anita . . ." he breathes, like my name hurts.

I shrug one strap off my shoulder, then the other. "Tell me you don't want this," I murmur. "You came because you heard the fear in my voice and your heart knew it belonged here."

His hands are on my waist before he even realises it, dragging me into him. His mouth crashes against mine, hot and desperate, the kiss anything but controlled. I moan into him, my arms wrapping around his neck, and I feel him groan into my mouth as I climb onto his lap.

"You make me crazy," he mutters, kissing along my jaw, down my neck. "I can't fucking think around you."

I reach between us, palming him through his jeans, and he jerks beneath me, biting down on a curse. His hands slide under my dress, gripping my thighs like he needs to *feel* me to believe I'm still his.

"Please," I whisper, kissing his jaw. "Just one last time." His face twists, anguish, desire, guilt all tangled together. He's shaking his head, but his hips are grinding up into mine like he can't help himself. "No one has to know."

"I can't," he says.

But he doesn't *stop* me as I kiss him again, deeper this time, and I feel him starting to give in. He unhooks my bra, thumbs brushing over my nipples, his mouth claiming mine like he's drowning.

We're a breath away from crossing that line.

And then there's a frantic knock at the door.

I freeze, and Atlas goes still beneath me, his breath ragged.

There's another knock, louder this time. "Anita? It's Tom. Open up."

Shit.

I scramble off Atlas's lap, pulling my dress up and dragging the zipper halfway closed. My heart is thundering.

"I called him," I whisper, panic rising. "When you didn't answer, I didn't know if you'd come. He's my solicitor."

Atlas stands slowly, running both hands through his hair, stepping back like he's just realised what almost happened.

The guilt crashes over him like a wave. It's written all over his face, etched into every line, every shadow. I feel it too, the fact I talked him into going against everything he believes in. *He's not a cheat.*

I step towards the door, but pause, turning back. He's looking at the floor, jaw locked, hands clenched into fists.

"Atlas—"

"I shouldn't have come," he mutters, voice low and wrecked. "This was a mistake."

ATLAS

My jaw is tight, breath ragged, hands twitching at my sides like they don't know what to do now that they're not on her body. My skin still remembers the way she felt. The sound she made when I touched her. The way her mouth knew exactly how to get my attention.

Fuck.

Her cheeks are flushed, but it's not embarrassment. It's grief. For what we almost did. For what we *still want* and keep pretending we don't.

I stare at the mess in the apartment. At the broken furniture. The chaos. It's safer to look at that than her.

The knocking comes again, and Anita jumps in fright, rushing to answer.

I turn to stare out the window. I'm a prick who almost fucked his ex on a pile of shattered glass while the girl I'm actually falling for waits at home, thinking I'm out doing club business. *Fuck*, I hate myself.

I close my eyes, pressing the heels of my hands to them.

Jesus.

What the hell is wrong with me?

Tom walks in like he owns the place, confident, collected, sharp suit and sharper stare. He clocks the mess immediately, then her, then me.

"Anita." His voice is calm but concerned. "Are you okay?"

She nods. "I'm fine now. Atlas got here."

His gaze shifts to me, lingering. "Atlas Rowe?"

I nod once, wary. "That a problem?"

He lifts his brows. "Not for me. You're with the Chaos Demons, right?"

I grunt a yes. It's not unusual for anyone in the field to know the club, we've been through our fair share of court rooms. And I can almost read his mind, even though his expression remains neutral. I'm the kind of man Anita *shouldn't* be involved with, especially not when she's vulnerable.

He pulls his phone out and starts snapping photos of the damage, every broken chair leg, every cracked picture frame. I can feel Anita watching me, but I don't look at her. I can't. My skin feels too tight, like I'm crawling inside it.

She cheated death tonight.

And I cheated on Rue.

Anita doesn't mean anything, right? It's just instinct, old feelings flaring up, my protectiveness spilling over. But the way my body responded to her? That wasn't just instinct, it was feelings and emotion. A need I can't seem to gratify.

It's something I've been trying to bury since Rue came into my life.

Now, all I feel is guilt.

Tom finishes his sweep and says something to Anita about uploading everything to his file, but I barely register it. I just keep staring at the spot on the couch where I had her in my lap. Where I would've taken her if the knock hadn't come.

She moves towards me after Tom walks into the kitchen, dropping his voice as he calls someone.

"I didn't mean to complicate things," she says softly, voice edged with something that sounds like regret.

I huff out a bitter laugh. "Too late for that."

She doesn't speak, and neither do I. The silence stretches, heavy.

"I told Rue I was doing club business," I mutter, more to myself than her. "Didn't even hesitate."

Anita folds her arms. "You're not a bad person, Atlas. We have history."

I look at her. She's still the same Anita I once knew, with a fire in her spine, but soft in ways she pretends not to be. And for a second, I wish we were back in that old world, where loving her didn't feel like betrayal.

But we're not.

And I don't love her the way I used to.

I love *Rue*.

I swallow the bitter taste rising in my throat and take a step back. "I can't do this again."

Her lips part like she wants to argue, but she nods instead. Slow, accepting, like maybe part of her already knew I'd walk away the second I came to my senses.

Tom reappears, sliding his phone into his blazer pocket. "Everything okay?" he asks, his eyes flitting between us.

I nod and head for the door, my mind already ten steps ahead. I have to see Rue and tell her the truth.

～

THE SECOND THE DOOR OPENS, I KNOW I'M FUCKED.

Rue stands there barefoot, arms folded tight across her chest like she's bracing for a storm. Except *she* is the storm, with her thunderous silence and eyes lit with rage. Her expression is blank, but it's the kind of blank that screams.

She doesn't smile. Doesn't say hi. Doesn't even move aside to let me in.

"Hey," I offer quietly, hands shoved deep in my jacket pockets. "Can we talk?"

She stares at me for a long second, then steps back just enough to let me through. I enter the flat taking a few deep breaths to calm the noise in my head.

She closes the door behind us, then leans against it like she needs it to hold her up and folds her arms over her chest.

"I lied," I mutter, avoiding her eye. "Just now, when I dropped you off."

"I know," she says bluntly, and my head snaps up. "I heard the call," she adds, "from Anita."

I inwardly groan. *Fuck.* The helmet must have connected. "Shit, Rue, I'm sorry," I rush out. Her expression stays stoney, her arms still tight over her chest. *Uninviting.* "I didn't know you could hear us."

"I gathered," she says, her voice full of sarcasm.

I shift uncomfortably under the weight of the situation. I don't know how to navigate this, how to make it right. It's not something I've had to face before. "I shouldn't have lied about it."

"But you did, so . . ." She shrugs. "You can't change it now."

I shrug feebly. "She needed me."

"Why didn't she call a friend? Or the police? Or literally *anyone* else?" Rue snaps. "Why you?"

"Because I've always been the one she calls when shit goes wrong," I say, my voice low, almost ashamed. "She was scared. Anthony had trashed her place. She needed me."

"And you couldn't just tell me that? You had to lie and pass it off as some club bullshit because you knew I couldn't question that."

"I fucked up."

"What else?" she asks, and our eyes meet again. "Well, there is something else, right?" I hesitate, my mind racing to create another lie, even though deep down, I know I should tell her the truth. "Just be honest, Atlas. *Please*."

Her tone punches me in the chest. *Pleading. Begging.* "I didn't go through with it," I whisper, my eyes back on the floor.

Her breath catches in a soft, pained inhale like something inside her cracks, but she doesn't cry. She doesn't break. She just stands there, rigid, barely blinking. "You sound like every man I've ever known," she mutters. "You stink of lies and secrets and . . . guilt."

"Because I'm not good at this," I cry. "I've never been in this situation before."

"Really?" she demands, arching a brow. "Because you're really good at the lying part."

"Rue, please," I whisper, my voice strained because of the lump clogging my throat. "I'm sorry."

"For what exactly?" she asks, placing her hands on her hips.

My fingers itch the tuck her stray hair behind her ear as it falls around her face. "She kissed me. *Again*. And I let her. *Again.*" I take a breath. "She took off her dress, *almost*." My head falls back, and I stare at the ceiling, hating the words as they leave my mouth. "And we nearly . . ." I bring my eyes to hers and almost crumble from the pain I see there. "But I didn't. I swear I didn't."

"Your words mean nothing," she whispers, wrapping her arms around herself again. "I don't know what's the truth and what's a lie anymore."

"I haven't had sex with her, Rue. It's you. Only you."

RUE

I stare at him in disbelief.

"It wasn't me an hour ago, Atlas. It wasn't me when you lied so easily so you could rush to be with her. Stop lying to yourself." I pause before adding, "And to me."

"I'm not a cheat," he mutters.

"You kissed your ex," I suddenly yell, taking us both by surprise. "Twice. She was practically naked in front of you, and what? You expect me to believe you didn't touch her, trail kisses down her body." My voice breaks with emotion. "You are a cheat, Atlas. You're just shit at covering it up."

"You don't curse," he mutters, frowning and I almost laugh at his words.

"That's your concern?" I ask on a cold laugh. "You're no different," I add. "From my dad, from all the men that hurt my mum. And I refuse to be second best to your ex."

He shakes his head, his frown cutting deep on his forehead. "Baby, you're not second best. I want you. I *need* you."

I pull the door open. "You should leave now."

"Rue, please don't do this. I'll make it up to you."

"No." It's firm and clear as I stare past him. "I'll make arrangements for Kasey," I add. "She'll be out of your hair in no time."

"That's not what I want," he mutters, stepping closer to me.

I move back from his reach. "There's nothing else to say," I mutter. "Just go now."

He steps over the threshold and turns to speak, but I slam the door in his face, twisting the key in the lock and resting my forehead against it. *That was the hardest thing I've ever done in my life.*

My phone rings out and I snatch it off the table, thinking

it'll be him calling from outside. Instead, it's Kasey's name I see on the screen.

"Hi," I say, forcing the sadness from my voice. "How are you?"

"Bad," she says. "Very, very bad."

"Oh?" I peek out the window to see Atlas mounting his bike. He places his helmet on and grips the handlebars, his head lowered like he's contemplating if he should leave or stay. "What's happened?"

"I just heard something I shouldn't have. And I want to tell you, but I'm scared it'll hurt you."

"If it's about Atlas, I know."

She's silent for a long minute. "What do you know?"

"That he's a liar and a cheat," I spit angrily. "That he almost had sex with Anita."

Silence again. "That mother fucker," she suddenly yells, and I pull the phone from my ear.

"Wait, that wasn't the thing you over-heard?"

"No," she cries. "Where is he, I'll kill him."

I groan. "Don't. He isn't worth it. What did you overhear?"

"Axel got a trace on Mr. D. Turns out he has connections that are close to the club."

"Really? So they know him?"

"Not exactly. His name is Damien Carpenter. And he's got a kid with Anita."

I process the words. "Atlas's ex, Anita?"

"The one and only."

CHAPTER 15

ATLAS

I stare at Axel open mouthed. "Damien Carpenter?"

"It should ring alarm bells," he continues. "It's Anita's ex-husband."

I frown. "Let me get this straight. Damien is the one looking for Kasey?"

"Yes."

"But he's a lawyer, isn't he?"

"Yep," says Grizz, tapping something on the laptop until the screen mirrors to the large screen on the wall of church.

"By day he's a lawyer, by night he's some kind of king pin with a taste for young hookers," Axel explains.

I stare at the picture of a middle-aged man in a suit and try to picture him and Anita together. "So why's he so intent of finding Kasey? He isn't short of money."

"He doesn't like to lose," says Grizz simply. "Especially to a woman."

"Maybe we can use this," I say, sitting down. "Anita is fighting for custody of their son."

They all stare open mouthed. "Anita has a kid?" Grizz asks.

"She keeps her private life to herself," I reply. "But he took her kid, and the hearing is coming for it to become permanent. If we could share this with her lawyer, maybe he can use it to discredit Damien?"

Axel nods. "Call her and share the news."

"Actually, can someone else do that," I mutter. "I'm trying to keep my distance."

Grizz smirks. "What have you done now?"

I push to my feet. "Let me know what she says." And I head out.

Kasey is waiting for me, pacing outside church like a little demon and I see it before it's even connected. Her fist catches my left cheek, and I wince. "Mother fucker," I hiss, holding my face.

"Why would you do that?" she cries, and her eyes are filled with mistrust.

"I'm sorry," I mutter, stiffening when Axel appears behind me.

"What the hell is going off out here?" he demands.

"He's a lying, cheating prick," she screams, jabbing a finger in my chest.

"Cool off," Axel orders.

"It's fine, Pres," I mutter. "I'll deal with it."

He eyes me for a second before nodding and going back into church.

Kasey folds her arms over her chest, just like her sister did, and follows me outside. She keeps her back to me, stopping by the wall near the garage.

"I fucked up," I begin. "I'm sorry."

"I liked you," she almost whispers. "I thought you were a good guy."

"Kase, I am," I say, my voice laced with regret. "I just . . . forgot myself."

"You forgot Rue," she snaps. "And how fucking amazing she is."

"I did," I admit.

She turns to me. "Why would you do that to her?"

"It's complicated. I've only ever known Anita for the longest time, way before we even became a thing. I've been so focussed on her that it's almost like a compulsion. She called and I ran. But I shouldn't have."

"If you still loved her, you shouldn't have gone near Rue."

I nod. "I know. But when Rue came along, she took me by surprise. And I couldn't ignore her."

"She wants us to leave," says Kasey, her eyes filling with tears. "She's trying to get money together to buy tickets to Ireland."

My heart stutters in my chest. The thought of them leaving breaks my heart all over again. "She can't go," I mutter.

"She'll never forgive you," she snaps. "Not now."

"I'll make her see how sorry I am."

"It'll never work. She hates cheaters more than anything."

"I didn't cheat, not really."

Kasey's eyes widen. "That there, that's the issue," she says angrily. "At least own what you've done. If Rue kissed someone else passionately, if she got half naked, is that still cheating?" I hang my head, my hands on my hips, trying to keep my cool cos the thought of my Rue, my sweet, innocent, Rue, doing that with another man, brings my blood to boil. "Exactly," she hisses.

I drag a hand down my face, jaw clenched, cheek still throbbing from her punch. I deserved it. Every damn bit of this.

Kasey doesn't move. She just watches me like she's waiting for me to tell her it's all a joke. That I'm not really a piece of shit that cheated on her sister.

"I know I messed up," I mutter, voice hoarse. "I know I don't deserve her."

"No, you *don't*," Kasey snaps, arms still tight over her chest. "You gave her hope, Atlas. And trust for someone like Rue, that's not something she gives easily. She finally believed that maybe not all men were liars or selfish or ruled by their dicks, and *you* proved her wrong."

My stomach knots. "I never wanted to hurt her."

"But you *did*. And then you stand here trying to explain it away like it wasn't cheating because your zipper didn't come down."

I look up, eyes burning. "I didn't sleep with Anita."

"You *almost* did," she throws back. "You went. You *wanted* to. And Rue heard your voice, heard you lie to her while she was still wrapped around your damn body on that bike."

I wince. I haven't stopped thinking about that. Her helmet. The call. My voice in her ear.

"And now what?" Kasey continues, stepping closer. "You're gonna beg? Promise it won't happen again? Try to convince her that she's different?"

"She *is* different," I say, teeth clenched. "She's everything."

Kasey's glare softens for a flicker of a second, and I know it's because she wants to believe that too. But she shakes her head. "She's scared, Atlas. She's not like me, she doesn't scream and punch. She just . . . shuts down. You broke something in her that's going to take more than apologies and sweet words to fix."

"You really think she'll leave?"

"She doesn't say things she doesn't mean."

My chest aches like someone's taken a crowbar to it.

"She made me promise not to talk to you. And here I am, being a total idiot."

"You're not," I say quietly. "You're a good sister. I just want a chance to make it right."

"You might not get one," she replies. "And honestly? I'm not even sure you deserve one. But for some insane reason, I want you to make her happy, Atlas. I want you to work."

It gives me a glimmer of hope. "I want that too."

"Then *act* like it," she hisses. "No more excuses. No more soft-shoeing around what you did. If you ever want a chance in hell of getting her back, you stop trying to look better and start *being* better."

She pushes off the wall and starts to head inside, but she pauses after a few steps and turns back. "Because if she cries one more time because of you? I won't just punch you next time."

I watch her disappear inside and release a long breath. *I have to make it right.*

RUE

I force myself into leggings and a hoodie, tying my hair back even though it feels like a wasted effort. My eyes are still puffy, and my head hurts from crying for most of the night, but if I stay inside any longer, I'll lose it.

The gym is half full and humming with that mix of endorphins and effort. I put my earbuds in, choosing something upbeat even though I feel anything but, and drag myself through a workout I barely remember. It's mechanical. Functional. Like brushing my teeth or tying my shoes. I just need to move.

Afterward, I walk to *Barley & Bean*, a coffee shop I don't usually use but decide it's best to change this part of my routine, just in case Atlas is hanging about. I order a flat white with oat milk, extra hot. The barista asks how I am, and I lie through my teeth. "Good, thanks. You?"

The coffee's too hot to sip, so I cradle it in both hands as I head out and walk the long way home through the park. It's quiet for a weekday. Just a few dog walkers and a jogger in the distance. The trees overhead rustle gently, sun poking through in places. It should feel peaceful.

It doesn't.

Someone's walking towards me. A man, older than me, maybe mid-thirties, wearing jeans and a wax jacket. There's nothing particularly threatening about him, but my gut clenches anyway. He's alone and smiling.

I keep walking, eyes forward.

"Hey," he calls out, closing the distance. "Sorry to bother you."

I glance at him, slowing my steps slightly. "Hi?"

"I just wondered, are you Rue? Rue Carter?"

I freeze mid-step. "Yes?"

He smiles again, too friendly, too deliberate. "Thought so. You look a lot like your sister. Kasey."

My fingers tighten around the cup, and I take a step back. "I'm sorry, do I know you?"

He shakes his head, still smiling like this is some joke only he's in on. "No, I know your sister though."

"Right," I say coolly. Every hair on the back of my neck stands up. I've never seen him before in my life. "Well, if you'll excuse me—"

"I was actually hoping you could pass on a message to her," he cuts in, tone still light but his eyes are sharper now, watching me too closely.

A tremor runs down my spine.

"I don't think I can help you," I say, shifting my weight and glancing around, there's no one nearby. No one close enough. "And I'd appreciate it if you stopped following me."

He lifts his hands like I've accused him of something. "Hey, I'm not following anyone. Just wanted to chat."

"Then you can do that through someone else. Goodbye."

I turn, heart thudding hard, and pick up my pace. I don't run, but it's close.

"Tell her *he's looking*," he calls after me. Not loud. Not aggressive. Just calm. Creepy. I don't look back. I don't *dare*. "And he's close."

I clutch my coffee so hard it shakes, walking faster and faster until I can see the end of the park, the main road, cars, *people*.

I've never wanted Kasey more in my life. Or Atlas. But I'm not calling him. Not after everything.

My hand is shaking as I dig my phone out of my pocket. I still don't look behind me, not properly. Just the occasional glance, trying to act like I'm checking the road or the time, anything but panicking. My coffee sloshes in its cup as I hold it awkwardly beneath my arm and jab at Kasey's name.

She answers on the second ring.

"Rue?"

"There was a man in the park," I say, breath hitching. "I don't know him. But he knew my name. And yours."

"What?" Her voice sharpens instantly. "What do you mean he *knew* my name?"

"He said he knows you. I've never seen him before, Kasey. He smiled too much. He was just . . . *wrong*. Then when I tried to walk away, he told me to give you a message. He said, *'tell her he's looking and he's close.'*"

It's met with silence before she asks, "Where are you?"

"Heading home. Just passed the Tesco by the east gate."

"No, don't go home." Her tone changes. Commanding. "Hold on."

I hear her shifting the phone, muttering quickly, and then another voice in the background. Male. Firm. *Axel.*

"Rue," she says again, more serious now. "Axel says go somewhere busy. A shop, anywhere with people. Don't go back to the flat and *don't* try to come here. We don't know if they're following you."

My stomach drops as I take another frantic look around. "I'm fine," I murmur, but even I don't believe it. My heart is still racing. My mouth is dry.

"You're not fine. I can hear it in your voice."

I duck into the Co-op on the corner, pretending to browse the meal deal fridge as I press the phone tighter to my ear. "I'm inside a shop," I say quietly.

"Good. Stay there. Axel's sending someone to come get you. Don't talk to anyone else."

"I hate this," I whisper.

"I know," she murmurs. "Just stay put. They'll be with you soon, okay?"

I nod even though she can't see me.

It's seconds before I see him duck into the shop, sending my heart into a panic. Atlas. His eyes search until they land on me, and something in them changes, like he was holding his breath until this exact moment.

He heads for me, and even though I'm relieved, I'm still pissed. "Is this a joke?"

"We don't have time for a discussion," he mutters. "We have to get you out of here."

"There must be twenty other biker's he could have sent . . ."

"And they would have asked for my permission first. Permission I was never gonna give, so Axel sent me, it was quicker."

I look past him as people enter the shop. I exhale. "Fine, whatever."

He holds out a hoody and I stare at it. "Put it on," he directs.

I hesitate, before reluctantly taking it and shoving my arms through. His scent wraps around me, causing a deep ache in my heart. Atlas reaches for the zipper and makes quick work of fastening it, before placing a cap on my head, and pulling the hood up. "We're gonna go out the front and get straight on my bike."

The thought of being on his bike again pains me, but I follow him anyway, keeping my head down as he throws his leg over the bike and starts the engine. I slide on behind and his hands curl under my knees and tug me close. He then guides my arms around his waist. "Press your cheek to my back," he instructs. "We're leaving the helmets off." I don't argue, pressing myself against his back and closing my eyes. Yesterday this all felt so thrilling, but today it just hurts. The sooner I'm home, the better.

We ride a short distance, before the bike slows and I open my eyes. I sit up straighter realising we're at the club. As he drives through the gates, one of the bikers closes them and chains the front.

He parks the bike alongside the rest and I notice there seems to be a lot more than usual.

I climb off as Kasey rushes out, throwing her arms around me. "Thank God you're okay."

I remove the cap. "Why am I here?" I whisper.

She glances at Atlas, slipping her hand in mine and leading me farther away. "Axel is putting the club on lockdown."

"What does that mean?"

"That we have to stay here until it's safe."

I frown. "It was just a guy. Maybe I overreacted."

"I told you they know who Mr. D is, right?" I nod. "Well, it seems he's a big deal. Until they've executed a plan, we're locked down."

I rub my brow in irritation. "And how long will that take?"

"I don't know. But Axel is sending someone to get your stuff later. You can work from the club."

I groan. "I can't teach English to my students with the club going on in the background."

"Axel promised he'd sort you a quiet space."

We go inside where Axel is waiting. "Office," he says bluntly, turning and heading there.

Kasey arches her brows at me before we follow. Atlas joins us, closing the office door as we sit down.

"What happened?" Axel asks.

"I was walking through the park and some guy approached me. He felt . . . off, unsafe." I feel Atlas stiffen at my words. "He approached me, asked if I was Rue Carter. When I said yes, he said he knew Kasey."

"What did he look like?" Atlas demands.

I ignore him, keeping my eyes fixed to Axel. "Then he asked me to give Kasey a message. He said to tell her 'he was still looking for her and he was close.'"

Axel's eyes flit to Atlas before he asks, "What did he look like?"

"Thin, middle aged. White. He wasn't out of place, just . . . odd."

"And those were his exact words?" he asks. I nod.

"Okay. I'm keeping the club locked down until it's safe."

"Isn't that an overreaction?" I ask. "He could have been an old friend of Kasey's."

"This goes deeper than Kasey. The guy we traced has other connections to the club."

"Anita," I mutter, and Atlas's head whips my way.

"I told her," Kasey admits.

"I have a meeting with her lawyer in five minutes," Axel continues. "Until I know more, I want you to stay at the club too. My dad wouldn't forgive me if I let anything happen to you or Kasey."

I give a slight nod.

"You can sleep in the room next to Kasey," he adds.

We head out of the office and Atlas rushes after me. "Can we talk?"

"No."

"Please, Rue."

"She said no," Kasey replies, taking my hand and dragging my upstairs.

ANITA

"I think he's overreacting," I say, folding my arms as Tom pulls up outside the Chaos Demons' clubhouse. "And what exactly could Axel possibly have *on* Damien? They don't even move in the same universe."

Tom puts the car in park, his jaw tense. "I don't know. But Axel said it could help, and I trust him."

"Do you?" I shoot him a sideways look. "Because yesterday you were lecturing me to steer clear of men like Atlas. Now you're personally chauffeuring me to their doorstep for safekeeping?"

"I had a conversation," he says simply. "Things have changed."

I stare at him, confused. "Since when are you on friendly terms with the club?"

Tom exhales like this has been a long time coming. "I've known Axel for a while. Longer than you think." His fingers drum on the steering wheel, then stop. "Maybe I was out of line yesterday. I saw something between you and Atlas. I didn't like it."

I blink. "What are you saying, Tom?"

Before he can answer, the passenger door swings open and Lexi grins at me like she's just won the lottery. "Welcome home."

I slide out reluctantly. "This isn't my home."

"Oh, come on, Nita. You love us, and we love you," she sings, tugging me into a hug that smells of leather, perfume, and danger.

Despite everything, I smile. "I guess it'll be good to catch up."

Axel doesn't waste time. The second we're inside, he takes us to the office. He closes the door, and the air shifts, heavier, more serious. We sit, but Axel doesn't.

"I'll get to the point," he says, tone clipped. "Damien's involved in illegal activity."

I straighten in my chair, a laugh catching in my throat. "Sorry, *my ex*, Damien? Damien Carpenter? The man who gets hives if his Champagne isn't the right temperature?"

Axel slides a photo across the desk. "That Damien. He's got a hitman looking for a twenty-one-year-old girl we're protecting."

I blink at the photo. It's Damien all right—expensive coat, arrogant tilt of the chin. I shake my head. "You must be mistaken."

"I'm not." Axel's voice is low but firm. "He thinks she stole from him, and now, he wants payback."

"Okay, well, how much money are we talking here?" I ask, instantly regretting how flippant it sounds.

"A few grand."

I frown. "That's nothing to Damien. He spends that on wine."

"He doesn't care about the money. He cares that she embarrassed him. That she made him look stupid. Men like Damien don't forgive that."

I lean back slowly, heart beginning to twist. "So, what, he's sending someone to hurt her? Because his pride's dented?"

"He's already sent someone," Axel says grimly. "A man approached Rue earlier today and told her to pass the message to her sister that Damien is looking for her."

The room spins a little.

I'd known Damien was cruel, calculated, even vicious when he didn't get his own way or he felt he was losing control of a situation. But outside of our marriage, he was always cool and calm. Everyone around us, always loved him. His charm. His charisma. Hell, it's how I fell into his trap.

"Wait, how does he even know Kasey?"

Axel takes a seat. "That's where I think we can help you." I wait for him to continue. "Atlas mentioned the custody case." I shift uncomfortably. "Couldn't you use this to get your kid back?"

I glance at Tom, who looks pensive. "Depends on what you have and if it's purely hearsay."

"He was sleeping with Kasey," Axel says bluntly. "For a long time."

"How long?" I ask warily.

"Well, let's put it this way, she was still in school when she met him."

I inhale sharply. "Underage?"

"It was on and off for years. He'd pick her up, have sex, drop her home. A few times, he introduced her to other men."

Tom leans forward. "He arranged that?"

Axel nods. "And he handled payment."

"Like a pimp?" I gasp.

"She got older, he lost interest in the sex side of things, but he did have her babysit a few times."

My mouth drops open in surprise. "What?"

"He would pay her to sit with the kid while he went off till all hours, sometimes even days."

"No, he wouldn't have done that."

"She could probably tell you more. But I'd say paying a prostitute to look after the kid rather than arrange proper childcare, might not look good."

Tom nods. "We might be able to use it if she'd give us a signed statement to say it's true. But I'm sure Damien would argue it's not true and say you'd paid someone to lie."

"But it could put doubt in the judge's mind," I add.

"Are there any police records?" asks Tom. "Anything that ties him to this other life you're saying he has?"

Axel shakes his head. "No. We're working on it."

CHAPTER 16

ATLAS

She's beautiful in ways that wreck me.

It's not just her face, though yeah, that smile could knock the breath from a man. It's the way she pushes her glasses up when they slide down her nose, the way she laughs with her whole body, like joy still surprises her. It's how her hair always escapes whatever clip or band she's used to tame it, falling into her face like it has a mind of its own. Like her.

Rue.

My Rue. Except she's not mine anymore.

"Earth to Atlas."

I blink, dragged back to the present by Grizz snapping his fingers in front of my face.

"What?"

He stares at me like I've grown a second head. "I've been talking to you for five minutes. Not a flicker. You're staring at her like you forgot how to breathe. Just go talk to her. Apologise."

"I've tried," I mutter, dragging a hand down my face. "You think I haven't tried? She hates me."

Grizz tilts his head. "She's hurt. There's a difference."

I glance back across the room. Rue's talking to someone—Lexi, maybe—but she won't look my way. She hasn't looked at me the same since I showed up at her door and told her the truth.

And god, if I could take it back.

Grizz walks off, muttering something about me being a hopeless bastard, and I stay rooted where I am. Not because I've got anything useful to do, but because I'm too caught in the guilt.

Then, Anita steps out of Axel's office, laughing at something Tom's just said. She looks good. Polished. Warm. Like she always does. And I hate that I notice. I hate it even more when she heads straight towards the old ladies gathered near the window, her voice already bright and familiar.

Rue's there. She's been mid-conversation, even smiling a little, soft and real, the kind of smile I've been aching to bring out of her again. But the second Anita joins the group, Rue takes a step back. Her shoulders tighten, and the wall goes back up.

Damn it.

I watch as Rue makes some excuse to Lexi and slips away, disappearing towards the back of the room without even glancing in my direction.

"Shit," I mutter.

Anita fits too well. She always has, making everyone feel like they've known her for years. She slips into the role like it's hers by right.

But today it feels like she's taken something that wasn't meant for her.

I cross the room and touch Anita's elbow. "Can I talk to you?"

She gives a nod and follows me away from the others. I catch Rue watching, but the second we make eye contact, she looks away.

"Are you sticking around?" I ask.

"Axel's put us on lockdown, do I have a choice?"

I shrug, stuffing my hands in my pockets. "It's just, Rue's here too."

"Oh," she almost whispers.

"And I told her the truth about what happened." She gives a stiff nod, looking down at the ground. "She's pissed, as you'd imagine. But with you here too, it's going to be hard to get her to trust me."

She frowns. "What are you saying, Atlas?"

"I want her to fit in," I mutter, "with the old ladies. If you're always there, she can't do that."

"So, you want me to not speak to anyone?"

I groan. "That's not what I'm saying."

"Then what are you saying?" she snaps. "Get to the point."

I exhale. "Honestly, I don't know. I just . . . you came out that office and swooped right in and she backed off. If I have my way, she'll be a permanent fixture around here. One of the old ladies."

She gives a knowing nod. "And if that happens, I won't be welcome around here anyway, right?"

"You know the rules, Anita. If she decides you can't be around, that's the way it'll be."

"And you'd let that happen?"

I hold her gaze. "If it meant keeping Rue? Yeah. I would."

She lets out a bitter breath. "Wow. Good to know where I stand."

Axel sticks his head out the office. "Atlas, can I have a word?"

I head in, leaving Anita to think over my words. Kasey is already seated. "What's she done now?" I ask with a groan.

"I haven't done anything," she snaps. "It's what he's asking me to do."

I take a seat beside her, and Axel sits behind his desk. "Kasey doesn't want to help Anita."

I sigh heavily, Scrubbing a hand over my face. "Because of what I did?"

"I don't care if she gets her kid back or not. She's a slag."

I wince at her words. "Don't call her that."

"What would you call it when she's getting half-naked in front of someone else's man?"

I glance at Axel uncomfortably. "This will help the club too."

"How?"

"Cos we're keeping you here so he can't get to you. It's all part of us dismantling his life."

"I'd rather we just kill him," she says, folding her arms over her chest. "Isn't that what you guys do?"

"Where did you hear that?" snaps Axel.

"Ignore her," I say. "She's read it in books and watched *Sons of Anarchy*."

He relaxes. "Look, I'm the damn President, and what I say goes."

She gives him an arched brow, and I nudge her. "Show respect," I whisper hiss, "or it'll be you he kills."

"I am not helping the woman who hurt my sister."

"It wasn't Anita's fault," I snap. "What happened is all on me."

"Why can't you just drag up the police report?" she asks, slumping back in the chair like a sulking teenager.

"Police report?" Axel repeats with interest.

She shrugs. "Well, yeah, I reported him."

I exchange a wide-eyed stare with Axel. "What exactly did you report?"

"The sex and stuff. I was a kid, and he wouldn't leave me alone. They didn't do anything, of course, cos who believes a scruffy kid off a council estate with a dad like mine. But they said they'd log it and look into it. I told them about the other men and how they picked me up from school." She sighs heavily. "They never got back to me. And he never mentioned it, so I don't think they even spoke to him about it."

"You never followed it up?" I ask.

She shakes her head. "Why would I? He left me alone a few months after, and when he asked me to babysit, I did it for the money. He never touched me after my eighteenth birthday."

"Why didn't you tell us you'd reported him?" asks Axel, picking up his mobile.

She rolls her eyes. "You didn't ask."

RUE

Anita laughs at something Grizz says, tossing her hair back like she's been part of this place forever. The guys around her —Grizz, Fletch, even Axel—are smiling, engaged, drawn in by her ease. She fits here, knows when to tease, when to flirt, when to listen. The kind of woman who doesn't hesitate.

I sip my Coke and try not to stare.

I wish I had that confidence. That natural ability to glide into any conversation and make it look easy. When I speak, my voice trembles. My jokes fall flat, and I never know where to put my hands.

I glance to the far side of the field, and I see him.

Atlas.

Leaning against the rail with a bottle in his hand, watching everything and nothing at once. His arms are folded, jaw tight, brow furrowed like he's halfway through an argument he can't win. Alone, for once. And for a split second, the ache in my chest is unbearable.

That used to be my place. Right there beside him, even if it was for just a short time. It felt right. He was my safe person.

My hand curls tighter around my drink. Because even now, after everything—after the lies, the betrayal, the heartbreak—my body still reacts to him like he's gravity.

But I'm not that girl.

I've spent my whole life watching women I love, fall for the wrong man and make excuses for him. I told myself I wouldn't be one of them. I told myself I'd be smarter. Stronger.

So, I square my shoulders and turn my attention towards the firepit, even as my heart whispers, *just one more look.*

"Rue," a warm voice cuts through my thoughts, "you alright?"

I blink then glance sideways. Duchess. One of the older women, her silver hair is swept into a braid, her smile lines deep from a life well-lived. She's holding a half-empty glass of wine and wearing a leather vest over a floral blouse like it makes total sense. Somehow, it does on her.

I nod quickly. "Yeah, just thinking."

She hums, clearly not buying it, but kind enough not to press. "Come sit with us. Xanthe's telling the story of how she met Fury."

I hesitate.

My eyes flick back to Anita, still laughing with the boys like she was born to do this, and I almost say no. But then Duchess reaches out and loops her arm through mine like she's already decided.

"Come on," she says. "If you're going to stick around for a few days, you may as well make new friends."

I let her guide me to the circle of lawn chairs by the fire pit, where a few other old ladies are curled up with drinks and stories. They greet me with easy smiles.

"Rue, right?" one of them asks.

I nod. "Yeah."

"Everyone," says Duchess, "this is Rue. I'm sure you all remember her from the barbeque a few weeks back, but she was here with Atlas." She proceeds to go around the circle and point everyone out. Lexi gives a small wave and pats the space beside her. I take it gratefully.

"Are you and Atlas . . ." Tessa trails off, waiting for me to answer. I give my head a shake. "Oh," she replies, giving Lexi a frantic glance.

"It's fine," I say, forcing a smile. "He just . . ."

"He almost shagged Anita," says Kasey, appearing like a lightning bolt and shoving her backside down beside me. "He doesn't deserve my sister."

I give an awkward smile, hating how honest Kasey is all the damn time, but equally relieved she's here to fill the silence.

"Oh, shit, Rue," mutters Lexi, giving my arm a gentle squeeze. "I'm so sorry."

"Is there no hope you two will sort things out?" asks Duchess.

I shake my head again. "No," I almost whisper.

"Well, forget him tonight," says Gemma, grabbing a

vodka bottle from the centre. She clumsily pours a shot and holds it out for me to take.

"Oh, I don't drink," I say.

"Because you're fighting demons or you have allergies?" she asks, her frown deep.

I almost laugh. "I just don't drink."

Kasey takes the shot and knocks it back. "Live a little, Rue. A few drinks won't hurt." She takes the bottle from Gemma and holds it to my lips.

The spirit fills my mouth and I almost gag before swallowing it down and wincing. "That's gross," I cry, coughing and trying to wipe my tongue with my fingers.

The women laugh, and eventually, I do too. It feels nice, so I take the bottle and down another mouthful. "In for a penny," I say, and they laugh again.

ANITA

The laughter from around the firepit grows louder. The old ladies are getting rowdy, their drunken laughter ringing out in the quiet of the evening air. I glance their way, watching the way Rue seems to have slotted right in.

Tessa nudges me gently with her shoulder. "She's actually really nice," she says. I hum in response. "I mean it. A little quiet. Shy, even. But she's warming to us."

"The perfect fit," I murmur. Bitterness scratches at my throat before I can swallow it down.

Tessa tilts her head. "What happened with you and Atlas?" she asks, voice soft but probing. "Kasey said you two almost slept together?"

My groan is instinctive, and I drop my head into my hands like I can hide from it. From me.

"I'm a cow," I say bluntly. "I tried it on with him. And the second he hesitated, I mean the *second*, I practically started stripping. If Tom hadn't shown up . . ." I let the rest hang. We both know how it would've ended.

Tessa's eyes go wide. "Why?"

I think about it then shrug like I didn't just feel my chest tighten. "Habit?"

She doesn't speak for a moment, then says, "Rue walked away. He told her everything, and she dumped him."

I glance towards the far wall. Atlas is sitting there with a bottle of beer dangling from his fingers, his eyes locked on Rue like she's the only real thing in the world. My stomach twists.

"I know," I murmur. "I don't even know why I did it. Jealousy, maybe. Or," my voice catches, "I just needed to feel wanted, Tess. Since Atlas, it's like I've been freefalling. And I know that was *my* choice. I walked away. But that doesn't make it any easier."

Tessa's quiet for a moment before she says, "You can't keep reeling him back in, Nita. Not if he's not your forever."

I nod, slowly. "The worst part?" I say, voice low. "He regretted it. Instantly. I could see it. He didn't even *want* me. Not really. He just . . . I don't know. We've always had this thing where we fall back into each other. Like muscle memory. Familiar and stupid."

"I think Rue made him happy," Tessa says gently.

"I know," I whisper. "I shouldn't have gotten involved."

"Maybe you could speak to her?" she suggests, cautious but sincere.

I let out a laugh, sharp and humourless, then realise she's not joking. "Tess. I can't."

"Why not? You could explain, tell her it wasn't about him. Tell her you're done."

My mouth opens, then closes. The truth is, I don't know what I'd even say. Or if I *am* done.

Tessa gives me *that* look, the one that says she sees more than I want her to, and nudges my arm again, this time firmer.

"You owe her that much," she says gently.

I swallow hard and nod, even though every part of me wants to walk in the opposite direction. But I rise, smoothing down my skirt like that'll help, and start heading towards the fire pit.

Rue's on the far side, perched on the edge of a seat with her knees tucked together and her fingers wrapped around a glass. She looks like she's trying to disappear, but there's a quiet strength in her stillness. Atlas is still watching her. I don't think she's even noticed.

She looks up as I approach.

Her expression doesn't shift. Not surprised, not polite . . . just neutral.

"Hey," I say, my voice quieter than I intended.

She doesn't answer, but she doesn't walk away either. I take it as a sign and sit down slowly, leaving space between us.

"I'm not good at this," I admit. She sips her drink, eyes fixed forward, but she remains silent. "I didn't come to excuse myself. I just . . . I wanted to say I'm sorry."

She still doesn't glance my way, but then asks, "Sorry for kissing him, or sorry I found out?"

I sigh. "Both. But mostly for hurting you. You didn't deserve that."

She turns her head now, eyes finally meeting mine. There's a flicker of emotion, not rage, not hate, just quiet disappointment.

I press on. "It wasn't about *him*, not really. Not in the way you think. I didn't try to take him from you. I just, I was lonely, and stupid, and hurting. I needed to feel like someone still saw me."

"That's not a reason," she says. "That's an excuse."

I nod, because she's right. "Yeah. It is."

She lets out a long breath, then finally sets her drink down. "Did you sleep with him?"

"No. Tom walked in before we . . . before it got that far."

She nods once. "So, you would've done it if you weren't interrupted?"

I wince, glancing to where Atlas is sitting and noticing he's rigid now, his eyes burning into me. "Maybe."

"Maybe, or yes?" she demands, and I realise she's not the shy, quiet nerd I thought, but she's got a fire inside of her, especially for Atlas.

"Whatever we had, it's done."

"Funny, he said the same."

"Exactly, because it's true."

"It doesn't matter now, the damage is done. I'm not sticking around so he can hurt me over and over."

My heart twists. "Atlas isn't like that," I say with sincerity. "I know it must seem like that to you, but he's the most genuine and honest guy you'll ever meet. And he messed up, we both did, but you have to understand, there's a history there for us."

"I don't have to understand," she snaps. "I don't care."

"If you walk away over this, you're making a huge mistake."

She scoffs. "Tell me, why didn't you two work out? If he's so great, why aren't you with him?"

"It's complicated."

She pushes to her feet, wobbling unsteadily. "You love him, and he loves you. Stop trying to kid yourselves and just get back together." She stomps off towards the clubhouse.

CHAPTER 17

ATLAS

Rue storms off, her heels clacking sharp against the floor. My stomach sinks.

I don't even think. I just move, straight over to Anita, who's still sitting where Rue left her, staring after her like she's trying to undo the damage with sheer will.

"What the hell did you say to her?" My voice is sharp, colder than I mean it to be, but I can't help it. The second I saw Anita cross the room, I *knew* it wouldn't end well.

"I was trying to help," she mutters, eyes flicking to me and away just as quickly.

"Well, don't," I snap. "You've done enough."

And then I'm gone. I catch Rue halfway up the stairs, her back tense, shoulders hunched like she's bracing for more bad

She turns, just enough to look at me over her shoulder, and rolls her eyes when she sees it's me.

Perfect.

"Are you okay?" I ask quietly.

"Was that down to you?" Her voice wobbles, and I see the sheen in her eyes, the way her mouth trembles. She's barely holding it together.

I shake my head. "No. It's my mess, I'd never ask anyone else to fix it."

She nods once then presses a hand to her stomach. "I feel sick."

"I've got you," I murmur, reaching for her hand and guiding her the rest of the way upstairs. She doesn't pull away, but she doesn't lean into me either. Just follows, shaky and silent.

We reach my room. I push the bathroom door open and flick the light on.

"You don't drink," I say gently, crouching beside her as she lowers herself to the tiled floor.

"I was joining in," she mumbles, already on her knees in front of the toilet.

Her words choke me, that quiet, stupid reason. Just trying to fit in, to belong.

"Can I get you anything?"

She shakes her head, still not looking at me. "No. Leave me alone." Her voice cracks as she tries to push the door closed between us.

I block it with my foot. "You can't lock it. Not if you're sick. I'm staying right here."

She doesn't argue. Just bows her head and breathes slow, like she's trying not to cry *or* throw up.

I stay by the bathroom door while she throws up, my hand

braced against the frame, listening to the awful sound of her retching. Every second of it twists something in my chest. I hate that I let things get this far. Hate that Anita opened her mouth. Hate that Rue is the one hurting because of our messy, complicated past.

Eventually, the room goes quiet.

I give it a beat before easing the door open. She's curled over the toilet, pale and damp with sweat, her arms limp at her sides. My heart squeezes.

"Hey," I murmur, crouching down and pressing my hand to her clammy forehead.

She doesn't answer. Her eyes are glassy, half-lidded, barely holding on.

Gently, I scoop her up into my arms. She doesn't resist, just sighs and lets her head fall against my shoulder like she's been waiting for this all night. Her body's soft and warm, despite the chill on her skin.

I carry her to my bed, kicking off my boots without bothering to untie them. She groans as I lay her down, and I hush her gently, brushing damp hair from her forehead.

"You're okay, baby. Just rest."

I undress her carefully, unzipping her jeans, sliding them down her legs, peeling her top away from her clammy skin. I grab one of my clean T-shirts from the drawer and pull it over her head, guiding her arms through like she's sleepwalking.

Then, I fetch a glass of water and some painkillers from the bathroom before sitting on the edge of the bed until her lashes flutter.

"Rue," I whisper, nudging her gently. "Hey, come on. Just sip some water for me. Take these."

She groans but lets me tilt the glass to her lips. She swallows the tablets with barely a grimace. Then she flops back down and rolls onto her side, pulling my T-shirt tight around her body like it's armour.

"Lay with me," she whispers.

I hesitate for a second. "You sure?"

She nods without opening her eyes. Then, she just scoots back and leaves space for me.

I climb in beside her, staying on top of the covers at first, afraid to assume too much. Her hand finds my chest, then travels down to my stomach, like she needs to know I'm really here.

"Can I ask you something?" she mumbles.

"Anything."

"What was it like? Being with someone like her?"

My throat tightens.

She opens her eyes then, just enough to look at me. There's no accusation in her voice, just quiet pain.

"Someone pretty. Someone powerful. Clever." Her voice shakes. "She's a lawyer, Atlas."

"Don't do that," I say, sharper than I mean to. I turn on my side to face her. "Don't make me listen to you cut yourself down."

She looks away, but I gently guide her face back to mine.

"She's not you," I say. "She's never been you. Rue, you're brave in ways most people aren't. You've got the kindest heart. The funniest sense of humour. You feel everything so deeply, even when it hurts. You make people feel seen. You make *me* feel seen."

She blinks, slow and heavy.

"And yeah, you're beautiful. You always have been. But it's not about that. Not for me. It's the way you scrunch your nose when you're trying not to laugh. The way you hold your breath when you're nervous. The way you never let anyone in, but you let me in."

Her lips part like she's about to cry or kiss me. I don't know which.

"I don't want Anita," I whisper. "I want you."

She leans in then, and our mouths meet in a kiss that's soft and aching and desperate. Like she's trying to believe me, one brush of her lips at a time.

She climbs over me, straddling my waist, her hands sliding beneath my shirt like she needs to feel my skin to stay grounded.

"Rue," I murmur against her lips, my hands settling on her thighs, trying to still her. "We shouldn't. You've been drinking."

"I know," she whispers. "But I want to remember this. I want to feel something good."

She kisses me again, deeper now. Bolder. Her body melts into mine, and it takes everything I have not to flip her off me and walk away, not because I don't want her, but because I want her too much to do this wrong, knowing tomorrow she might regret it.

But she's looking at me like I'm the only thing keeping her afloat, and I don't have the strength to let go.

So I let my hands roam over her body, up my shirt and over her breasts. She gasps, arching forward and pressing her core against the outline of my erection over my jeans. I grip her hips, encouraging her to keep moving, rocking against me until the friction sends her spiralling over the edge.

Her cheeks are flushed pink and her eyes sleepy as she falls against my chest. I wrap my arms around her, pulling the sheets over us. And for the first time in days, I relax. Rue is in my arms, right where she belongs.

RUE

I wake with a start and realise straight away I'm not at home. Yesterday comes flooding back and I groan, rolling onto my side to see Atlas's side empty. I sigh with relief. *Thank God.* And then I push to sit, looking around for my clothes.

I grab my jeans and pull them on, I whip off Atlas's shirt, right as the door swings open and he waltz' in with a smile. It fades when he spots me half dressed.

"Morning," I almost whisper as I pull my top on.

He places a tray on the bed and the smell of pastries hits me, making my stomach growl out loud with hunger. "I got us breakfast," he says, his eyes full of mistrust.

"I'm gonna grab something with Kasey," I say, picking up my shoes. "Thanks though."

I head for the door, and he steps in front of me, blocking my exit. "Wait, what's going on?"

I stare down at the floor. "Thanks for looking after me last night, Atlas, but that's all it was. I was drunk."

"You asked me to hold you," he snaps.

"Again, I was drunk."

"You came on my jeans," he snaps, and I feel my cheeks heat with embarrassment. "You practically begged me to fuck you."

I bristle at his words. "And you're so easy when a woman begs," I snap.

He relents, sighing. "I just thought . . . yah know, maybe we'd turned a corner."

"You nearly had sex with your ex," I snap.

"But I didn't."

"Only because you were interrupted," I yell. He stills. "Anita told me that you only stopped because Tom arrived."

"Everything I said last night was true. I am falling for you."

His words cause more pain, and I inhale sharply, placing a hand over my chest. "We're over." I rush from the room, slamming the door behind me.

∼

THE AIR IS COOLER NOW, LACED WITH THE HUSH OF LATE evening. Crickets chirp somewhere in the long grass, and the tree above me rustles every so often, its branches swaying gently like it knows how fragile I feel.

I sit cross-legged on the grass, my palms pressed flat to the earth like I'm trying to ground myself. Everything is still. But my mind is racing.

I should feel better. I should feel something more than hollow. But there's a quiet ache behind my ribs that hasn't let up since I left his bed.

I don't regret it. Not really. I just don't know what it *means*. If it was comfort or connection, if it was a goodbye or if I was just too drunk to remember all the hurt.

I hug my knees to my chest, watching the dark outline of the club through the trees. There's laughter from inside. Music. Clinking bottles and the occasional roar of a bike engine.

None of it feels like mine.

Then I hear footsteps, soft ones, deliberate. I don't look up. I already know who it is.

Atlas doesn't say a word.

He just kneels beside me and sets three things on the grass: a blanket, thick and worn, a coffee mug, steaming, and a book, *my* book, the battered copy of *The Night Circus* I've read a hundred times, the one with my scribbles in the margins and the loose spine I once tried to fix with tape.

I blink down at the items, my chest tightening.

He doesn't touch me. Doesn't even try. Just lingers there for a beat, like he's making sure I'm really okay.

Then, quietly, he walks away.

And I break, not in a painful, falling-apart kind of way, but in the way a person softens when they're seen exactly as they are.

I wrap the blanket around my shoulders and press the coffee to my lips. It's perfect, and exactly how I always order it, with a hint of vanilla syrup.

Even when I can't find the words, Atlas seems to hear what I don't say.

~

I WAKE TO THE SCENT OF HIM. IT'S A SUBTLE HINT OF leather and smoke and something warm, like cedar, but it wraps around me before I even open my eyes.

For a second, I think I'm still outside. Still under the tree with the night pressing down around me. But then my fingers shift, brushing against sheets instead of grass, and I feel the weight of a blanket tucked around my shoulders.

I blink slowly into the dark room. I reach for the lamp on the nightstand and click it on. The glow floods the room, soft and golden, and my breath catches in my throat.

Atlas is asleep in the chair by the window.

His arms are folded across his chest; his head tipped back against the wall. One leg is stretched out in front of him, the other bent just enough to suggest he didn't mean to fall asleep. There's a book resting on the arm of the chair, *my* book, the spine splayed open like he'd been rereading the parts I've underlined.

He must've carried me inside and tucked me in. My heart twists in my chest.

The sight of him hits me hard, not because he looks good (he always does), but because of what it *means*. Because he didn't leave me out there. Because he came to check on me and then took care of me.

He *stayed.*

Even when I didn't ask him to.

Especially when I didn't ask him to.

I sit up slowly, the blanket falling from my shoulders, and I just watch him. Letting myself take in every quiet detail. The crease between his brows. The slight twitch of his fingers like he's dreaming.

I move quietly, careful not to wake him. The blanket slips from my shoulders as I stand, and I gather it in my hands, walking it over to where he sleeps.

He looks uncomfortable in that chair, he's too tall for it, and his neck is tilted at an awkward angle, but there's something peaceful in his face. His chest rises slow, steady breaths, his lashes casting soft shadows over his cheekbones.

I drape the blanket over him, tucking it around his arms and shoulders. He doesn't stir.

I should stop there.

But I don't.

I hover a moment longer, my heart thudding wildly, a war raging behind my ribs. My head is screaming at me to walk away, to leave this thing alone before it ruins us both again.

But my heart?

My heart begs for one stolen second.

He'll never know.

So I lean down, slow and hesitant, until my lips brush his.

It's feather-light, barely a kiss at all. Just a breath of contact, a silent confession he'll never hear. I linger there, like I can pour everything I never said into that one moment. Like I can give him this tiny part of me without ever having to explain it.

And then I pull back.

Only, before I can take a step, his hand shoots out and closes around my wrist.

I gasp, startled, and meet his eyes.

He's awake.

Not groggy. Not confused.

Awake.

And watching me.

His eyes burn into mine, dark, steady, unreadable. He doesn't say a word. Doesn't ask why. He just *looks* at me, like he's trying to read every thought I've ever had.

My breath catches, frozen between apology and panic.

Then slowly, gently, he releases me.

I stand there a beat too long, my skin tingling where he touched me.

Without a word, I turn and slip into the bathroom, clutching the edge of the sink as I try to catch my breath.

My heart is racing. *What did I just do?* He wasn't meant to know. To catch me. I groan. I stare at my reflection in the mirror. "You have to get a grip," I whisper at myself.

By the time I step back into the bedroom, he's gone. The chair is empty with the blanket draped neatly over the back, like he was never there.

I should be happy he left without a word. But I can't deny the ache burning deeper in my heart.

ANITA

"I don't think this is a good idea," I whisper, my voice barely audible over the clink of cutlery and low restaurant chatter. We're seated by the window, too exposed, too bright. My palms are already damp.

"We're laying our cards on the table," Tom replies, calm and unmoved as ever. "Giving him a chance to back out of the battle."

I glance towards the door, and my stomach knots. "What if he's got something worse on me?"

Tom doesn't flinch. "Like?"

I open my mouth, then close it again. I don't *know*. That's the worst part. With Damien, the truth is elastic. He bends it until it strangles you.

"He's been known to make stuff up," I mutter.

"I've requested a female judge," Tom says, folding his napkin with irritating precision. "She's new but sharp. Not the type to be bribed or bullied. She'll stick to the evidence."

"So, why are we doing this?" I ask.

He turns to me fully, his gaze direct. "Because if he's bluffing, this is where he'll flinch."

I don't get a chance to respond before a voice cuts through the air.

"Anita."

I jolt, head snapping up.

He's early.

"Damien," I manage, trying to sound neutral. My spine stiffens as he slides into the chair opposite me, dressed like he's walked out of a boardroom—clean, controlled, poisonous.

A waitress materialises beside him. "Can I get you a drink?"

"No, thank you," he says without looking at her. "I won't be staying long."

The second she disappears, his eyes fix on mine. He doesn't even glance at Tom.

"What do you want?" he asks, crisp and cold like a slap.

I clear my throat, nerves tightening around my vocal cords. "How's Leo?"

"Get to the point," he says, voice flatter now. *Impatient.*

Tom leans forward slightly, finally drawing Damien's attention. "We wanted to be upfront. Some new information has come to light. We're giving you the chance to respond before it goes through the courts."

Damien's gaze flicks to him, sharp and dismissive. "Such as?"

"Kasey Green," Tom says evenly.

It's brief, but I see it—the faint twitch in Damien's jaw, a flicker of recognition in his eyes. He knows the name.

"Who?"

Tom chuckles, low and humourless. "Let's not insult each other with that. I don't have time for games."

Damien drums his fingers on the table. *Tap. Tap. Tap.* He's rattled, yet trying to cover it with arrogance.

Then, casually, like tossing a grenade with a smile, he turns back to me. "Are you still hooking up with the biker, Anita?"

Tom doesn't rise to it. "Do you have evidence of that?"

"Do I need it?" Damien replies, smirking slightly. "Your client doesn't have the cleanest reputation."

Tom laces his fingers together and rests them calmly on the table. It's a calculated move, done with quiet authority. "Yes, Mr. Carpenter, you *do* need it. Because this time, we're doing things by the book. No backdoor judges. No fabricated scandals. Just facts."

Damien's expression falters. Only for a second. But it's enough. "I see you've been taken in by my wife."

"*Ex*," Tom corrects without missing a beat.

Damien huffs a dry laugh. "Ex-wife. Trust me when I say, she will make a fool of you in that courtroom once I present what I've gathered."

Tom doesn't blink. "Judge Griffin is meticulous. And fair. I look forward to hearing what stories you've crafted. I'm confident the truth will speak louder."

For once, Damien has no clever comeback.

I glance down at my hands under the table, pressing my fingers together until they ache. This is it—the beginning of the war.

But for the first time in a long time . . . I don't feel alone.

He finally stands, yanking his suit jacket into place and straightening his tie like he still has control of something.

"I'll see you in court," Damien mutters, his voice tight with the effort of keeping his temper in check.

And then he's gone, the door swinging shut behind him with more force than necessary.

For a beat, I just sit there, staring at the empty space he left behind. The tension still clings to me, like static after a storm. But then it cracks and something warm blooms in my chest.

I turn to Tom, barely containing the rush in my voice. "Oh my god, you were amazing," I breathe, grinning wide. "He didn't know what to do. I've never seen him so . . . *lost for words*."

Tom allows a small smile, but it's measured, the kind of smile you earn from him, not the kind he hands out.

"He's not used to being challenged," he says simply, reaching for his coffee. "Especially not by someone who knows the law better than he does."

I lean back in my chair, exhaling the tension I hadn't even realised I was still holding. "I needed that," I admit. "To see him flinch."

"You needed to see he bleeds like everyone else," Tom says.

I nod, and for a moment I let myself enjoy the silence. The weight of Damien's presence has lifted, and in its place, there's just me and Tom. Calm, capable, quietly victorious.

"Thank you," I say, more sincerely this time.

Tom's eyes meet mine, steady and professional, but there's a softness there too. "You're the one doing the hard part," he replies. "I'm just helping you make it stick."

My smile fades a little, shifting into something steadier. "Still," I say, "it feels good to have someone on my side who isn't afraid of him."

Tom finishes his drink and sets the mug down with a faint *clink*. "He should be afraid of *you*, Anita. He just doesn't know it yet."

I bite my lip to stop the smile from spreading. "You have a way with words," I murmur, letting my gaze drop.

But then he reaches out, takes my chin between his fingers, and lifts my face to meet his. His touch is light, careful, but his eyes burn into mine with something that feels like awe. Like he's looking at a woman who matters.

"I'm not saying anything you don't deserve to hear," he says softly. "I'm just doing what every man before me *should* have done, reminding you who you are."

I blink, my heart stalling.

"Somewhere along the way, you forgot," he goes on, his voice barely above a whisper. "But I didn't. Not for a second."

The air shifts. I lean in—not fully, not boldly—just

enough to let the possibility hang between us. To see if he'll close the space.

His eyes flick to my mouth, and I swear he sways closer for half a second. My breath catches.

But then he clears his throat and pulls back, letting his hand fall away with a quiet sigh. "We should probably get out of here," he says, his voice rougher now. "Before I forget I'm your lawyer."

He smiles faintly, but it doesn't reach his eyes. I nod, almost lost for words as I push to my feet, my mind racing with what just happened . . . or almost happened.

CHAPTER 18

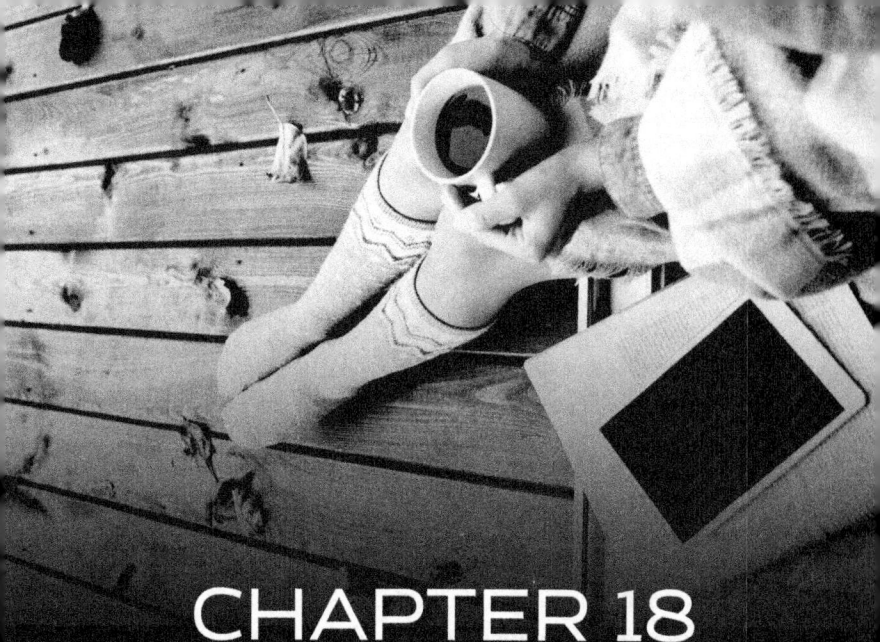

ATLAS

"Is it supposed to make that sound?" Grizz asks, eyeing the coffee machine like it might explode.

"It's heating up," I mutter, frowning at the blinking lights like they've personally offended me. "It's fine."

Axel leans against the counter, arms crossed, smirking like he's watching a rom-com instead of me trying to set up the world's most unnecessarily complicated machine. "So let me get this straight, you spent how much on a coffee machine?"

"Does it matter?"

"Depends. Is this to impress us?" He gestures between himself and Grizz. "Because if so, I take oat milk."

Grizz chuckles. "You don't even drink coffee these days, man."

"Yeah, but if Atlas is making it, I might start."

"Both of you shut up," I mutter, fiddling with the milk frother nozzle. "It's for Rue."

There's a beat of silence, then Kasey's voice pipes up from the doorway. "You're gonna have to do more than a cappuccino to get back in her good books."

I glance up. She's leaning on the frame, arms crossed, watching me like she's amused but not unkind. Her eyes flick to the coffee machine, then back to me. "She's still very mad."

"I know."

"And sad," she adds, pushing off the door frame and stepping closer to inspect the shiny gadget.

"I'm working on making that right," I say.

I go back to the buttons, heart thudding harder than I'd admit. The stupid machine hisses again.

"What even is that thing?" Grizz asks, peering at the instruction booklet I've got folded beside me. "Looks like it could launch a satellite."

"It makes her coffee just the way she likes it," I say, sharper than I mean to. "She can't leave the compound, so I figured . . . I'd bring it to her."

Axel whistles. "You kiss one lawyer and now you're compensating with appliances."

I shoot him a look. "That's not what this is."

"Sure it's not."

"I messed up. I know that. But I'm starting again with her, behaving how I should have in the beginning."

Kasey moves into the kitchen and grabs a mug from the shelf. "She doesn't stop looking for you when you're not in the room. But if you tell her I told you that, I'll end you."

I give a small smile, thankful she's trying to help me. Having her on side is half the battle won.

Axel reaches for the machine just as it lets out a high-pitched beep. "You reckon this thing's gonna kill me?"

"Touch it and I'll break your hand."

He grins. "Ah, there's the romantic we know and love."

I ignore him and pour the first coffee. It's got the swirl. The foam. The vanilla syrup.

It's not an apology. But it's a start. It's stupid, *probably*. She might not even take it.

But I carry it anyway.

The clubhouse is louder than usual, someone's music is playing down the hall, and girls are laughing near the pool table. But all I see is her.

Rue. She's curled up at the table with Lexi, her knees tucked to her chest like she's guarding herself. I don't think she even knows she does it.

I step through the doorway, mug in hand, and then I hear her and my heart sinks. "Atlas!"

I turn to glance in Anita's direction. Her voice slices the moment clean in half. Too cheerful. Too much. I pause, barely, then keep walking.

"Can I talk to you a sec?" she calls out again, her heels tapping behind me.

"No." I don't turn. Don't flinch. Just keep my eyes on Rue.

She sees me. Her back stiffens, then her hands freeze mid-fidget. She's wary, cautious.

I slow as I reach her, the mug held steady.

"You said you missed the coffee at that place near your flat," I say quietly, aware of Lexi watching like she's front row at the theatre. "I figured I'd try and bring it to you. Just how you like it."

Rue doesn't answer. Doesn't even reach for it.

She just looks at it. Then at me.

That pause, the stretch of it, hurts more than it should. But I don't move. I wait. She has to come to me. Her terms. Her pace.

Her fingers finally wrap around the cup. The way she holds it, careful like it's a delicate thing, it makes something in my chest ease.

"Thanks," she whispers.

I nod. That's all I get. But that's enough, for now.

I turn to leave, and Anita's standing by the doorway still. Her arms crossed, her smile long gone.

I don't stop because I can't have Rue see me talking to the woman I cheated on her with, but she follows me into the kitchen. "I only wanted to tell you that you were right. Damien does know Kasey."

Axel looks up, and I'm glad Kasey is still in the room to witness every second, so no one can get it twisted. "I told you," I say, "but you need to update Axel now on this shit. He's handling it."

I see the way my words crush her, but she gives a slight nod and turns to Axel instead. "Me and Tom met him. He didn't admit to it, but he knew Kasey. His eye flickered the way it does when I'm too close to the truth."

"Good," says Axel. "It's what we wanted."

"Now, what?" she asks.

"Now, we pay him a visit." He glances at me. "Let's call church."

She startles at this. "Wait, you can't."

Axel laughs. "I can do what I like, Nita. I'm the President around here."

"But what if Leo's there?" Her voice is laced with panic. I gently touch her shoulder, and she begs me with her eyes.

"He won't be," I reassure her. "I promise, Leo won't witness anything he shouldn't."

"Can I come?" asks Kasey, popping a biscuit into her mouth like none of this is remotely scary to her.

"No," I say firmly.

"But it's me he's after."

I ruffle her hair, the way she hates. "Which is why you're staying here, so we know you're safe." She scowls, and I head out to round the men for church.

∽

THE PLACE SMELLS LIKE OVERPRICED WINE AND INSECURITY.

I clock Damien the second we step inside—back corner, laughing too loud at whatever his date just said. He looks relaxed, confident. Like he's not dragging a trail of mess behind him.

Not for long.

The hostess blinks at us, clutching her tablet like it's a cross. "Can I help you gentlemen?"

Axel gives her that slow grin that usually means someone's about to cry. "Don't worry, we ain't staying long and we're not gonna make a mess." He shoves a roll of bank notes in her hand. "Hold off calling the police."

She gives a nervous nod, pocketing the cash.

The clink of cutlery and the low hum of conversation follow us as we cross the restaurant, three wolves in a room full of deer.

Grizz sees the opportunity first. A waiter with a tray of drinks steps into his path. He sidesteps, but not enough to avoid him, just enough to make it look like an accident.

The tray tips. Red wine *explodes* across Damien's table. His date squeals, loud and dramatic, as it soaks her pale designer dress.

Grizz throws up his hands. "Well, shit. Look what I've done."

The woman stares at her ruined dress in horror.

"I know a cleaner who's real good with stains," Grizz offers with a wicked grin. "Or you could just take it off now. I won't look. *Much.*"

She gasps, turning on Damien. "Are you going to do anything?" she screams.

"That wouldn't be wise," I say with a smile. "Now, leave."

She's gone in a blur of expensive perfume and angry heels.

Axel slides into her seat like he owns it. I rest a hand on Damien's shoulder when he tries to rise, not hard but heavy enough. He sits. "Smart choice."

"I should have you thrown out," he snaps.

"You should sit still and listen," I say.

Axel pours himself a splash of wine from Damien's bottle, swirling it lazily. He doesn't drink it.

"We're here for a friendly chat," Axel says, his tone light. "Kasey Green. Sound familiar?"

Damien's expression barely flickers, but I see it. Recognition. Guilt.

"She didn't steal your money, so you're gonna call off the search party," he continues.

"She took my money," he growls.

"A few grand," I hiss. "That's pocket change to you."

"And a ring," he snaps, trying to shrug me off. I grip firmer, glancing at Axel, who doesn't let the new information change the narrative.

"I'm telling you it wasn't her," he says firmer this time.

Damien's mouth twists. "You think I give a shit what your little club thinks?"

"You should," I say. "Rue and Kasey are under our protection now. You go near them, even hint at messing with them again, and it's not the law you'll need to worry about."

Axel leans forward. "You're not the biggest fish in our pond, Damien." He smirks. "In fact, you're just a tadpole swimming amongst the sharks."

"It's twice her name's come up in twenty-four hours. First, my ex-wife mentions it, and now you," says Damien, relaxing again. "Is that coincidence or are you fucking her?" he asks Axel.

"When I plan to take someone down, I always have a back-up plan," says Axel. "You should remember that."

"She won't get Leo back," he rages.

Axel grins, pushing to his feet. "It was nice to meet you, but let's not cross paths again."

As the others head out, I lean closer. "And it was me," I whisper. "I was the one who fucked Anita, and man, she loved every second of it." I slap him hard on the back and head out.

RUE

I'm half asleep when someone taps on my bedroom door and a second later, Atlas peers around it. "Hey, can I borrow you for a second?"

I push to sit, glancing at the clock. It's almost nine but it's so noisy downstairs, I doubt I'll be sleeping properly any time soon, so I stand. "Sure, what's up?" I ask, hating there's still tension between us.

"Follow me," he says, turning and heading back down the hall.

We head up to the next floor, right to the end where

there's a locked door. He produces the key and unlocks it, glancing back at me as he opens it. "Trust me?" he asks.

I nearly turn back. Because I don't trust him. Not yet. As if he realises all too late the impact of his words, he winces. "It's a nice surprise," he mutters.

He leads me up a narrow metal staircase, his hand hovering like he's ready to catch me if I trip, though he doesn't touch me. At the top, he unlocks the rooftop door with a key I didn't even know he had.

And then he pushes it open. Warm light spills out.

I blink.

The space is transformed. String lights zigzag between rusted metal beams. There's a thick old rug on the ground and two giant beanbags with mismatched cushions in the middle. A couple of lanterns flicker at the corners. Someone's dragged a little firepit up here, not lit yet, but the promise is there.

And in the centre, like it's waiting just for me, is a crate with a coffee mug perched on top and a stack of books next to it. Old, worn paperbacks. Covers with cracked spines and creased corners. My fingers itch to grab them and examine them.

I step out slowly, my boots crunching against gravel.

"You did all this?" I ask, glancing at him. He shrugs, trying to play it cool, but he's not fooling me. His jaw is tight, like he's bracing for me to hate it.

"No one comes up here," he says, rubbing the back of his neck. "Figured you might like the quiet. And the coffee machine was a bust, so I made a fresh one the old-fashioned way. The books . . . I, uh, asked the lady at the second-hand shop for help. Told her you like the kind of stuff with messy emotions and complicated girls who think too much." He gives an unsure laugh.

My throat tightens. I don't know what I expected from him. But it wasn't *this*.

"I like it," I say, so quietly I'm not sure he hears me.

He nods once, like that's enough, and starts to turn back towards the stairs.

But something in me panics at the idea of him leaving. This man, with too many sins and not enough softness, has just given me a place to breathe.

And I don't want to breathe alone.

"You can stay," I blurt, heat rushing to my cheeks. "If you like. I mean, you don't have to. I just—"

He stops and looks at me. And for once, he doesn't smirk, doesn't joke. "I'd like that," he says.

He comes back and sits on the other beanbag without a word. Close, but not too close.

I drag the books onto my lap. "How did you know how much I love old books?"

"I paid attention," he says simply, and my heart swells a little more.

"One day, I'll have a room full of books," I say dreamily. "It'll smell of paper and dust. And it'll be quiet, just like up here."

We fall silent again, and then he says, "I need to tell you I'm sorry."

I look over, startled. He's not looking at me. He's watching the skyline, his arms resting on his knees, fingers knotted like he's holding himself together. "I shouldn't have started anything with you while things were still messy with Anita. I tried to pretend it was over, but the truth is, I was still figuring it out. And that's not fair to you. You deserve more than someone who's 'figuring it out'."

My chest tightens. He shifts slightly, finally looking at me. "I'm sorry I kissed her . . . twice. And that I almost slept with her. It was wrong on both of you. I regret it so deeply, I can't even begin to explain. I have no excuses or reasons, but please know I'm sorry and if I could take it all back, I would."

"Why?" I whisper and he frowns. "Why would you take it back?"

He thinks over my words. "Because hurting you is one of the worst things I've ever done, and trust me, I've done some terrible shit. But seeing the way you look at me now, the hurt and mistrust," he sighs, shaking his head, "it brings me to my knees, Rue. It keeps me up at night. And the worst thing is, I can't change it. I can't fucking take any of it back because the damage is done."

I sit very still. I can hear the wind tugging at the lights above us, the creak of the roof beneath our weight. My fingers tighten around the spine of the top book. "I ruined what we had for old habits and bad choices. It was a mistake, a huge one. Hurting you will be the one thing I'll never get over."

Something in his voice makes my throat ache. Because he sounds . . . broken. I don't feel like he's angling for forgiveness, there's just a raw emotion surrounding him right now, and it feels genuine.

"I don't expect you to forgive me," he says after a moment. "But I needed you to know. You didn't imagine any of it, Rue. What was between us, it was real. And I'm sorry I wrecked it before it had a chance."

I swallow, the burn behind my eyes building. And then he stands up and brushes his hands on his jeans. "I'll leave you to your books."

He turns towards the door, and something snaps inside me.

"Wait," I say, the word out before I can stop it. "You're just gonna dump all that on me and run?"

He freezes then turns halfway. His brow lifts a fraction, caught off guard.

"Don't I get a chance to speak too?"

He exhales, like he'd been holding his breath. "Of course," he says quietly, and takes a slow step back. "I just didn't want to pressure you. Or make things worse."

I shift the books off my lap and stand up, crossing my arms over my chest, not to be defensive, but to hold in the storm twisting inside me.

"You're right, you have hurt me," I say, voice steadier than I feel. "You broke something I didn't even realise I'd handed you. And I hated you for it. Not because you kissed someone else, but because I let myself believe you were different."

He nods, eyes on me. He doesn't flinch, doesn't try to interrupt. He just listens.

"But then you did all this." I gesture to the rooftop, the books, the lights, the effort. "And I'm not saying it fixes things. It doesn't. But it makes me hate you a little less."

That gets a flicker of a smile from him, barely there. "I can live with that."

"I'm not saying I trust you again," I add.

"I wouldn't expect you to."

"But I'm not done talking to you either," I say, softer now. "And I don't want you to go."

He studies me like I'm something precious, something he's scared to touch. "I'll stay," he says, "if you want me to."

I nod once. "I do."

He lowers himself back to the beanbag, and I do the same, heart thudding a little louder than it should.

ANITA

"Call off the pitbulls," yells Damien the second I answer his call. "Or so help me, I'll—"

I hold the phone from my ear. "Careful, you'll give yourself a hernia yelling like that." It feels easier to be confident when I know I'm winning the battle.

"I will drag you through that courthouse," he screams. It's also satisfying knowing I'm getting to him.

"You already are."

"Is this what you want for our child?" he asks.

"I want the very best for Leo," I state.

"And you think that's with you?" He laughs, it's cold and empty.

"Yes, Damien, I do. I'm his mother."

"You're nothing, sweetheart. A scrubber who fucks bad boys like they're going out of fashion."

"Remind me again how old Kasey was when you first had sex with her?" I keep my voice even, and Tom fist pumps the air with a huge grin. I glow under his praise. "At this point, I'd like to offer you regular contact," I say firmly. "Agree to Leo living back with me, and I'll be reasonable, which is more than I can say for how you've behaved."

"I'll be speaking with your parents, Anita. Without their backing, you don't stand a chance."

He disconnects, leaving me staring at the phone still in my hand.

"You did great," Tom rushes to say.

"He's right," I almost whisper. "What judge would give me my child if my own parents think Damien is the better option?"

He sits on the seat opposite my desk.

"Win your parents over," says Tessa from her desk. I glance over. "You're their daughter, remind them."

"They hate me, Tessa. Everything I do pisses my father off."

"What would make him happy when it comes to you?" asks Tom.

I think over his question. "If I went to work for my father's company."

He winces. "Well, that can't happen."

"Exactly. He'd also be kinder if I was to marry right."

"Right?" he asks.

"As in not a biker," says Tessa with a smirk.

"Or any criminal, for that matter," I state, arching a brow in her direction. "He would only really be impressed with a lawyer or some rich guy with a golfing membership." I laugh, shaking my head. "He's a pompous prick."

"I have a platinum golfing membership," says Tom simply.

My cheeks instantly burn with embarrassment. "Oh, shit, I didn't mean—"

"Relax, Nita," he says with a laugh. "I'm saying, invite him to dinner and I'll charm him."

I frown, but Tessa jumps in before I can respond. "As her boyfriend?"

My head whips up. "Tessa," I cry.

Tom laughs again. "Exactly."

My eyes flick to his. "What?"

He rounds the desk, taking my hand in his and gently pulling me to stand. "Invite your parents to dinner this evening. We'll impress them together."

I inhale, holding my breath as I stare longingly at his lips. His little smirk tells me he's on to me, and then he slides my mobile into my hand. I blink, glancing at it. "Eight o' clock in

The Ivy. My treat." And then he gives me a chaste kiss on the cheek before turning and marching right out of the office.

I stare after him, my mouth half-open. "Well," says Tessa, blowing out a puff of air, "that was . . . unexpected."

"Right?" I whisper.

"Is he serious? Is it a real date?" she asks.

I shrug because I have no idea. I thought my feelings were from confusion. I haven't exactly been making the best choices lately. It was only the other night I tried to seduce Atlas. I groan. "He's just being nice, right?" And I stare at her baffled expression. "Because I'm a hot mess right now."

"Either way, this might help, and you need to get them on side before Damien tries."

I nod, typing out a text to my father.

> Me: Hi, can we have dinner this evening at the Ivy, eight?

His reply comes instantly.

> Father: What's the occasion? Premature celebrations of screwing your kid's life up?

> Me: I'd like to explain it all.

> Father: Fine. See you at eight.

CHAPTER 19

ATLAS

The sun's barely up when I knock on Rue's door.

She blinks up at me from the doorway, hair a mess, hoodie hanging off one shoulder. "What time is it?"

"Time for me to take you somewhere," I say, holding up the spare helmet. "You said you like mornings. Quiet ones."

She eyes the helmet like it might bite her. "Where are we going?"

"You'll see."

She makes me wait while she gets changed, which, honestly, I'd wait all day for, and then she finally steps out, pulling her hoodie sleeves over her hands, hesitant but curious.

The ride is short, maybe twenty minutes, just outside town. The road winds into a wooded trail I scouted a few days ago, the kind of place where you don't hear cars, just wind and birdsong. I park the bike near a grassy clearing where I set everything up this morning. A picnic blanket, takeaway coffees, and a couple fresh pastries I know she likes, and most importantly, a worn copy of *Persuasion*.

Rue stops in her tracks when she sees it.

"You did all this?" she asks, barely above a whisper.

I shrug, trying not to grin like an idiot. "You like quiet, and books, and coffee done right."

She walks slowly to the blanket and kneels, fingers brushing the cover of the book. "This is my favourite Austen."

"I know," I say, sitting beside her. "Thought maybe you'd read some to me."

She looks at me, and then she does something I wasn't ready for. She crawls over and curls up in my lap like she used to. Head under my chin, knees drawn in, the softest sigh escaping her lips as her body relaxes against mine.

It's the first time she's touched me since everything went to hell. I don't move, don't speak. Just hold her, heart pounding like a war drum.

Her voice is muffled against my chest. "Can you read it to me instead?"

I swallow hard and nod. My fingers shake a little as I open the book, but I find the page and start.

"You pierce my soul. I am half agony, half hope," I read, my voice rougher than I want it to be.

Rue doesn't move, so I keep going, my thumb gently stroking the edge of the page where her hand rests.

"Tell me not that I am too late, that such precious feelings are gone forever."

My throat tightens, the line hitting a nerve. She shifts a little in my lap, her fingers curling lightly into my shirt. "I hate that I still feel things when you're near." Her voice startles me. It's barely a whisper but it echoes around me.

I stop breathing for a second, her honesty slicing through me like a knife. Her cheek is against my chest, and I can feel her heart pounding. Or maybe that's mine.

I tilt her chin up, forcing her to look at me.

"I'm glad you do," I say, low and rough, "because I feel everything, Rue. Every second I'm near you. Every second I'm not. I ache for you."

Her lips part, but no sound comes out.

"I hate myself for every moment I made you doubt how fucking much you matter to me. And if it takes the rest of my life to prove that, I will."

I shift beneath her, the book balanced in one hand and the other wrapped around her protectively. I scan the words and begin to read the next line.

"I have waited for this opportunity to tell you that—"

Rue kisses me. There's no warning, no words, just her lips pressed to mine in a slow, unsure kiss. I feel my whole body tense, scared she'll realise any second that this is a mistake and pull away. But her fingers pull my shirt tighter into her fists as her body turns slightly more towards me. The book slips from my hand with a thud, and my fingers tangle in her hair, tilting her head back and taking control of her mouth.

She pulls back, her eyes staring wide and unsure. "I don't . . . I don't know why I did that," she stammers.

My heart slams faster in my chest while I stare back at her silently, praying she doesn't pull away with regret. "I'll take whatever crumbs you'll give me," I murmur. "But make no mistake, I'm starving for all of you."

She inhales sharply as her eyes soften slightly. I feel her pulse pick up where my fingers brush her wrist. But I make no move to kiss her, not wanting to rush her and scare her away.

"What are we doing here?" she eventually asks.

"I told you, enjoying the quiet."

She smiles. "No, I mean us, what's happening here?"

I pause, thinking over her words. "I'm hoping I'm showing you how things could be."

"Atlas, you're a biker," she says, as if that's news to me. "Reading Austin in the woods, dates on rooftops . . . that's not you."

"It's who I want to be for you."

"But that's just it," she says, gently placing a hand against my cheek. "I need you to be yourself, Atlas. How can I decide if we'll ever work, when you're not being true to yourself?"

I lean into her touch without thinking, eyes locked on hers. There's something raw in her voice, something that cuts through all the noise I've been carrying around.

"I am being myself," I say quietly. "This," I gesture around us, to the blanket, the book, the quiet space I carved out just for her, "this isn't some performance, Rue. It's not pretend."

She looks down, fingers sliding away from my cheek.

"I know I don't fit your idea of me. Hell, I probably don't fit anyone's idea of how a biker's supposed to act. But you think I haven't always craved this too? Something soft. Something quiet. Someone who sees past the leather and noise."

She meets my gaze again, slower this time, and I reach for her hand, threading our fingers together.

"Don't mistake what I do for who I am. I can be rough. I can be violent when I have to be. But I can also sit in silence with a woman who makes me feel like I've finally come home." I squeeze her hand. "This is me. You're not changing me, Rue. You're just giving me the space to be the parts of myself I never thought I was allowed to be."

Her eyes shimmer like she's trying to blink back whatever she's feeling.

Then, softer, almost like she's testing the weight of it: "So, this isn't about trying to win me back?"

I smirk, brushing my thumb over her knuckles. "Of course, it is. I'd tear down the damn world if it meant earning a second chance with you. But I'm not pretending to be someone else to do it. I'm showing you all of me, even the parts I keep buried."

RUE

His words do something to my insides, and I'm hit with that nervous excitement I always get when I think of Atlas and the way he gets under my skin. I shift, placing my hands on his shoulders before throwing my leg over him so we're facing one another. "So, if I agreed to give this a second shot . . ." I pause, enjoying the glimmer of hope I see in his eyes. "What do you envision our future will look like?"

His hands cup my backside, tugging me farther up his lap. "Peaceful," he says, brushing his nose against mine. "Real," he adds, his eyes staring deeply into my own. "Ours."

I want to believe him, everything in me wants exactly what he's offering, but there's a small part of me that still can't bring myself to trust him.

I lower my forehead to his, closing my eyes like it might steady the thud of my heart.

"You say all the right things," I whisper, "and I want to fall into them, into you. But what if you break me again?"

His hands still on my hips, the only movement between

us now is the slow, shared rhythm of our breath. I hate that he doesn't rush to answer. Hate it and love it. Because it means he's thinking, not just saying what I want to hear.

"I can't promise I won't mess up," he says eventually, his voice gravel soft. "But I'll never lie to you. Never betray you. I'll spend every day showing you you're it for me. I've never wanted anything the way I want this . . . *us*."

My throat tightens. The version of me that used to be so cautious wants to back away, wants to protect herself. But the other version, the one he's coaxing out of hiding with every soft look and small gesture, leans in, brushing my lips against his.

His breath hitches, and then he tilts his chin just enough for our mouths to slot together in the softest way—not desperate, not rushed, just . . . sure.

And for a second, I let myself believe that maybe, just maybe, this could work.

When we finally pull apart, I rest my hand over his heart, steady and strong beneath my palm.

"I need to go slow," I murmur.

"You set the pace," he says. "I'll be right here."

I lay my cheek to his chest, enjoying his warmth, when the sound of boots scuffing gravel jolts me upright.

Atlas goes still beneath me.

We both turn at the same time.

Eight men stand at the edge of the clearing.

Uninvited. Unsmiling. Unfamiliar. My pulse spikes instantly, instincts screaming.

Atlas shifts me off his lap and rises slowly, placing himself between me and them. His whole-body changes. The soft, steady man from a second ago replaced by the one I've imagined. Broad. Coiled. *Lethal.*

"Can I help you?" His voice is calm, but there's a warning beneath it.

The man at the front stands tall, broad, and he's dressed like he belongs on a battlefield, not in the woods. He takes a step forward. His lip curls as he glances past Atlas and straight at me.

"We're here for the girl."

My breath catches. *Me. They're here for me.*

Atlas doesn't move, doesn't flinch. "No," he says. "She's not going anywhere."

The man smirks like he expected that. "You don't want this to get ugly."

Atlas steps forward. "Then walk away."

The man nods. It's an unspoken order and suddenly, the other seven are moving towards us.

Atlas swings, hitting the first one hard enough to drop him. But it's eight against one, and he gets two more good hits in before they drag him down. I scream his name, fighting to get to him, but someone grabs my arm and hauls me back.

"No!" I shout, thrashing as the man yanks me away from Atlas, who's now on his knees, blood dripping from his lip, arms held by two men while others lay into him.

"Rue!" he shouts, struggling against them. "Let her go, you f—"

The leader steps forward and punches him hard in the gut, and the sound Atlas makes rips through me like a blade.

"Take her," the man orders.

"No! No, please . . ." My voice cracks as rough hands shove me towards the trees.

Atlas lifts his bloody face, staring right at me. "You have to go with them, Rue, but I'll find you."

I kick out, screaming angrily as I'm dragged away. It

makes no difference, and as I try to turn back to see Atlas, a sack is placed over my head and everything goes dark.

ANITA

I sit straighter, and Tom places his hand over my own on the table. "Relax," he whispers. "It's going to be okay."

"You don't know my parents," I mutter, looking towards the entrance for the hundredth time.

"I've met my fare share of money driven arseholes, Nita. I'll win them over."

I half smile, loving how optimistic he is. "What is this, exactly?" I ask, because the question has been playing on my mind all day.

He grins now, relaxing back in his seat and snatching up the wine menu. "A chance for you to see the life I can offer you." I frown, surprised by his words. "Nita, I've been crazy about you since . . . probably the first day I ever set eyes on you. But you're not like other women," he states, smiling fondly, "and I had to be the man you deserve before I put myself on your radar." He looks past me. "We'll talk later. They're here."

My head whips round as my heart slams harder. I'm unsure if it's from his confession or the fact my parents are walking towards us.

I stand clumsily, almost pulling the tablecloth with me. Tom stands too, reaching past me to shake my father's hand. "George, it's great to see you again," he says, his shake firm. Then he moves past me, fixing his eyes on my mother. "And you must be Carol," he says fondly, kissing her cheek. "I've seen you many times at various gatherings but never had the chance to meet you officially."

Mother looks startled, smiling as he kisses her other

cheek. "You look amazing," he continues, pulling out a chair for her.

My father eyes the Champagne. "Are we celebrating?" he mutters, sitting beside Mother.

I glance nervously at Tom because I have no idea why he ordered the four-hundred-pound bottle either. "I haven't even told Anita yet," says Tom, taking his seat as he waves the waiter over to open the bottle. "But I made partner today at Jackson and Holden."

I gasp, my hands flying to my mouth in shock. The firm is huge, one of the biggest around here, and I know my father is secretly jealous of the owner, Amber Jackson.

"That's amazing," I cry as the Champagne cork pops. I throw my arms around him, and he drags me closer, placing a lingering kiss to the side of my mouth. I feel my cheeks flush and bite my lower lip to control the smile. "Well done," I whisper.

My father stands again, shaking Tom's hand. "Great news. Congratulations." My mother follows.

The waiter fills four flutes and passes them out before disappearing.

"Now, all I need is Anita to agree to marry me," he says, his tone teasing as my head whips in his direction. "And, of course, to meet Leo, then my life will be complete."

"Marriage?" Father repeats, his brows furrowed together. "She's never even mentioned you."

"He was kidding," I mutter, forcing a tight smile.

"I'm not," Tom says, looking my father dead in the eye, "but that conversation will take place over golf, yes?"

This gets my father's attention. "You play? I've never seen you at Hadfield's."

"My loyalty lies with Marsdon's," says Tom, and my father's eyes almost light up. "My friend owns the place, and I'm a platinum member. I can get you in there anytime."

Father sits straighter, and I can tell by his face as he nods that he's impressed. "Marsdon's is always full," he says. "I've been trying years to get in there."

Tom smiles. "Consider it done," he says, lifting his glass and holding it in the middle of the table. We all clink and take a sip.

~

I STARE AFTER MY PARENTS AS THEY HEAD TO THEIR WAITING car, still in disbelief. They didn't throw a fit, didn't question my life choices.

And they appeared to love Tom.

His hand grazes the small of my back, his touch warm and possessive, and I turn to him, my lips curving with surprise. "That went surprisingly well."

"I told you there was nothing to worry about." His voice is a low murmur against my ear, and then he takes my hand, slotting his fingers through mine with a casual intimacy that makes my stomach flutter. He begins to lead me towards his car, and I glance down at our joined hands, half confused, half delighted.

It feels right.

Even if I don't know what 'it' is.

"And I managed to get us on the golf course first thing tomorrow," he adds as we reach the car. "Which means I can distract your dad if Damien tries to call. And, hopefully, by the time they speak, I'll have convinced him how solid we are."

My smile falters as I climb in. "But when he finds out the truth . . ."

Tom leans in, close enough that I feel the warmth of his body wrap around me. He reaches across to gently tug the seatbelt around my chest, his hand brushing the swell of my breast, not accidentally. His face hovers inches from mine, his mouth a breath from my own.

"The truth?" he asks, his voice low, coaxing.

My pulse spikes. "That we're not . . ." I murmur, eyes flicking to his lips, to the way they part slightly like he's already halfway to kissing me.

He doesn't let me finish. "I already told you the truth, Nita," he whispers.

Then his lips are on mine. Soft at first, a little unsure. But when I don't pull away, he takes what he wants. What we both want.

His hand cups my cheek, angling my face to deepen the kiss, and his tongue slides against mine with slow, hungry precision. My fingers clutch the front of his shirt, my body leaning into his, desperate for more.

By the time he pulls back, my breathing's a mess and my mind's not far behind.

He grins like he knows exactly what he's doing to me then shuts the door and rounds the car. I blink after him, stunned.

When he slides into the driver's side, he throws one hand on my bare knee, squeezing slightly, and starts the engine with the other.

"We'll take it slow," he says, eyes still on the road. "I know this is a surprise to you. But make no mistake, Anita, I wasn't putting on an act back there. I'm all in if you'll have me."

His tone is even, but the weight behind his words lands in my chest like a thud. He's dominant, yes. Bold. A little cocky. But there's something else simmering underneath.

Conviction. He's not playing. And, despite everything, that turns me on more than I care to admit.

The sudden shrill of my phone breaks the heat between us, jolting me.

I yank it from my bag. "Axel?" I murmur, glancing at Tom.

"Take it," he says, his fingers flexing on my knee. "It might be about Damien."

I nod and answer the call, putting it on speaker.

"Hi, Axel."

"Have you heard from Atlas tonight?" His voice is tight, tense.

My spine straightens. "No . . . should I have?"

"He was supposed to be here for church. He didn't show."

I frown. That's not like Atlas. Not at all. "Is that a huge problem?"

"I tried to call. His phone rang out, several times."

My frown deepens. Atlas would never ignore a call from his President. None of them would.

"You think he's been arrested or something?"

"That was my first thought. But if he hasn't reached out to you, he can't have been." He's right, my number's his emergency contact for legal representation. If something had happened, I'd know.

"Where was he last?" Tom asks, sharp now. His fingers are no longer casual on my skin.

"He took Rue out on the bike," Axel replies. The name still stings a little, but not like it used to. Not with Tom sitting beside me. "And Kasey tracked Rue's phone," Axel adds, "but it was off."

A flicker of unease crawls up my spine. "Oh," I say, more to myself than anyone, thumbing through my phone. "I have a tracker too. Atlas put it on both our phones months ago."

I've never used it. I'd forgotten it existed until now.

I load the app and tap his name, and a location pings.

"He's nearby," I murmur, glancing at the woods ahead. "A wooded area. That turn-off . . .there." I point it out to Tom, who doesn't hesitate. He veers the car down the lane, his jaw clenched.

"I'll send you the location," I say quickly, flicking it over to Axel.

Tom follows the tracker down a narrow, tree-lined track, the car bumping gently over the uneven road. The sun has dipped low enough that the woods feel darker than they should, shadowy and still.

"There," I say, spotting the gleam of chrome tucked behind some overgrowth. *Atlas's bike.*

Tom pulls in fast, cutting the engine. The silence that follows is deafening.

My phone rings again. It's Axel. I answer before the first ring finishes. "We found his bike. It's here."

"Don't go in," Axel snaps. "Wait there. I'm sending a crew. It could be a setup."

My heart slams against my ribs. "A setup?"

"Just wait for backup," he insists. "Ten minutes, Anita. Don't do anything stupid."

But I'm already out the car, sprinting, because ten minutes is too long.

"Anita!" Tom calls after me, but I don't stop. I can't.

The trees close in fast as I break into the woods, leaves crunching underfoot, branches clawing at my jacket. My breathing turns ragged, but I don't care. I keep pushing through the underbrush, drawn by something deeper than instinct.

Fear. Love. Guilt.

I stumble into a small clearing and freeze.

Atlas lies on the ground. *Unmoving.*

A brutal gash bleeds down his temple, his leather cut torn at the shoulder. His arms are spread wide, like he fell mid-fight and stayed down.

"No," I whisper, the word barely audible as I rush to him.

I drop to my knees beside him, hands trembling as I press my fingers to his throat. *Come on, come on, come on.* There, a pulse. Weak, but it's there.

"Atlas," I breathe, leaning over him. "Hey . . . hey, open your eyes." My fingers cup his jaw, trying to steady him, to wake him, to do something. But he doesn't move. "Shit." My eyes sting. "What the hell happened to you?"

Tom crashes through the clearing seconds later, cursing when he sees him. "Christ," he mutters, crouching beside me. "We need to get him out of here. Now."

"I don't want to move him, what if he has a neck injury?"

Tom exhales, scanning the trees. "Then we hold tight and keep him stable."

I nod, brushing the blood from Atlas's temple with my sleeve. My chest aches just looking at him. So strong, so proud, now broken and unconscious in the dirt.

I reach for my phone with a shaking hand, hitting redial. "Axel," I say the second he answers, "he's down. He's unconscious but breathing. We're in the clearing behind the ridge, about fifty metres from the bike."

"We're almost there," he says. "Hold tight, and keep your eyes open."

I end the call and stare down at Atlas, biting hard on my bottom lip.

Tom puts a hand on my back again, grounding me. But I can't look away from Atlas.

"Just hang on," I whisper, pressing my forehead gently to his for a second. "You don't get to leave me. Not like this."

CHAPTER 20

RUE

The world blurs past in shadow and steel.

I don't know how long we've been driving. My wrists ache from the cable ties cutting into my skin. There's a sack over my head, thick and scratchy, muffling every sound but the growl of the engine and the low, clipped voices of the men who took me.

My heart pounds hard enough I can feel it in my ears. I tried to scream once, back on the trail, but one of them slammed a fist into my ribs and told me if I did it again, they'd hurt Atlas more.

More. That shut me up.

Atlas. Please let him be alive.

The van slows. Gravel crunches beneath the tyres. A heavy gate groans open, then slams shut behind us. My lungs tighten.

A door slides open, and someone grabs me roughly by the

arm, yanking me out. My feet scramble for the ground as they drag me forward, disoriented, shaking.

The sack is ripped from my head.

I blink hard against the sudden glare of fluorescent light. We're inside some kind of warehouse. Concrete floors, high ceilings, and the air smells like oil and stale sweat.

I don't recognise any of the men.

But then, standing at the far end of the room, beside a battered leather chair and a small table holding a crystal glass, is a man I've only ever seen in a picture.

Damien.

His shirt is crisp white, sleeves rolled, cufflinks glinting as he lifts the glass to his lips and takes a sip of something amber. He looks exactly the same as I imagined—tailored, cold, smug.

Only his eyes are different. Colder, sharper.

They assess me as one of the men from behind me, shoves me forward a few steps. "You look nothing how I imagined," he says thoughtfully.

"Funny," I mutter, "You look exactly how I imagined."

He laughs, it's cruel, matching his expression. "You are just like your sister, only plainer. Almost innocent looking."

My mouth goes dry. My chest tightens, but I don't give him the satisfaction of seeing me crumble.

"What do you want?" I manage, forcing my voice to stay calm. "If this is about the money—"

"Oh, Rue," he says softly, almost pitying. "This isn't about the money anymore, it would be so much simpler if it was." He gestures and one of the men cuts the ties on my wrists. My skin throbs, red and raw. I almost collapse, but I force myself to stay upright.

"It's about unfinished business."

I glare at him. "With Atlas?"

A flicker of amusement crosses his face. He steps closer, slowly circling me like I'm some exhibit on display. "You made yourself important to people I'm trying to break. That makes you . . . useful." He takes a sip of his drink. "I took a step back and thought about all the people I want to fuck up, and I realised the one person that they all have a connection with, is you."

"I'm not afraid of you," I lie.

"Good," he says smoothly. "Because fear would make this boring. And I want to enjoy what's coming."

He turns to the others. "Put her somewhere safe. And make sure she knows the rules."

One of them grabs my arm, dragging me backwards again. I struggle, kicking once, twice, but it's no use. Damien doesn't flinch. He just watches, smiling faintly.

"He'll come for me," I scream. "He'll find me."

"Hold on to that," he says, his voice laced with amusement. "It's so much more fun when you have hope and I get to see it leave those pretty little eyes."

And then the door slams behind me and I'm met with darkness. But even in the pitch black, one thought roars in my chest.

Atlas will come.

He has to.

ANITA

The machines beep steadily, cruel in their calm. I've been listening to that same rhythm for hours now, memorising every rise and fall of the numbers on the monitor as if willing them to stay steady could somehow bring him back.

Atlas hasn't stirred. Not once.

I'm curled into the visitor chair beside his bed; my coat

draped around my shoulders like a blanket. The harsh fluorescent lights have long since given me a headache, but I can't bring myself to leave. Not while he's like this.

Tom hasn't left either.

He's still here, sat in the corner with his legs stretched out and arms folded across his chest, watching me in quiet silence like he's guarding us both. Every now and then, he brings me coffee or puts a gentle hand on my back. He hasn't asked for anything in return.

I glance at him now, my eyes sore from crying, my voice hoarse when I speak. "Do you mind?"

He raises an eyebrow. "Mind what?"

"That I'm here," I say softly, nodding towards Atlas. "That I'm sitting at the bedside of a man I once thought I loved."

Tom doesn't answer straight away. He just stands, walks over to me, and crouches beside the chair until we're eye-level. "Do you still love him?"

The question lands like a stone in my chest. Not because I don't know the answer, but because I thought maybe I'd been avoiding it.

I turn my gaze to Atlas. His face is still, a bandage on his temple, bruises blossoming along his jaw. I thought we had shared love, just a dysfunctional kind where I couldn't commit because of Leo and Damien, but now I see it was all excuses. Because now when I look at him now, I don't get that excited butterfly feeling in the pit of my stomach, I just feel . . . sad.

Sad for what we were. For what we could never be.

"I care about him," I murmur, tracing the line of Atlas's hand with my eyes. "I always will. He was important to me once, in a way that felt permanent." I pause, and then I shake my head. "But, no, I don't love him."

Tom exhales slowly, and when I glance back at him, there's a faint smile tugging at the corner of his lips.

"That's good enough for me," he says simply, standing and pressing a kiss to my temple. "I'll go grab us something hot to drink. Maybe something sweet. You look like you need both. And I need to call your father and rearrange golf."

My throat tightens, but not from grief this time. It's something warmer. Softer. A love with possibilities, a love that doesn't hurt.

"Tom?"

He turns in the doorway.

"Thank you. For staying."

He nods. "Always."

ATLAS

The world returns in fragments. A beeping noise. Too loud. Too steady. The hum of fluorescent lights. Voices, low and muffled, like they're underwater.

Pain finds me next. A dull throb behind my eyes, sharp pressure at my ribs. I try to move and immediately regret it.

"Don't push him. Let him come to slowly."

That voice. Female. Familiar.

I blink against the harsh ceiling light and turn my head a fraction towards the sound.

Anita.

She's here.

I groan softly, and the motion draws her eyes to mine.

"Atlas?" she says gently, her voice thick with relief. She's beside the bed in a second, her hand gripping mine. "Hey, you're okay. You're safe."

Safe. That word doesn't sit right.

I force my throat to work. "Rue." My voice is cracked,

barely a whisper, but it's enough to shift the mood in the room. A shadow crosses her face.

Tom is there too, standing back, arms folded, watching with a furrowed brow like he's ready to step in if I try to rip out my IV and go hunting.

"We found you unconscious in the woods. No sign of Rue."

I try to sit up but a bolt of pain lances through my side and I grunt, falling back with a curse. "They took her."

"We know." Anita squeezes my hand. "Axel's already got everyone looking. We'll find her, Atlas."

"No." I shake my head, fury bleeding through the fog. "She was terrified. I have to get to her."

At that, Tom moves closer, his jaw tight. "Relax, you took a good knock to the head."

My eyes flick between them. "Get me out of this fucking bed."

"You're not strong enough," Anita says, panic creeping into her tone.

"I don't care." My voice hardens, breath catching on every word. "I'm not lying here while Rue is fuck knows where, alone. Scared."

"About time you woke up," comes Kasey's sarcastic tone. I shift my eyes in her direction as she approaches the bed holding a coffee. "Enjoy nap time?"

"I have to find her," I repeat.

"Yeah, you do," she says firmly. "I'll let Axel know you're heading home." And she takes out her mobile and steps out the room.

"Atlas, I really don't think this is a good idea," Anita begins.

"I didn't ask," I snap, shifting onto the edge of the bed and pushing to sit. I groan as pain rips through me. "Fuck," I hiss, and Anita steadies me, her hands on my arm. Everything around me spins and I briefly close my eyes. When the dizziness subsides, I take a breath and pull the tape off the drip in my hand. I carefully slide the needle out and throw it on the bed. "Get me back to the club," I order. "Now."

CHAPTER 21

ANITA

The second we pull into the compound, Atlas disappears straight into Church, slower than usual but still stubborn as hell. He's barely been out of a hospital bed, but he's already throwing himself into strategy. *Typical.*

Tom slips his hand into mine, anchoring me, his thumb tracing small circles across my knuckles. "He'll be okay," he murmurs, trying to reassure me.

I shake my head. "You heard what the doctor said. They haven't ruled out a bleed on the brain. He shouldn't even be *standing*, let alone charging into their little war room."

Tom draws me in gently, brushing his lips against mine, his voice a soft murmur against my skin. "I love how much you care about these guys," he says. "Even when they drive you insane."

Before I can reply, my phone rings.

My heart sinks the second I see the name on the screen.

Damien.

I let out a frustrated breath. "It's him."

Tom's hand tightens in mine. "Answer it. Ignoring him will only cause problems."

I hit speaker and lift the phone, already dreading his voice. "Now isn't a good time," I snap, trying to keep my tone controlled.

His smug voice cuts through instantly. "I suppose you're in a flap over lover boy."

My whole body goes still. Tom's arm slips from around me as he steps away, already heading for Church to inform the guys.

"What?" I ask, my voice barely above a whisper.

"The biker," he clarifies, laughing like this is some kind of joke. "Last I heard, he wasn't in a good way."

My stomach lurches. I follow Tom across the room, watching him tap on the Church door and duck inside.

My voice hardens. "And what the hell do you know about that?"

His chuckle makes my blood run cold. "Jesus, haven't you figured it out yet? I've had his bitch for nearly twelve hours."

I stop dead. The air leaves my lungs in a rush.

No.

No, no, no.

I step into Church blindly, the men all turning to look at me as I place the phone on the table. "You have Rue?" I say, every word scraping out of my throat.

"That must've stung," Damien says. "When he dropped you for her. She's got that soft thing going on. Sweet. Innocent. Not your usual competition."

"I don't understand." My voice trembles, and I hate it.

"You never did," he spits. "That's half the problem. Kasey took my money. Atlas took my wife. And now you want to take Leo? You all think you're untouchable."

"So you took Rue to punish us?" My mind is racing, but nothing makes sense. "This is about Leo?"

"No. This is about power," he snaps. "Rue means everything to the biker. And the biker—he still means something to you, doesn't he?"

I flinch.

"Here's how this goes," he continues, low and cruel. "Drop the fight for Leo. Get me my money back. Do that, and I let the girl go. If not . . ." He pauses. And that pause says everything. "If not, I'll make her pay. Again. And again. And again. Until I get what I want."

The line goes dead.

I stare at the phone like it might explode, the world muffled under the roar in my ears.

No one speaks.

I can't breathe.

Tom steps beside me, his hand coming to my back, but I barely feel it.

This is all him. *Damien.*

And if I don't stop this, if I don't figure out how to fix what's broken, Rue's going to suffer for everything.

I lift my eyes to Atlas, who's already halfway out his seat, his jaw clenched so tight, I'm surprised his teeth don't shatter.

"We need a plan," I whisper, my voice hoarse.

RUE

The room is silent except for the ticking of the old pipes

attached to the ceiling, and the soft shuffle of my own restless pacing. It's cold, damp, and reeks of mildew. There's a thin mattress in the corner and a single, bare bulb that buzzes overhead. No windows. Just walls and silence.

My throat aches from thirst. My lips are cracked. They haven't given me water in hours, maybe longer. I've lost track of time. My head throbs from where someone knocked me sideways getting me out of the van. My hands shake, but I ball them into fists to stop the tremble.

And I need to pee.

I press my thighs together, rocking slightly on my heels, but I can't hold it much longer.

Swallowing what's left of my pride, I walk to the door and knock.

Nothing.

I knock again, louder. "Hello? I . . . I need to use the bathroom."

Silence.

Then a few heavy footsteps approach. The door creaks open, just a few inches. A man peers through the gap. One of the ones who dragged me out of the van. Crooked nose. Yellow teeth. The same dirty hoodie he wore when he laughed as I cried.

"What do you want?"

I force myself to speak, even though my voice comes out hoarse. "Please. I need to go. To the bathroom."

He disappears without a word, and for a second, I think he's gone for good. But then the door opens wider, and he shoves something into the room, a bucket.

A fucking bucket.

I blink at it, unsure if this is a joke.

"You've got five minutes," he says. "Make it quick."

He doesn't move.

I wrap my arms around myself. "Can you . . . turn around or something?"

His grin stretches wide. "Nah. I'm good right here."

Shame floods my chest, hot and suffocating.

I don't move.

"I said five minutes," he snaps, stepping farther inside.

I freeze, heart thudding so hard I can barely hear. Every bone in my body screams not to do this, but my bladder won't wait.

So, I turn away, shaking, dragging the bucket into the farthest corner, trying to shield myself with my back. My hands tremble as I pull down my jeans.

He laughs behind me. A sharp, ugly laugh that makes my skin crawl.

Tears sting my eyes, but I don't let them fall. Not here. Not in front of him. Not when I need every ounce of dignity I've got left.

When I'm done, I stand slowly, not turning around. My breath hitches as I whisper, "Are you proud of yourself?"

"There's no shame in pissing," the man drawls, lifting the bucket with a greasy grin. "Some freaks *pay* to watch that shit." His eyes rake over me, slow and revolting. "Hell, I'd let you piss on me."

I stiffen, jaw clenched, stomach churning.

"What the fuck's going on?" a voice snaps from the doorway.

The man jumps, spinning on his heel. Damien steps into view, calm but cold.

"Girl needed the bathroom," the man mumbles, hurrying out with the bucket like a rat escaping a trap.

"Apologies," Damien says, stepping into the room like he

owns the air in it. "The amenities aren't five-star." He smirks, tucking his hands into his pockets. "How's that hope holding up?"

I glare at him. "I don't even know why I'm here."

He tilts his head. "Sure, you do."

"No, I really don't," I snap, heat rising in my throat. "I've done nothing to you."

"But you're connected, Rue." His voice softens, mockingly gentle. "To Kasey, to Anita, and especially to *him*."

I shake my head, exasperated. "So, what?"

He sighs like I'm being difficult. "Your sister stole from me. Anita's trying to take my son. And Atlas," his eyes narrow, "took my wife."

I freeze. "This is about revenge?"

"No," he says coolly. "It's about leverage." He steps closer. "Anita loves your biker, and if he asks her to back off for *your* safety, she will."

My heart stutters. "Atlas would never ask her to do that. He's not like you."

Damien chuckles. "That's the problem with men like him. Honourable. Predictable. Easy to manipulate." His eyes gleam. "So, if he won't ask her to stand down, well . . . maybe you'll be less valuable than I thought. And hope?" He leans in, just enough to make me flinch. "Hope fades real fucking fast when no one comes."

He walks out, slamming the door behind him.

ATLAS

The door creaks as I push out of the club and into the dying light. The air's cooler now, carrying that scent of dust and oil, summer rain somewhere in the distance. I drag a hand over my face and inhale deeply, trying to keep it together. Rue's gone, and the weight of not protecting her, is sitting heavy in my chest.

Footsteps approach, soft and hesitant. I don't turn.

"You okay?" Anita's voice is quiet but tight, like she's holding something in.

I nod once. "No," I admit, "but I will be."

She stands beside me in silence for a moment, arms crossed, staring out at the gravel lot like it holds answers. "I never meant for any of this," she says suddenly, her voice cracking. "This is my fight with Damien. It's my mess. And now, he's pulling Rue into it, and you—" She stops herself, like if she says more, it might all unravel.

I glance at her. "Stop."

Her brows furrow. "Atlas—"

"This isn't your fault." My voice is steady, firm. "Damien's the kind of man who'll use anyone to get what he wants. You didn't choose this war. He brought it to you."

Tears well in her eyes, and I see the guilt eating her alive. "You keep fighting for Leo," I tell her. "You hear me? That kid deserves better than a man like that for a father. You're his safe place, Nita. Don't let anyone make you feel bad for wanting to protect him."

She nods slowly, wiping under her eyes. "Thank you."

We fall quiet again, and I glance sideways at her. There's history between us, old, frayed, but still threaded with something tender.

I clear my throat. "You and Tom?"

She blinks at me. "What?"

"Is there something there?"

A beat passes. Her lips twitch into a soft smile. "Yeah. There is."

I nod, letting it settle in my chest. It doesn't ache like I thought it might. In fact, it feels right.

"I'm happy for you," I say, meaning it. "You deserve good things, Anita. Someone who shows up for you. Don't let fear make you push it away."

Her eyes shimmer again. "You really mean that?"

"Yeah," I say. "Grab it with both hands."

The silence between us shifts. Not heavy, not awkward, just full of things we've said, and things we no longer need to. I squeeze her shoulder gently, turning to head inside.

I can already feel the rumble of engines firing up inside me.

It's time to get my old lady back home where she belongs.

I go back into church, the weight of my presence pulling all eyes my way.

My brothers are already gathered around the table, maps and burner phones scattered. Tom trails in behind Anita, and Kasey's already here perched on the edge of a chair, arms crossed tight, eyes full of fear.

Outsiders. In church.

If anyone needed proof this shit was serious, it's that. We don't let outsiders in, not even the women we love. But no one says a word, all too focussed on what we need to do.

I walk to my place at the table and rest my hands on the wood, letting the silence settle before I speak. "I'm claiming Rue," I say firmly. It's not the way I planned to announce it, hell, I haven't even had a chance to discuss it with Rue. But if she's mine, the club will go above and beyond to get her back.

"You heard the man," says Axel, slapping me roughly on the back. "His old lady's been taken, and we gotta get her back."

Fletch leans forward, his jaw tight. "I've got a list of

every place he's been known to frequent. Every bar, every office, damn, we even got his friends and family on this thing," he says, turning his laptop towards me. I scan my eyes over it. Nothing stands out.

"There's another week before the custody hearing," says Tom.

I shake my head. "She can't wait a week. She'll never last that long."

"And who knows what he'll do if he think's we're not following his demands," adds Kasey, wrapping her arms around herself.

"He thinks if Atlas tells me to back off, I will," mutters Anita, glancing my way.

I shake my head. "Not happening."

"There's no guarantee he'll even hand her over if that happens," says Axel. "He ain't gonna leave her able to speak and tell the police what he did."

"We bring her home. And then we help Nita get full custody of Leo. That bastard should never see him again," snaps Kasey.

"But you can't do anything to him before the hearing," says Tom. "It'll look to suspicious." He fixes me with a stare that tells me he's gonna make sure Anita wins the battle and Damien never upsets her again. "If we run his plates, it's possible ANPR systems have him driving to and from the place he's keeping Rue."

"I know a guy," says Fletch, pulling out his mobile and stepping from the room.

"We're going to rattle his cage," I say, tapping the table. "Make him panic. He wants us quiet and desperate. Instead, we make noise. We show him what it feels like when you come for someone who's ours."

Grizz nods, cracking his knuckles. "It's about time."

"We go to every place, including his office, and make noise," Axel orders. "Tell everyone we want to speak to him. Get them all worried."

I look around the table, at these men I trust with my life. Then I say the words that start everything.

"Let's bring her home."

CHAPTER 22

RUE

Damien paces in front of me like a storm about to break. His phone rings again, shrill and relentless, and he hurls it across the room with a roar.

"*Fuckkkk!*" he bellows, raking both hands through his hair like he wants to tear it out. "Those fuckers are pushing me too far! I've got every bastard I know calling me, telling me they've been looking for me."

"You underestimated how angry Atlas would be," I say quietly, my voice just loud enough to cut through his chaos. There's a tremor there, but I force the words out anyway. "You thought he'd roll over."

He spins, and the slap comes so fast I don't see it. My cheek explodes with pain, and I stumble back, crashing to the floor, the back of my skull slamming into concrete. Stars bloom in my vision.

I gasp, fingers brushing the spot. It's wet. *Blood*.

Before I can move, Damien lunges. He pins me, his face hovering inches above mine, breath hot and sour with rage. "Or maybe *he* underestimated *me,*" he growls, "and just how far I'll go to ruin every single person he loves."

My pulse races. I swallow it down, try to think clearly. "I thought this was about Leo."

Damien doesn't answer with words. Instead, he drags his nose slowly along my neck. I go rigid beneath him, my stomach turning.

"I can see why he likes you," he mutters, voice dark and low.

"Loves me," I whisper, lifting my chin with whatever defiance I have left.

He smiles, but there's no warmth in it. "But not enough to give up Anita."

His words sink deep, sharp and cruel. I feel the sting in places I don't want to admit. I press my lips together, ignore the ache in my chest, and keep my voice cold. "You don't deserve to keep Leo."

His eyes flare, and his hand shoots out, wrapping around my throat, not squeezing, but enough to remind me he could.

"You don't know anything about me," he growls.

I meet his gaze, unblinking. "I know you're using Leo to punish Anita. That you're terrified she'll win, and that's why you're doing this. One day, Leo will see you for what you are. And when he does? He'll hate you."

His grip tightens for a second.

Then, slowly, he lets go, standing over me with a sneer. I cough, my lungs burning, but I don't look away.

"You'd better pray he finds you before I ruin you," he mutters.

I MUST'VE DRIFTED OFF AT SOME POINT, CURLED UP ON THE thin mattress, aching and cold, my head throbbing with every shallow breath. My body feels leaden, heavy with fear and fatigue, but something stirs me.

A noise. Distant, sharp.

Metal screeching. Voices shouting. Footsteps pounding closer.

I jolt upright, heart hammering, just as the door bursts open.

"*Rue!*"

Kasey.

She's there in the doorway, eyes wide, frantic. I blink up at her, disoriented. Is this real?

"Oh my god." She crosses the room in two strides, dropping to her knees beside me. "You're okay. You're okay." Her hands are trembling as they cup my face. "Come on, we have to go, *now.*"

She hauls me up before I can speak, her arm wrapped tight around my waist. I stagger, the pain in my skull making everything spin, but I cling to her and let her pull me towards the corridor.

The hallway is chaos, with broken furniture and smashed glass. There are shouts from outside, boots pounding against concrete.

"Kasey, what's—" I croak, but she's already dragging me past a half-open door. I freeze.

Through the crack, I see Atlas. Not the calm, steady man I know.

He's a storm.

His fists rain down on Damien, over and over, with blood coating his knuckles, his forearms, Damien's face barely visible beneath the mess. There's something primal in the way Atlas moves, a rage that looks like it's been burning for years.

ATLAS

I don't even feel my knuckles anymore.

Just the dull shock of bone hitting bone, the sting of blood, his and mine. Every punch is for Rue. Every blow is for the fear I saw in her eyes as they took her from me, leaving me helpless on the ground.

"You think you can take what's mine?" I snarl, grabbing Damien by the collar and slamming him back down. "You think using a kid makes you a man?"

He coughs, chokes on blood, and still manages a crooked smile.

I see red. My fist draws back again . . .

And then I feel it, like a shift in the air. I stop cold, the breath catching in my throat. Slowly, I turn my head.

She's there.

Rue.

Half-lit by the hallway light, standing barefoot and bruised, her hair tangled, her eyes wide with disbelief.

She's real.

She's *here*.

My heart stumbles.

I drop Damien, letting him fall like the scum he is.

All the rage drains from me like a snapped thread. I take a step forward, hand still sticky with blood, but I don't reach for her. I don't deserve to, not yet.

Her mouth parts like she wants to say something, but no sound comes.

I'm not even sure I'm breathing.

"Rue . . ." Her name falls from my lips like a prayer.

And then the sound of a choked sob leaves her throat as she stumbles towards me, throwing herself against me. I wrap her in my arms, ignoring the pain in my body as she wraps her legs around me and holds me tight. "You came," she sobs into my neck.

"I told you I would," I reply, my voice breaking with emotion.

The door slams behind us, and I hear heavy boots stomp in.

"Jesus Christ, Atlas," Grizz growls. "Tom said not to leave a *visible* mark."

I glance down at the bloodied mess that is Damien, sprawled across the concrete. "Didn't hear that part," I lie flatly, still holding Rue like I'll never let her go again.

Grizz exhales a long breath, muttering something under it, but he doesn't push.

Rue lifts her head, eyes red-rimmed and glassy. "Take me home," she whispers.

I nod, already moving towards the door, cradling her like she's the most precious thing I've ever touched.

"To the club," she adds, softer now, and it guts me.

That one small word—*home*—it tells me everything. Even after all of this, she still wants to be with me.

~

Rue stirs, mumbling something in her sleep, and I'm on my feet before I even realise I've moved. Pain lances through my ribs. Broken or bruised, I don't know. I didn't stay long enough at the hospital to hear the verdict.

She comes first. *Always.*

She blinks up at me from the bed, her eyes still puffy, her voice barely audible. "What time is it?"

"Early," I say, brushing a strand of hair from her face. "You're safe. Go back to sleep."

She tries to sit up, but I place a hand gently on her shoulder, easing her back down.

"Don't even think about getting up."

"I need to pee," she whispers, voice raspy.

I press a kiss to her forehead. "Okay, fine. Bathroom and then straight back. Doctor's orders."

"Doctor or biker?" she mumbles with a tired smile.

I grin despite myself. "Same thing."

I help her to the en suite, staying outside the door but ready if she needs me. Every movement she makes feels like a stab to the gut, not from pain, though I've got plenty of that, but from helplessness. From knowing I couldn't stop what happened.

When she's back in bed, I settle the blanket around her and perch on the edge of the mattress, watching her eyes flutter as sleep tries to claim her again.

"You don't have to hover," she says softly, eyes closed.

"Yes, I do."

"I'm okay now."

"No, you're not." I smooth my thumb over the purple bruise on her cheek. "And that's okay too."

She goes quiet, and I think she's drifted off again, but then she whispers, "You didn't rest either."

I ignore the comment. "Tessa tried to bring you tea earlier. I sent her away."

She smiles faintly. "You're screening my visitors?"

"Damn right I am. You get tired fast. Too fast." My jaw clenches. "And if one more person tries to hug you or ask you how you feel, I'll lose what's left of my mind."

Her eyes open, meeting mine. "You're in pain too."

"So?"

"So, lie down. Next to me. Just for a bit."

I hesitate. My body's screaming, but I don't want to risk jostling her, hurting her by accident.

She sees it in my expression and pats the mattress beside her. "Please, Atlas."

That's all it takes.

I lie beside her carefully, and she shifts just enough to press her cheek to my chest, curling into me like she belongs there. And God help me, she does.

I exhale, wincing as pain shoots through my ribs, but it's worth it just to feel her breathing steady against me.

Her voice is a breath in the dark. "You didn't stop looking for me."

"Never."

"Even when you were hurt."

I press a kiss to her temple. "Even if I was on my death bed." Silence falls between us, but it's the kind that soothes. "I love you," I add, holding my breath. The light sound of her snores fills the room, and I grin. "Of course, you're asleep," I whisper out loud.

ANITA

Atlas has gone into full protection mode. No one gets in to see Rue, not without going through him first. So, when Tom suggests pulling him aside to talk about the upcoming hearing, I know exactly what he's doing.

And I let him.

Because I need this chance.

I'm not even sure if Rue wants to see me. After everything that's happened, after everything Damien's done, I wouldn't blame her if she didn't. But I have to try. I need to at least attempt to repair the damage, or I'll never be able to move forward.

I wait in the bathroom, heart pounding. The second I hear Atlas's voice agreeing to head to church with Tom, I slip out, moving quickly and quietly into his bedroom.

I close the door behind me, and when I turn, she's awake.

Rue is staring at me from the bed, pale and still, like she's not sure if I'm real.

I offer a weak smile, my throat dry. "Hey," I say gently. "How are you?"

I perch on the edge of the mattress, careful not to jar her. Up close, the bruises on her neck look darker, angrier. Guilt twists in my stomach.

"I'm so sorry you got dragged into all of this," I say quietly. "Damien . . . the custody fight . . . none of it should've touched you."

Rue's mouth tugs into the ghost of a smile. "Kasey's the one who poked the bear, Anita. Don't take all the credit."

A breathy laugh slips out of me, surprised and shaky. Then my face sobers. "There's something else."

She waits.

"I know I've said this all before, but I've had time to think it over. To understand my actions. The night I kissed Atlas . . . I was a mess. I didn't even see it then, but I was clinging to him because he felt familiar. Safe. A habit I couldn't kick." I wet my lips, shame burning. "I told myself it was real, but it wasn't. It was me being lost and selfish, and it hurt you."

Rue studies me for a long moment. The silence feels endless.

"At least you figured it out," she says at last, voice soft.

I swallow hard. "I regret coming between you. I can see

how he looks at you, Rue, like you're the first true thing he's ever had. I'd never want to take that from either of you."

Her shoulders relax a fraction. "Thank you for saying that."

"I mean it," I whisper. "Atlas is happier than I've ever seen him. And that . . . that's because of you."

For the first time since I entered the room, her expression eases into something like peace. She reaches for the water on the nightstand, sips, then sets it down.

"He loves you," she begins, and when I go to protest, she holds up her hand, silencing me. "As a friend. And I get it, you two have history. I don't want to come between that friendship either, but you cross that line again, and I'll make sure you never set foot near him. Okay?"

I bite my lower lip to hide the smile. She's protecting him and I love that. I nod. "Understood."

"Are you going to win the custody case?" she asks.

I look to the floor. "Tom seems to think so."

"And you don't?"

"I want to have faith," I admit, "but Damien has so many tricks up his sleeve, I'm scared to believe I can."

"You have the entire club behind you. Over fifty men and women who are gonna treat Leo like a nephew. You have everything to offer him, and Damien has nothing but aggression and anger. Believe it, Nita. He's coming home."

I smile, tears gathering on my lower lash. "Thank you for being so understanding, and for being nice to me."

The door opens, and Atlas fills it, his eyes narrowing in on me.

"You're his friend," says Rue, her eyes going to his, "and so you're mine too."

CHAPTER 23

ATLAS

As if I couldn't love her even more, then she goes and says shit like that. I wait for Anita to leave before crawling over Rue, pinning my hands either side of her thighs and landing a kiss on her lips. "Fuck, what did I do to deserve you?"

"Same," she murmurs, trying to take the kiss deeper. I pull back and she growls in frustration. "Damn it, Atlas, I won't break."

I grin, resting my forehead against hers. "It's not you I'm worried about."

She laughs, "No?"

"I know how you get when you're all pent up like this," I say, my tone teasing. "My ribs are still healing." I carefully turn onto my back and place my hands behind my head. "I'm delicate."

She throws her leg over me, placing her hands on my

chest and staring down at me. "You just relax," she says, popping the button on my jeans. "I'll do all the hard work."

∼

3 days later . . .

I SIT ON THE COLD WOODEN BENCH, MY SHOULDERS TENSE AS the judge clears her throat. The room's quiet, thick with anticipation, but Anita doesn't flinch. She sits straight-backed beside her lawyer, eyes fixed ahead, hands clenched in her lap. There's something calm in her, like maybe, finally, she believes she deserves to win.

The judge begins to read the evidence aloud, and I glance over at Damien across the aisle. Smug prick hasn't smirked once since the hearing started.

He damn well knows he's lost.

"The court acknowledges substantial evidence of neglect on the part of Mr. Carpenter," the judge says, her voice unwavering. "This includes documented instances of leaving Leo Carpenter, a thirteen-year-old child, under the sole care of a minor, Ms. Kasey Green, on multiple occasions."

I see Anita's jaw tighten. She never wanted to drag Kasey into this, but Damien forced her hand. We had to make sure this went her way.

The judge continues, tone harder now. "While the investigation is ongoing, the court cannot ignore Mr. Carpenter's recent arrest for engaging in a sexual relationship with Ms. Green, who was fifteen at the time. Regardless of criminal findings, this behaviour demonstrates a gross lapse in judgment and an unsafe environment for Leo. And we must not ignore that whilst the investigation is ongoing, Mr. Carpenter has been suspended from his job."

Damien shifts in his seat. If he thought he could charm or threaten his way out of this, he's finally learning otherwise.

But it's the next part that hits me in the chest.

"Given Leo's age and maturity," the judge says, glancing down at the papers in front of her, "his wishes have been taken into account. When asked where he felt safest and happiest, Leo expressed a clear preference to live with his mother, Ms. Anita Jenson. He described her home as calm, stable, fun, and loving."

Anita's hand flies to her mouth. She just closes her eyes for a beat, like she's exhaling all the weight she's been carrying.

It's over.

The judge looks up. "I believe she will provide Leo with everything he needs. She has proven herself time and time again, and I fail to understand why this has taken so long. I can only surmise that Mr. Carpenter has abused his position in this court, a position he currently does not hold. I also note that Ms. Jenson has reconciled with her parents, building a stronger support network. Sole custody is hereby granted to Ms. Jenson, with supervised visitation for Mr. Carpenter pending further investigation."

She looks up, fixing Damien with a steely gaze. "Mr. Carpenter, the court cannot overlook the serious allegations of coercive control and what can only be described as sustained emotional intimidation. Should the ongoing investigations result in findings against you, the court will strongly consider revoking any future contact rights."

The moment we step out the courtroom, Anita hurries towards us, her eyes already glistening.

"Thank you so much for coming today," she says as Rue wraps her in a tight hug. "Having you both here made all the difference."

"Have they said when Leo can come home?" Rue asks, pulling back.

Anita nods, joy breaking across her face. "Today. I can collect him from school this afternoon."

"That's incredible, Nita," I say, meaning every word. "You did it."

She nods, voice thick. "My boy is coming home."

Tom appears beside her, sliding an arm around her shoulders. "Told you not to worry," he murmurs, kissing her temple.

"Well done," I say, holding out a hand. He shakes it firmly.

"And you have to bring Leo to the barbecue tomorrow," Rue adds, smiling. "Everyone's excited to meet him."

Tom nods. "I think he'd like that. Sounds like a great idea."

RUE

The sun's starting to dip, casting the yard in warm gold as laughter spills around me. The scent of grilled meat still lingers in the air, mixing with smoke and beer and something sweet from the dessert table. Kids are running wild between bikes, men are yelling over card games, and someone's turned up the music.

It's been a good day. A really good day.

I sink deeper into one of the old outdoor couches, my drink sweating in my hand as I watch Kasey throw her head back laughing, flicking a paper plate at one of the guys who teased her. Her hair's up, her boots are dusty, and for the first time in a long time, she looks . . . light. *Free*. Like maybe she's finally let go of all that weight she used to carry around.

I smile to myself, letting it all sink in.

Atlas is somewhere nearby. I can feel him even when I don't see him. It's like that now. This quiet awareness between us. We've slipped into a rhythm that feels easy, like we've been doing this for years instead of weeks. He still watches me like he can't quite believe I'm real, and I still catch myself staring when he isn't looking, my heart leaping every damn time.

But we haven't talked about the future. Not really.

My flat still exists. My toothbrush is probably dry. But the thought of going back there . . . it feels hollow. Like rewinding time to a version of me I've outgrown. Everything I want is here—his shirt in my drawer, his scent on my pillow, and he touches my lower back when he walks past like it's second nature now.

I want to stay.

I just don't know if he wants me to.

The cushion dips beside me, and I don't even have to look to know it's him. Atlas stretches an arm along the back of the seat, letting his fingers brush my shoulder, and I lean into the touch like a sunflower chasing light.

"You see Leo out there?" he asks, his voice warm with amusement.

I smile, nodding towards the yard. "He's been glued to Axel all afternoon."

"Kid fits right in. Axel even let him have a go on his bike. Well, just sitting on it, but still." He chuckles. "Didn't stop Leo from revving it like a maniac. Think he's already planning which patch he'll wear."

I laugh, picturing it. "God, Anita would have a heart attack."

"I dunno, she seems more relaxed now," Atlas says, his gaze drifting towards where Anita stands with Tom near the grill. "She looks happy. They all do. Her, Tom, Leo, they make a good team. Solid. Like a proper little family."

There's something in his voice, something soft and a little raw. My chest tightens.

"You ever want that?" he asks suddenly, eyes back on me now. "Kids?"

The question steals my breath for a second. But I nod. "Three."

His brows shoot up. "Three?"

I laugh. "What? I know I'm quiet, but that doesn't mean I want a quiet house."

He shakes his head in awe, a smile tugging at the corner of his mouth. "Damn. You keep surprising me."

I nudge him. "Your turn."

His voice lowers, lips brushing close to my ear. "I want a lot. But only with you."

My heart thunders as he pulls back just enough to look me in the eye.

"I don't want there to be a single day when you're not round with my babies. I want you barefoot in my shirt, pregnant and swearing at me because I'm not rubbing your back."

I laugh, half breathless, half melting. "Your comment is outdated, but also quite sweet. Do you think I'll look good pregnant?"

He grins, dark and hot and full of meaning. "I think you'll look sexy as hell."

He kisses me then – slow, deep, like the world's stopped turning for a second. My fingers curl around the edge of his cut, grounding myself, because I can feel the words bubbling up, and for once, I don't want to bury them.

When we break apart, I say it quietly. "So, does that mean you want me to stay?"

His brow furrows.

"I mean, really stay. My lease is up next week. If I need to renew it –"

"You're not renewing shit," he growls, voice low and fierce. "You're not leaving my side, Rue. Not again. Not ever. You're mine, and hell itself couldn't keep me from you now."

My heart trips over itself. I'm still trying to catch up when he stands suddenly and claps his hands together to get everyone's attention.

Oh no.

"Atlas," I hiss, tugging his hand, mortified.

But it's too late. The yard quiets, all eyes on him.

"I've got something to say," he announces, voice carrying. "This woman right here," he yanks me gently to my feet "She's it for me. She's not just my girl. I'm making her my old lady."

The crowd erupts, cheers, whistles, laughter, and someone yells, "It's about damn time!"

I'm blushing so hard I'm sure I'm glowing, but when Atlas turns to me, those blue eyes locking on mine, all I can feel is love. *Fierce. Forever.*

I'm home.

THE END

Acknowledgments

Thank you to all my wonderful readers—you rock!

Social Media

I love to hear from my readers and if you'd like to get in touch, you can find me here . . .

My Facebook Page
My Facebook Readers Group
Bookbub
Instagram
Goodreads
Amazon
I'm also on Tiktok

Printed in Dunstable, United Kingdom